MW00414446

All char

fictitious. Any resemblance to actual persons, living or dead, is entirely coincidental. The names, incidents, dialogue, and opinions expressed within are products of the author's imagination and are not meant to be construed as real. Nothing is intended or should be interpreted as expressing or representing the views of the CIA, DARPA, DHS, SIS, or any other department or agency of any government body. Nothing is intended or should be interpreted as expressing, or representing the views of MIT, Sapienza University, or any institution of higher learning.

Originally paperback edition September 2021
Second paperback edition, May 2022

Book design by Rod P. Couser | Cover
Photo 33855555 | Academia © Frannyanne | Dreamstime.com

ISBN 978-1-7376917-6-1 (Hardcover)
ISBN 978-1-7376917-0-9 (paperback)
ISBN 978-1-7376917-1-6 (eBook)

Prologue

The air within the room was cold and unmoving as Gilberti Ricci sat motionless in his old leather chair, patiently waiting for the heat to take hold. He had been waiting for several hours now, but this part of the *Universita delgi Studi Di Padova*, the University of Padua, was hundreds of years old. Any attempt to provide warmth to this room had long been ruined by the added walls and doors placed there by necessity rather than efficiency. The truth was heat simply could not find its way there.

Dressed in layers of wool, he shivered as he rubbed his gloved hands against his trousers. Although it was daylight, the blinds were drawn, and the room was dark except for a small ray of light at the long edge of the drapes. As he slowly rubbed his legs, his mind escaped the icy darkness, and he took another moment to consider his current impasse.

Gilberti had been born fifty years before in Treviso, Italy, just sixty kilometers from Padua where he now lived. His parents knew their oldest son had a very special mind and offered educational opportunities to him, which were rare at that time. After *Scuola Secondario Superiore*, (high school), he was accepted to the University of Padua, one of the oldest universities in the world.

Adapting easily to the academic environment, Gilberti barely noticed when Padua became the main command station for the Italian Army when they entered WWI in 1915. With university backing, he avoided war service. But two years later, following the battle of Caporetto, Gilberti, studying safely in the university library, never heard the mortar fire that destroyed his childhood home, killing his entire family.

Guilt-ridden, he withdrew into his studies, and quietly graduated alone, two years later with his Laurea, then the equivalent of a doctorate, from the school of arts in Physics.

To ease himself back into normalcy, he took his first job as a non-tenured assistant at the university and began to spend considerable time with Sonia Baldi, a shy but brilliant study partner. As a scientist herself, Sonia understood Gilberti's quirky mind, and they were soon married, and had a son, Bortolo. With Sonia and Bortolo, Gilberti had a stronger sense of purpose.

Gilberti's field of study was electromagnetics, and he was influenced by the predictions and findings of other physicists and noted theorists of his field such as Maxwell, Heaviside, Hertz, Birkland, and Strømer. In those early years, he was fascinated by the visual phenomenon, the Aurora Borealis, named by Galileo after "Aurora" the Roman god of morning. Like his contemporaries, Gilberti believed these electrons and protons from the sun could be captured to create energy.

Although an amazing time to be a physicist, this was tempered by a rapidly changing political landscape inside Italy. Although Gilberti took little notice, it became impossible to escape the growing fascist movement, and soon all university professors were required to become members of the National Fascist Party. Some silently cursed its curtailment of free thought and cultural independence, but most swore allegiance to the regime. Many, including Gilberti, viewed this as a requirement of their profession rather than an extension of their personal politics and beliefs.

That changed dramatically with the passing of Italy's racial laws in 1938 and the subsequent expulsion of Jews and others from public office and higher education. Losing valued colleagues angered him and made him realize the fascist movement was entirely wrong for him. Conflicted, he and Sonia considered leaving Italy, but it was clear they were financially and emotionally bound to the university.

Shortly after Italy ended its war with the allies on the signing of the Armistice of Cassibile, Germany invaded the north of Italy, creating the Italian Social Republic. Once again, the entire Venice region, which included Padua, was transformed by war and Nazi command began interrogating universities for war-based ideas. It was this recent turn of events that found Gilberti sitting without hope, wondering why he had not left when he had the chance.

He had formalized his new research when pro-Mussolini and Nazi officials arrived at the university and approached him. Although he attempted humility, they became infatuated with the thought that his ideas of atmospheric energy could be weaponized, and they approached the University Rector to enlist Gilberti's cooperation. The rector sympathized with Gilberti, but knew that while the Nazis were asking now, they would soon demand his cooperation. The realization to Gilberti was that his research had placed his family, the university, and his students at risk, which he could not accept.

Having previously shipped his research in secret, far away from the university, Gilberti wept as he mouthed a longing goodbye to his beloved Sonia and son Bortolo. Silently cursing the cold, his hand shaking, as he placed a small pistol next to his amazing mind and pulled the trigger.

Packard's Corner, Boston, Present Day

Sara Ricci sat at her small kitchenette, eating cold pizza while reviewing an equation on her tablet computer. Glancing at the corner of the screen, she saw the time and suddenly jumped up off the chair. Grabbing her backpack, she yelled to herself, "Shit, I'm going to be late again," and ran out with a half slice of pizza in her mouth heading east, towards the Boston University Bridge.

Born in Horsforth England, Sara was the only child of Italian parents, Giovanni and Annini Ricci. The family had come to the UK from Verona, Italy, but moved back to Milan when Sara was at the awkward age of thirteen. Fortunately, she was bilingual given that her parents, while immersed in English at work, usually spoke Italian at home.

A dedicated and hard-working student, Sara handily completed her undergraduate degree in geoinformatics, and her master's two years later in physics. She had always considered a doctorate, a prerequisite for any career as a chief scientist, or academia, and with her parents' blessing, she applied to six top universities.

Sara had prepared herself to expect tough choices, but was humbled and surprised to only receive acceptance at the University of Rome or Sapienza and MIT. She ultimately chose the MIT and moved to the United States.

Now, two years later, she was almost running as she went east on Albany toward the Francis Bitter Magnet Laboratory. She entered the building quickly, almost running into two students coming out whose eyes were glued downward to their phones.

"Sorry, guys, in a hurry," she said between breaths.

"Ah, what?" said the first as he stopped and looked up only to cause his friend to run into the back of him, who shouted, "Hey dude, not cool, you can't just stop." As they argued, Sara hurried towards the stairs, going up two steps at a time. She never used elevators, always choosing the exercise of the stairs instead.

Today, she was giving a class on electromagnetic design, and like many doctoral candidates, she had offered to teach undergraduates to defer expenses, but admittedly, she didn't really care for this. As she flew into the small room, she noted the clock reminding her she was seven minutes late.

A few of the students were standing and began looking for a seat as she came in saying between breaths, "Sorry everyone," making her way to the front. She flew a quick hand through her long brown hair and started. "So, we left off last week talking about the relationship between magnetism and electricity. As we have discussed previously, it was Oersted who discovered that a wire containing an electric current, when placed above a magnetic needle would cause the needle to deflect ninety degrees. Remind me: why did it do that?" She looked at the students, expecting the worst. In her view, none seemed to care much about electromagnetics, hence her frustration with teaching.

A freshman said confidently from his chair, "The constant source of electricity in the wire produces a magnetic field around the wire core. This disturbs the magnetic field of the earth's magnetism present in the needle."

"Okay, good, but why did it do that?" she replied, trying to see what he really knew beyond the textbook answer.

He froze, but a girl next to him quickly stood and answered. "I think that the Frenchman, André-Marie Ampère, concluded that magnetism is the circulation of electrical currents at right angles to the axis joining the poles of the magnet. In Oersted's experiment, the deflection, therefore occurred ninety degrees from the length of the wire." She looked apprehensive and sat down, looking at Sara for approval.

"Correct, but what does that statement actually mean? The deflection occurred ninety degrees from the length of the wire?" Sara replied, baiting them.

The room did not erupt in eagerness as some students pondered the answer and others looked around for help. Sara said firmly, "Come on people. You have to invest yourself in this to understand. There are magnetic reactions all around us, but they don't matter because most often, the magnetic field is coming from electrons that are spinning wildly around the nucleus of atoms." Waving her hands about in the air to give the sense of objects swirling around with wild abandon, the class laughed. "Why? Because they are all colliding with one another, canceling out their forces. There is no unification. No way for positive or negative currents to dominate. I'm asking why?"

The room was silent, but she was happy to see the young women who answered the previous question rise to the occasion. "Because as you describe it, the electrons are all spinning in random directions. Magnets, because of their natural properties, arrange molecules so that their electrons spin in only one direction. I think it is that movement that creates a magnetic force flowing out of the north and south poles of the magnet. It is also the reason that two like poles will resist each other, but two opposite poles will attract each other."

"Nice job," Sara said, satisfied, "And yes, that is precisely the reason. Although once thought of as separate phenomena, electricity and magnetism are now known to be components of the unified field of electromagnetism. Particles electrically charged interact with an electric force, while charged particles in motion produce and respond to magnetic forces as well. Today we are going to put that all together in the lab to make our own crude, but effective, electro-magnet."

Sara grabbed her backpack and motioned to the door, "Let's head down to the workshop in 11B, and grab your stuff; we are not returning to this room." As they walked, she was not thinking of her fledgling students, but questions for her own doctoral preliminary exam, which would arrive soon. Her open-book test started later that day.

2

Milan, Italy

Giovanni Ricci looked at his watch and thought of his daughter Sara, now preparing for a class, or perhaps studying for her preliminary exam. He noted it was just after 4:30 p.m., which meant it was 10:30 a.m. in Boston as he poured some wine for himself and his beautiful wife, Annini. She looked tired, but he said nothing. A stay-at-home mom much of her life, Annini started to write children's books when they lived in the UK. Back then, Giovanni assumed this was just something to do, a way to pass time. But her books became quite popular, and now, twenty-seven books and a children's weekend morning cartoon later, she was making considerably more money than he.

He had just returned from a trip to Venice as part of his job with an insurance company based in London. Giovanni brought his glass of Damilano Barolo Cannubi 2010 to his nose. This exceptional wine from the village of Barolo in the Piedmont region was made of rare old vine Nebbiolo grapes, which over time changed to an almost brick-orange color.

"It is good to be home, my love," he told Annini, as he smelled the exotic blend and lowered his glass toward a toast.

11

"It is always good to have you home," Annini replied as she clicked her glass to his, "but I have fun when you're away." She smiled and lowered her eyes.

"Fun working, you mean. I wonder how our special girl is doing."

Sara was the pride of her parents, especially her dad. In her awkward teen years, Sara was very tall, very skinny, and loved school. This made her a target of harassment at school, and he began to call Sara his special girl. He said it to make her feel special and, while still true, it was more of an endearment now.

"She is no doubt wondering how to pay for school because her father buys such expensive wine," Annini added, still smiling.

Giovanni looked down and laughed. "I seriously doubt she is thinking any such thing, although perhaps her mother is. My guess is she is preoccupied with her upcoming exams. When we last spoke, she seemed unnaturally nervous."

"It is understandable. This preliminary exam must be passed for her to move forward."

He nodded and took another sip. They sat silent for several minutes before Annini said softly, "My love, I need to lie down. Don't be alarmed, I am fine, only tired." She walked slowly to their bedroom.

Giovanni thought of Annini's cancer and their decision to keep this from Sara. Although he felt it was the right decision, he hoped that when the time came to tell her, she would see it that way. He also reminded himself again that he had to be strong and believe that his beloved Annini would be fine in the end. Taking another sip of wine, he again thought of his Sara, hoping she was having a great day.

Four thousand miles away, Sara was walking back toward her office from the physics and plasma building where she had just briefly met with Dr. Adrian Zimbrean, her thesis chair. She felt a rush of energy come through her. She didn't stop, just smiled, and knew her mom and dad were thinking of her.

Doctorial efforts have differing requirements based on the field of study. In Sara's case, MIT required choosing a thesis chair, creating a thesis committee, submitting a plan of study, and two years of coursework, all of which Sara had completed. What remained was her preliminary examination or "prelim," research and experiments, the completion of her doctoral dissertation and finally, an oral defense of that dissertation to her committee. This was the first day of Sara's prelim.

The preliminary examination was the committee's way of determining if Sara was adequately prepared to start research and experimentation on her thesis. It was also a rite of passage. If she passed, she would move forward, but if she failed, there was no next step until she passed.

Sara's field of study was electromagnetism, and her thesis was on beamed energy, or more directly, the ability to use powerful microwave beams to move objects in space from earth. She had sent her committee a reading list based on this, and in the folder she was now holding were the questions each had submitted and given to her shortly before by Dr. Zimbrean.

Backpack in hand, she nervously entered her small compact office and closed the door as she flipped a small sign she imprinted with, *Please Do Not Disturb.* As she sat, she slowly used a breathing technique to calm herself and glanced at the clock. It was now just after 4:00 p.m. Friday and she had until end of business on Monday to complete the "open book" answers. Intending to do most of the work here, away from distractions, she had stockpiled a small assortment of foods, canned drinks. She even included a bottle of wine and finally gathered the courage to open the folder.

Her committee had not minced words regarding the challenge of the questions. There were no easy ones, as they were all related to her ability to prove or disprove her theory. One even asked, "Why are you choosing this as your thesis?" Her immediate thought was, *great, just great!*

She anxiously reached for her water flask without looking and promptly knocked it over. Water immediately spilled everywhere as she panicked and grabbed the folder, just seconds before it would have been ruined. "Come on, Sara, get your shit together!" she yelled to herself. "It's just a test."

Despite the rocky start, Friday evening quickly became Saturday. She carefully, but methodically, considered her responses. Becoming more confident, Saturday flowed even faster into Sunday as she wrote the obligatory response to each question. By Monday morning she had completed all the responses, pledging herself to proofread the essays for the rest of the day to assure this was her best work.

Satisfied, she scheduled an appointment with Dr. Zimbrean at 4:20 p.m., his last appointment of the day, before uploading the paper into her student portal.

Romanian born, Dr. Adrian Zimbrean, was tall and lean, with an unassuming appearance that suited him given his preference to blend in and not be noticed. Although some thought of him as aloof, Sara knew he was renowned for his prior work in electromagnetics and could help her in ways others could not. He had a way of guiding her with a modicum of words.

As she walked into the foyer to his office, his assistant Maggie Zimmer wasn't there, so went to his open door. She chuckled at the sight. There he sat, deep in thought surrounded by clutter as every conceivable void in the room was filled with books or stacks of papers.

As she coughed to get his attention, he looked up. "Ah, Sara, it is good to see you looking refreshed. Come in, come in."

She forced a smile, trying to hide how exhausted she really was as she handed him the bound version of her answers as a formality. "I have been preparing for this day for close to a year and accept the possibility that I might not pass. But I trust you and my committee and will learn from your judgment. Thank for your time and I look forward to hearing from you."

He smiled, knowing the robotic and practiced comment was a sign of her nervousness. "Sara, when we have reached a conclusion, I will summon you to this office, or perhaps just call. For now, rest after a job well done, and we will talk again in three to four weeks." He reached out his hand, which Sara shook, signaling that the meeting was over.

As she walked back toward home for some much-needed sleep, her cell phone buzzed, and she reached into her dated and worn hobo bag, pulling out her phone. On the screen was a new text from her roommate, Lisa Payne: "Sara, sitting here in the pub and just saw you walk by. Done with your prelim? Want a drink before heading home?" Lisa was a first-year master's student in geology, and she and Sara had been housemates for the last two years.

Having just passed Ashdown House, one of the many graduate residences on campus she decided she deserved it, and turned as she texted her back: "Pretty wiped, but that would be great. See you in a few minutes. Thx."

Sara turned around and walked back to the building before she headed towards the back where the Thirsty Ear Pub was located. Walking into the pub, she saw Lisa waving next to an empty seat and after a quick hello, they both sat and got the attention of a server. They both ordered a red wine and talked about small stuff before Lisa asked, "So how was it, really?"

Sara thought to say it was no big deal, but Lisa was a great sounding board, so she opened up a bit saying, "Emotional."

"Wow, that is the last response I would have expected from you, robot girl." She laughed as she regularly teased Sara about her stoic mannerisms under stress.

"Hilarious. No, seriously. Unlike a normal test where I can make up for any error in a subsequent effort, my fate is now entirely in the hands of the committee. To pass the test and move forward, I need all of them to grant me meets or exceeds expectation. If just one doesn't, I'll have to retake that part of the test a second time, and the next test isn't until March putting my program on hold for six months. I'm just not used to being this vulnerable."

"What's your gut say?"

She responded instantly. "Nailed four, missed one." She took a sip of her wine. "I can't possibly know what they know with a combined hundred-twenty-five years of knowledge among them, so I could only answer from my few years of study. I just hope they trust me enough to let me move forward."

Lisa looked up, smiled, and said with confidence, "I'm sure you'll do fine."

The conversation changed to the weather and to Lisa's upcoming off-campus project that would take her into the field in Arizona for two months. Sara was jealous, as she really disliked the upcoming Boston weather. Finishing her wine, she rose to leave. "Lisa, are you staying or going home?"

"I'm going to stay for a bit and see if any cute guys arrive."

"Got it. Thanks for the wine and words of encouragement. I needed both." With that, she turned to walk home to get some needed rest.

3

MIT Campus, Boston

Sara entered her small office two weeks later and as she sat down, she hit play on her ancient MP3 player. As the sound of *Chasing the Dragon* by the Dutch band Epica filled the small space, she reached for a stack of applications from master's students who had applied for her research assistant position. To complete her research phase, she was going to need help.

Having given all applicants a quick read, she surmised that anyone at MIT was likely to be to the right of the bell curve intellectually. Instead, she focused more on candidates she could work with and had separated the applications into two stacks; those who seemed worthy of a face-to-face interview, and everyone else. So far, she wasn't comfortable with anyone she had interviewed, but in a few minutes; she was going to meet with Nathen Chase, a first-year master's student she had worked with a few times in the past and had even taught at one point the year before. She pulled out his application, resume, and a short bio from the university.

Nathen was twenty-five and had been born in the Philippines to American dad Richard Chase and Filipina mom, Darna Bautista. Dad had been a Navy Seal and returned to the United States with Nathen following his honorable discharge. They settled in Kalispell, Montana, but mom had stayed in the Philippines.

As she looked at Nathen's hobbies, most involved the outdoors. He was an avid hunter, biker, hiker, and runner, so clearly, he was the athletic type. As she read on, she chuckled as Nathen apparently had a partial football scholarship for his undergraduate. Sara knew little of American football and wasn't even sure if MIT had a football team, but apparently they did.

She also didn't know that he had first applied for geology, but his major was changed quickly in his freshman year to earth, atmospheric, and planetary sciences. She made a note, wanting to understand the reason for the change, when her thoughts were disrupted by a powerful double knock at the door. "Come in."

Nathen's frame filled the doorway, and she forgot how tall he was. She glanced quickly at the attractiveness of his blended features and put down his application.

"Hi, Nathen, good to see you again. Please come in and sit down."

He did, and she continued. "We know each other somewhat, but for the sake of process, we'll talk for a few minutes and then head to the lab. Sound okay?"

He replied in a friendly but monotone voice. "Sure, that is fine."

"Nathen you have obvious skill as a student, but might I ask, what made you change your major from geology to earth, atmospheric, and planetary sciences the first year of your undergrad studies?"

"Ms. Ricci..."

She immediately stopped him. "Please, it just Sara."

"Sara it is. Although I had a partial scholarship, I chose geology because it was my best chance of getting accepted. I love the outdoors and thought that geology would allow me a lot of outside lab time. Once I got here, the exposure to so many really smart people made me realize my interests went deeper. My advisor suggested earth, atmospheric, and planetary sciences to prepare for geophysics. It's a lot harder for me, but I have no regrets."

"I noticed that when your father left the military, you moved back to the United States. Do you recall much about the Philippines?"

"Sure. I was only four or five when we left, but we've gone back several times, and I still talk to my mom now and again. It's nice there, but there's no comparison to Montana."

"Is your mother a scientist?"

He glanced up surprised, "Yes, as a matter of fact. She is a biologist and works for Petron Corporation on biological solutions to oil spills and cleanup. She's quite the free spirit and she and my dad still have a thing for each other even though they are rarely together. What made you ask about my mom?"

"I only asked because your interest in science wasn't entirely explained by your father's career. What are the reasons you're interested in my assistant position?"

"Although I have some financial support, I come from a place with beauty that money can't buy, but here in Boston, I can't even afford ugly. So, the first reason is I need some spending money." That caused Sara to laugh, as it really was expensive here.

"Sorry, that was funny. Please go on."

"The second reason is harder for me to admit, but... I kind of need a mentor." He paused for a moment and then continued after easing forward in his chair. "Sara, my guess is you have always been smart, probably at the top of your class, and probably haven't really had to work for it. Your brain is just wired SMART. As I work on my master's, I constantly have to push my knowledge base, but unlike you, I can't do that just because I want to. I need to be around those that can help me see through the fog. In the few times we have worked together, I was impressed by how quickly you can make complex things so understandable. I guess I need that and thought this would be a win-win for me."

"Well, thanks, and while I disagree this is easy for me, I understand how unique minds work at different speeds and how working with others can help immensely. To be honest, Nathan, I have some concern. Arguably, my thesis might be relational to your current knowledge, but it could also overwhelm you."

If Nathen felt any insecurity, it wasn't obvious. "As I understand it, I am helping you setup experiments and didn't think I needed to be at your level intellectually. If I missed something, then you are correct. I have wasted your time." He rose, which made Sara feel she had been too direct.

"Nathen, a doctoral program at MIT is a giant leap forward for anyone, including me, so I need help, too. All I'm saying is I can't spend lots of time educating you on the basics. You understand what I am trying to say, right?"

Nathen, still standing, looked at Sara and then sat down. "I would never hinder your progress. How about this? Try me for a month without pay, and if I don't work out, I'll leave happy because I got to work with you, and you didn't have to spend a dime."

She laughed. "That is unnecessary, but tell you what; let's go to the lab."

As they left the office and rounded the corner, Nadia Sadir, a freelance journalist for the MIT weekly newsletter, came within inches of running right into Sara. Nadia and Sara knew of each other, but had never become friends. It was even safe to say they really didn't care for one another.

Nadia froze as they came body to body and almost smacked heads. "What the hell, Sara. You almost ran right into me!" As she locked eyes on Sara, she glanced over at Nathen and then smiled.

Nathen looked down. "Hi Nadia, sorry we were heading out to the lab. Didn't mean to startle you."

"Oh Nathen, hi, how are you?" Nadia replied in a sugary voice. "You were fine, by the way. It was Sara here who was in my lane; obviously, she hasn't adjusted to American traffic direction."

"Nadia, always good to see you," Sara responded, "and to the uninformed, Italians drive on the same side as Americans, only faster." As she walked away, she said over her shoulder, "Nathen, let's go. We still have a lot of ground to cover."

He went after her waving goodbye to Nadia who watched them leave, thinking to herself, *why is he with her?*

Once they finished going through the public areas of the magnetics and fusion centers, Sara was actually impressed. Despite only one semester into his masters, he had obviously spent a great deal of time in the lab. She turned to him as they were leaving, "Nathen, I'll call you in a few weeks since by then, I'll know if I passed my Prelim. Obviously, if I didn't pass, I won't really need an assistant."

He turned and laughed. "I know you'll pass, and it would be an honor to work with you. Talk to you next week."

Thursday morning Sara eased into her normal routine of a quick run, a quick shower, limited make up, and comfy clothes. She said goodbye to Lisa and walked with purpose to the Mud Room, a small but unique coffeehouse on the corner that really knew how to make un-American coffee.

To be fair, when it comes to coffee, the drip variety popular in America does not really exist in the less tourist centric areas of Italy. The closest equivalent is the Americano, which was created for US servicemen during WWII, and, big surprise, most Italians don't drink Americanos. The heartbeat of all Italian coffee drinks is an espresso shot and in Italy, it is simply called "*un caffè*" or a coffee. *Espresso* in Italian means "fast," so the basic translation of an espresso is a fast coffee. The Mud Room does this very well, and today Sara needed a double.

The barista that day was a student at Boston University, and she could only assume he thought of himself as quite a flirt since he went out of his way to talk to her.

He looked up, saw her, and smiled. "The usual, Professor?"

"Once again, I'm not a professor. I'm a PhD student, and yes, please."

"And what is it you study again? It's like laser beams, right?"

"No." She shook her head at yet another attempt to describe her work to him. "I'm studying the ability to send microwaves into space to move objects there, using an onboard receiver that can capture the beams from earth."

"Right! Well, we have a microwave here. Have a seat and I'll 'beam' your expresso to you," as he laughed. Sara simply rolled her eyes and moved over to the pickup line, too tired to explain.

When she had finished her cup, she headed off to campus and was barely there when her phone buzzed, and, glancing at the caller ID, she saw it was Zimbrean. Shit. She paused before taking the call. She took a deep breath and answered.

"Sara, I hope you have a minute," and without waiting he went on, "This call would usually begin a week or more from now, but yours was an interesting review. As you know, you received five questions instead of four because I submitted one myself. You did well on the others with one score of meeting requirements and three scores of exceeding requirements. It was the fifth question where you stumbled and because of that, I'm hesitant."

She said nothing, so he continued. "Sara, these storied halls have seen some gifted scientists, and knowing a few of them, they usually fall into three categories: lucky, gifted, and remarkable. I exalt you and believe you are gifted, but you could be remarkable. The problem from a purely physics point of view, is that you hold yourself back—always choosing easier paths."

Sara absorbed his words as he continued, "My question was trying to test your ambitions and frankly you did not meet *my* expectation. The dilemma I face is that holding you back will not likely change your response. There is something inside you that gives you pause, an unwillingness to reach the point of potential failure. I can only imagine that you, possibly self conscientiously, pursue topics you already know you can do. I think you need to stretch the boundaries of your thinking in order to achieve your real potential."

He paused again for the words to be absorbed before finishing. "Given that I have no idea when, or if that might happen, I have hedged my bet and passed you, with the understanding between us, that I expect more from you. I will send you the written responses and please read them and take time with each member of your committee to understand any comments or concerns. Do you have questions for me, Sara?"

Sara sat holding the phone still processing the conversation, when he said, "Sara, are you there?"

She snapped out of it. "Yes, of course, Dr. Zimbrean. I was just processing your words and no, I do not have questions." She stopped to breathe, which he mistook for her being done.

"Well, if that is all…"

"I thank you and the committee for your support," Sara said quickly, "and I hope we can meet to expand on your concerns." She paused before adding, "To your earlier comment, I think you would be surprised, Dr. Zimbrean, to discover how many remarkable people got that way because they were also lucky."

He chuckled, saying nothing as he hung up. He liked that about her. She was spunky. On the other end of the call, Sara, satisfied with her response, smiled and immediately called her parents. She had passed!

4

Isle of Skye, Scotland

Maximillian Drummond looked out of the large windows of his impressive residence on the Isle of Skye in the northwest of Scotland. On this second largest island after Lewis and Harris, the grandness of the Scottish Highlands met the formidable Atlantic Ocean. The result was dangerous beauty, and the exact reason he built his residence and private offices there.

Although far from his company's main campus on the grounds of Gatwick airport near Crawley, West Sussex, England, Maximillian found he could run his corporation from the Isle of Skye most of the time. For his private business, he had built a small company on the lower floor, almost entirely into the bedrock, and then built a residence on top of it. From the highway looking toward the ocean, only the large single-story residence could be seen. Only from the ocean one could see the glass offices of the private company below.

He watched the seas, which were positively wild now, and glanced over at Angus Adair, his short, stocky, and absolutely brilliant senior analyst.

Maximillian had at his disposal both legitimate research teams and covert research teams. The legitimate team stayed within the laws of Scotland and the host location on intelligence, collecting public information on topics Maximillian thought important. The covert team, led by Angus, had free rein to hack any source and even use his private security team to obtain insider information and secrets.

"What do you have for me?" Maximillian asked.

"Sir, we peeked into the MIT server for doctoral students but found very little," Angus replied. "There was a recent addition by a young lassie named Sara Ricci. She has submitted a plan of study for her PhD, and although she has not yet prepared a final research question, she has a great deal of interest in beamed energy."

"And why is this important?"

"The name might have escaped you, sir, but she is related to the 1930s era scientist, Gilberti Ricci. According to our research, this topic could refer to what he was secretly working on when Nazi Command demanded Gilberti work for them on a weapon of some sort at the beginning of WWII. He was subsequently killed, supposedly by the Nazi's, but his personal research papers were never found. Given the Germans' interest, I would conclude he was working on a weapon of mass destruction."

Maximillian smiled. "Interesting, but what does this have to do with her?"

"Perhaps nothing. But all families have secrets and perhaps she has access to his research."

"Yes, that is possible. Continue to monitor her work periodically. Is that all?"

"Yes sir. As I said, not much."

Angus rose and took his leave as Maximillian smiled, thinking of the high-level contact he now had in place at the Defense Advanced Research Projects Agency or DARPA in the United States. Perhaps they could find out more regarding this young scientist. If it was a weapon, they would know.

Maximilian, who never went by the abbreviation "Max," was born in Edinburgh, Scotland, in the summer of 1954, a year of considerable rain and limited sunshine, perhaps explaining his love for dark, stormy weather. His parents, Malcolm, and Alana had one older son Blaney, and daughter, Innis. After Maximillian's birth, they had another daughter, Bridget, who was still alive, although Innis and Blaney had since passed on. Innis to cancer and Blaney from an industrial accident.

As a child, Maximilian was an exceptional student, far above his classmates and more often than not, his educators. Although parents Malcolm and Alana were both self-taught, they insisted Maximillian attend university, and he quickly received his undergraduate in mathematics from the University of Edinburgh. The following year, he was accepted to the Department of Metallurgy and Science of Materials at Oxford.

Malcolm had been immensely proud to have a son at Oxford, and used it to justify Maximillian's many quirks. Considering Scottish law, which usually considered the oldest son, his successor, Malcolm viewed Maximillian in this role more than the eldest, Blaney. He also saw the Oxford pedigree as a means to raise additional capital, all of which perplexed him when Maximillian left his studies after just one year, saying that he was bored. It made absolutely no sense.

The family business was the brainchild of Malcolm as founder and managing director of the Malcolm Ridge Engineering Co., LTD., a small textile machinery company in Leith, northeast of Edinburgh. Malcolm had taken over the company when the owner died suddenly with no living relatives. Then, the company only repaired textile machines. Being a self-taught engineer, Malcolm quickly designed and built a small family of machines with special attention to solving the design failures of machines by others that they often repaired. Once complete, they sold their new robust machines under the rebranded company.

On his sudden departure from Oxford, Malcom urged Maximillian to join the family business, but Maximillian refused, the implication being the company was not worthy of him. Malcolm was utterly shocked, as his son had never suggested the company was something that he was not proud of, but Malcom saw this as a slap in the face. This was his life's work and he and Maximillian slowly became estranged from each other. In fact, only Bridget would talk to him outside of holidays.

Never one to look in the rear-view mirror, Maximillian was seemingly unaffected and found early financial success in product development and strategy within energy related multinationals in the North Sea. He would often consider bold ideas and vision that the managing directors and boards never would have imagined.

Back home in Leith, Malcolm was quietly proud of his son's success but had difficulty accepting that he could work seamlessly for people he didn't know but would not help his own father. In truth, Malcolm erroneously viewed Maximillian as an engineer. He wasn't. He was a mathematical genius with a fondness for strategy and finance.

This conflict came to a head in 1982 when both parents died in a plane crash, and company bylaws placed Blaney in charge of the company.

Blaney had an excellent engineering mind and was quite capable with his hands but was entirely out of his depth in finance and leadership. To his credit, Blaney quickly met with Maximillian minutes after the funeral and begged him to come into the business, but Maximillian politely refused once again. Believing there would be too much conflict between them, he suggested Bridget be hired on to help. She had worked in the company off and on for many years and was savvy in business, some would even say, ruthless.

Together, Blaney and Bridget made the best of the company, but textiles were becoming a dying art form. Even tourist dependent Scottish clothing manufacturers often imported much of the overall materials from Asia. That caused the number of machines needed to produce cloth to shrink every year. And it didn't help that the Malcolm Ridge machines simply never broke down, so replacement machines and lucrative spare parts were the smallest subset of their falling annual turnover.

Six years had passed since Blaney had taken over the company, and things would soon change significantly. It was a balmy evening in May 1988, when Maximillian arrived at the factory works one night to walk the grounds and feel his father's presence. It was difficult for Maximillian to accept that others felt he had treated his father poorly in life. Just because he had not wanted to attend Oxford, or work in the family business, never meant he didn't love his father. He simply couldn't understand why others construed his behavior toward him as disdain or disrespect.

Entering the grounds that night, he could feel his father's presence, but it was quickly interrupted by a sound to his left and as he turned, he noticed one outbuilding was lit; someone was working late.

His first thought was to leave as someone there all but ruined his reason for coming, but he was curious. Instead, he walked to the building and through the window saw his older brother, Blaney, in heavy work clothes, operating an enormous press. He decided to say hello and walked around to the entrance door.

As he entered, he said, "Working late, Blaney?" but there was no acknowledgment, so he said again, closer now, "Working late Blaney?" but again there was no acknowledgment. He noticed Blaney had wax in his ears for sound protection. He stood silent until at last Blaney looked up startled, saw him, and stopped the machine.

"Fancy seeing you, brother," he said as he pulled out the earplugs and withdrew the heavy steel shape.

"Just stopped by to say hello to Dad. I do that from time to time, but don't rationally understand why. He is dead and certainly not here."

Blaney paused, surprised his brother had momentarily sounded human, but decided he was not much interested. "Well, I have a deadline on this piece. It's due to ship in just three weeks, so enjoy your walkabout, and please let yourself out." He and his brother had never been close.

As Blaney went to place the wax back in his ears, Maximillian noticed the guards on the press were unattached and asked Blaney, "I thought you couldn't run the press with the guards down."

Blaney looked at him annoyed, "We have to remove them for these large parts because otherwise you cannot affect the side of the yoke. This part must be turned several times and we don't have a press that allows that, but this one is large enough if we have a larger area to work in. We put them back on afterwards."

Maximilian understood, thinking to himself, *Blaney would never consider buying the right machine for the job.* He waved to Blaney to continue as he walked away, looking at the various stages of the building process. All were unchanged from his childhood and there did not appear to be rhyme or reason to the layout of the works relative to the logical sequence one might employ to build a complex device. He paused for a few seconds and eventually walked back toward Blaney. He really could sense his dad now and knew he wasn't happy with the current state of the factory works. As Maximillian walked toward the press, he was now directly behind Blaney. Not premeditated, he simply pushed Blaney him forward into the machine as the enormous press head came down. There was a muted yell followed by a sickening crunch and then silence as the press ended its cycle and rose back up to its stop.

Maximillian looked down at the nearly headless remains of his brother and then up and around the works, as if he wasn't sure what to do next. Putting his hands in his pockets, he just walked out the door and headed to his car, thinking, *you were right, Dad. Nothing has changed, no innovation or productivity improvements at all. Bridget and I will fix this, I promise!*

In line with Scottish law, Maximillian inherited the business on Blaney's death, which was ruled an accident. It was rumored he had considered selling, but he saw an entirely different version of the company. With his sister, Bridget, MDE Enterprises, was created and taken public ten years later. The former textile machinery company in Leith was now a major industrial conglomerate.

The holdings of MDE Enterprises comprised MDE Aerospace in London, which manufactured drones, small aircraft, and parts for commercial aircraft. On the same grounds was a related company, MDE Defense, who manufactured military drones and tactical systems for weapons, including launch devices, stealth capabilities and systems that connected electronic weaponry. MDE Commodities mined exotic rare earth metals from a boutique mine in Madagascar, and a mine off the coast of Antarctica. The newest company was MDE Trust, a company in Edinburgh, Scotland, that designed and protected electronic components and infrastructure within companies to avoid service interruption and damage from electronic spikes and electromagnetic pulses. It had been one of Maximillian's private companies but was folded into the public company just six months prior.

Each company was an extension of the others, and Maximillian and Bridget owned thirty-nine percent of the company stock, with an estimated net worth of just under six billion euros. They also had a controlling interest in an additional eleven percent, which was held by a family trust and key employees. Money was clearly not one of the Drummond's concerns.

5

Giovanni looked at his wife, Annini, after hanging up with an exuberant Sara who had just told them over the speakerphone about passing her preliminary exam thus receiving her the much-needed post-prelim status. They were melancholy, however, as her research and dissertation would last two years or more. At some point, they would have to tell her about Annini's cancer, which had been diagnosed three months earlier and based on the tumor size, was moving towards the dreaded fourth stage.

Annini spoke first. "I know we keep waiting for a good time to tell her, but at every turn, her pace speeds up, and I fear a good time may never come. I am being optimistic, Giovanni, but I must see my daughter before the end."

"Let's not discuss the end. That is in God's hand. Of course, I understand, and while I cannot swallow your stoic resolve, I would be devastated further if you couldn't see her. Let her define her research methods, and we'll tell her before she formally starts her research phase. Agreed?"

"Yes. Let's have a delicious glass of your expensive wine." Annini forced a smile.

Sara had just finished preparing for the next day's undergrad lessons when she called Nathen. She appreciated his ability to think forward, and he seemed to get her, something Sara did not encounter often, especially from men.

The phone rang but Nathen did not answer. Seconds later, an automated text appeared on Sara's phone: "In the lab and will call back soon." Cell phones were not allowed in certain labs, so she understood.

Her cell rang twenty minutes later, and it was Nathen. "Hey Sara, how are things? Any news?"

Having had few people to talk to about the good news, she responded excitedly, "Yes. That's why I'm calling. I passed; can you believe it? My chair posed the impossible question, and he only reluctantly moved his vote to acceptable so I could pass. I have some work to do to please him, but he just wants me to challenge myself. I'm looking forward to getting the actual written appraisals so I can see the strengths and weaknesses."

Almost rambling now, she continued, without allowing him a chance to respond, "And if you're still interested, I very much need an assistant. You seem to be a quick study and understand me, which is refreshing; most people don't. Anyway, this is my way of saying you would be great, so can we meet to discuss?"

Nathen chuckled at her rare, animated tone. "I knew you would pass, and I'm thrilled for you. I can meet after 6 p.m. today. How about the pub?"

"That sounds great. I'll see you there."

"Now that I have a job, the first drink is on me," Nathen replied, laughing.

Sara was seated in her small, highly organized office as she pulled up the appointment calendar on her tablet, intending to plan the next few weeks. There was a knock on her door, and the handle jiggled clockwise as the door opened. She had seen the man who walked around before, but didn't actually know him. He was attractive in a rugged way, and she didn't think he was a student. He was older, perhaps he was with security, she thought.

"Excuse me, but I thought it made sense to introduce myself, as we might have interactions in the future. I'm Jason Sykes, the DARPA liaison here at MIT." He held out his hand.

Shaking his hand, she said, "DARPA, as in the United States Government's Defense Advanced Research Projects Agency?"

"Yes, Ms. Ricci."

She immediately stopped him. "Please, it is just Sara."

"All right, fine, Sara. I wasn't sure if you knew of it, but given your field of study, I guess that makes sense. Anyway, I live in Virginia, but spend almost all my time here at Harvard or MIT."

"Ah, so you are a fellow scientist?" Sara asked.

"No, not actually. I have my MS in Materials Science and spend considerable personal time in nanotechnology as a hobby. After completing officer training in the Army, I spent time in Iraq and Afghanistan before getting involved in a project with DARPA. I have been working with them since my honorable discharge."

"Well, I know little of your army, but how does one follow DARPA projects at two of the top schools in the world if you don't yourself understand the science?"

"Sara, you might have misunderstood my role. I am not following the projects; I am following the scientists."

Skeptically, Sara looked at him. "I don't understand this."

"Sara, many of these projects are secret, which can expose scientists to various forms of espionage and unwanted contacts from bad actors of foreign governments and corporations. I'm here to protect them to assure they are unharmed and not attracted to these influences. If they are, I can bring in support to neutralize such problems."

"Such things never occurred to me, but this makes sense." She smiled and then frowned. "But what does this have to do with me?"

"Well, nothing at this moment. This is just an introduction, but I work closely with the campus security and several weeks ago, one of their graduate program servers was hacked. Even at MIT this happens from time to time, and the perpetrators used an embedded search engine to seek keywords which led them to your files, files they may have copied. While I understand you have not yet entered your research phase, we became concerned simply based on the attempt."

"Why am I just hearing this now? Why didn't someone say something to me?" Sara barked, surprised and feeling violated.

"Well, to be honest, it took a while for the MIT cyber security team to understand they had been hacked. Then they had to notify the university administration which opened other concerns and you're finding out within just a few days of that. Just know that I have your back and you should meet Myeong Yoon of the MIT cyber security team to discuss your file security protocols."

He stood now as if to leave and handed her a business card. "Sara, there is no reason for alarm, but here is my contact info and if you sense anything or even feel something is off, call me. That's what I'm here for."

She stood and looked over at him holding the card and said, "Thank you and I'll treat this seriously, but I just never imagined having to worry about such things." She reached out to shake his hand, which he firmly reciprocated, and exited her office.

Outside the building, Jason pulled out his cell phone and dialed his boss, Ralf Müller, the Assistant Director, Microsystems Technology Office at DARPA. He needed to give him a heads up on some pressing projects and he mentioned the hack into Sara's work in part because it was simply on his mind.

6

The Defense Advanced Research Projects Agency (DARPA) was created in 1957 following the Russians Sputnik satellite program. It had caught the United States government off guard and they vowed never again to be surprised and more to the point, never to be in second place in advanced technologies. Their present mission was to develop breakthrough technologies for Department of Defense (DOD) capabilities within their six mission-focused departments.

At their headquarters in Arlington, Virginia, Ralf Müller and five other Assistant Directors sat around a large conference table, as each went through their weekly updates of projects. Ralf himself was in charge of the systems side of intelligent micro-systems and components for a variety of end uses, among them: electronic warfare, directed energy, and advanced reconnaissance.

He had just finished his prepared presentation when he added in closing, "A few weeks back I mentioned a possible revisit to a former project involving beamed energy in the upper reaches of the atmosphere. A doctoral candidate at MIT that I was interested in, is considering such research, but was hacked three weeks ago. According to my source, the people responsible targeted doctoral files looking for keywords, Atmospheric, Beamed and Energy. They have no idea what if anything was removed or copied, but they are looking into it? Until I know more, I simply find the timing of my interest and the hack troubling. Unless there are questions, that completes my update."

Ralf was preparing to sit when to his right, Dr. Bernard Cummings, his equal over Tactical Technology said, "A hack at MIT?"

Ralf replied as he walked to sit down. "Yes, strange, but in a world of smart people, institutions get constant threats to the tune of thousands per day, of which, even at MIT, I guess, a few get through. This one was masked as a power fluctuation, but that is all I know."

"Do they know who did this? Have they been able to trace it back to any specific region? Do we have some idea who we're dealing with?"

Perplexed at the exchange, he replied, "Dr. Cummings, I have no idea, and this is their problem, not ours, as this scientist is not under grant to us. I brought it up only because I registered an interest, and there was a hack at almost the same time, on the same student, and on the very nature of research that perked my interest."

"Well," continued Bernard, "I think you should have Sykes get deeper into this to see what can be uncovered. I find this troubling."

"Yes, so do I. That's why I brought it up," he said as he sat down thinking, *that was really strange; why would he even care?*

A few days later, Jason and Sara sat with Myeong Yoon in the MIT cyber security office trying to find out what, if anything MIT knew about the hack itself? As they entered, Jason introduced Sara, and they sat next to Myeong's computer desk.

Jason took the lead. "Myeong, has your team been able to trace back anything on the doctoral server hack last month?"

Myeong spoke good English, but you had to pay attention as she answered, "Very good bad guys. They covered themselves well and leave no trace. If they come in again and use the same method, we have a spider that will attach itself to them and, if not swept off on their end, it will tell us more."

"So, this same team, same method has not been seen before?" Jason replied.

"No."

Sara asked, "Myeong, what can I do, or should I do to protect myself and my research?"

"Miss Sara there is not much for you. We don't know who this was, and it is just lucky your information matched the search request. Is this the correct word, Lucky? No, I do not think this is about you. Your work is not part of secret programs and you just passed exams, so not yet a big fish. You understand, yes?"

"Yeah, I got it. I'm a nobody, but thanks for your time," Sara replied as they both got up and walked out laughing, as Myeong sat wondering what she had said that was so funny.

Back in her office, Sara was reviewing her class notes for the following day and, once done, she turned on her MP3 player to *Lost in Paradise* by Evanescence. The old iPod was no longer supported by its manufacturer, but she kept it for two reasons. First, her mother had given it to her a few years into her undergraduate effort. When she turned it on, it reminded her of how excited she had been and the resulting smile on her mom's face. It was almost uncanny that it brought back that image every time she turned it on, and she cherished that. The second reason was far more pragmatic. Despite newer alternatives, replicating her extensive library of five-thousand-plus songs was a luxury of time she no longer had.

Settling in, she began to review literature related to her thesis, Beamed Energy. Drinking some water, she numbly looked through the countless headings, clicking on those that interested her, when suddenly, her eyes froze, and a look of concern spread across her face.

Sara's thesis was looking into microwaves beamed from earth to space to move objects that had been outfitted with a receiver that could receive the beam. This concept was not new, and conceptually it worked, although most of the energy was lost because of the vast distance the beam had to travel. Most satellites operated in the low earth orbit, or about one-hundred-eighty miles above earth. The reason the beam lost much of the energy was that the microwaves scattered and crisscrossed each other over that distance.

Sara had predicted those losses could be improved if the beam were collimated. A fancy word that simply meant that if those same microwaves were sent through a lens or collimator, the waves would exit parallel to each other, not crossing each other. In theory, this might solve the distance problem.

As she read on, however, it appeared two researchers at Tsinghua University in China had just dispelled this. They were experimenting with far-field or radioactive region transfers using a microwave beam, which they had collimated to avoid losses. Based on their math, however, they had concluded the collection systems still needed to be massive and that large energy losses would still exist. They even said the losses likely meant this was not economically viable. Unlike others, they had used a collimated beam, but got the same result.

Sara called Nathen and left a message briefly explaining the issue and asked if they could meet the following day. Within a few minutes, Nathen called, "Sara, what the heck, somebody beat you to it?"

She replied, "Well, perhaps. Using beaming microwaves is far from groundbreaking, but a modern paper that arrives at the same conclusion as the past, but with a collimated beam, means back to the beginning for me. I need to test the math and assumptions used to determine if this is the same as I intended."

"Okay, do you want to start now or wait until tomorrow?"

"I don't mean to drag you away at a moment's notice, but now would be great. I'll never be able to sleep until I understand this, and we might even call the Tsinghua team if we start early."

"Not a problem. I'll bring a few munchies to bide us over. See you in thirty minutes," he said as he hung up the phone, packed up and headed to her office.

Once he arrived, they reviewed the math and concluded that the paper was well done, but it contained several assumptions, some of which were vague. Sara had texted the two researchers and luckily one texted back and said he could talk to them at 8:00 a.m. his time or 8:00 p.m. in Boston, which was less than an hour away. When the time came, Sara setup a web call and after twenty minutes of discussion, she considered their approach and math solid. While not an absolute cancellation of her thesis, it was darn close, and she would have to tell Zimbrean.

Sara looked over at Nathen. "I wonder if Dr. Zimbrean will be at all surprised. Maybe he already knew this, and that prompted him to want me to move into bolder research."

"I don't think so, Sara. I think he wants you to invest yourself as a theorist instead of limiting yourself to applied physics."

Sara looked at him a bit surprised, but only said, "Perhaps. I'll find out tomorrow, but thanks for the help and have a good night." They both got up and walked out to a very empty hallway and went home.

Sara met with Zimbrean the next day in the late afternoon and explained the paper, although, as she predicted, he did not seem surprised.

"I was not aware of this particular research, although I am aware of the groundswell around these concepts. As I have mentioned before, Sara, you are capable of much more and, given that this new Chinese research places your original thesis in doubt, you can now reconsider. I'll leave you to that and look forward to seeing what you propose to the committee." He stood with a slight smile.

Sara thought his response was harsh but started back for the lab, thinking once again that Nathen appeared to be right. Dr.

Zimbrean wanted her to focus on larger and grander theories, and he had all but told her the original concept was dead. Discouraged, Sara headed home.

7

Packard's Corner, Boston

Over an expresso at the Mud Room at the end of the week, Sara was reviewing the online addition of the MIT newsletter when her eye caught an article from Nadia Sadir. She read through it, and immediately knew it was about her and glanced up to see if anyone was looking at her. Of course not, nobody seemed bothered. While never mentioned by name, this was about her lost thesis. The article suggested that an unnamed doctoral student would go back to the drawing board because she had done a poor job reviewing research literature in her field. That was grossly unfair, but clearly the lasting impression of the article. *Great,* thought Sara, *what the hell else could happen?*

As she left the Mud Room and headed up Essex Street to the bridge that would take her over the Charles River to MIT, her phone rang. It was her dad, and she answered, "Hi Dad, how are you? How's Mom?"

"Sara, are you in class?"

"No dad, I'm walking over to the lab now, but I have a long walk. You sound tired. Are you okay?"

"Sara, I am fine; this call is about your mom."

Alarmed by his tone, she said, "Dad,... what happened?"

"This is so difficult, my special girl, but your mom has cancer, stage three pancreatic cancer, and she wants to see you just in case."

Sara stopped walking and was now shaking and about to cry, "Dad, what do you mean just in case? How long has this been going on? Did she just find out?"

"Please, Sara, let's not concern ourselves with timing, but yes, we have known for a little while, but we're hesitant to concern you. Now seemed like a good time since you have not started your formal research. This is not a cancer that is easy to detect, and you know how much your mother hates doctors of any kind."

Although she could barely ask, she did anyway. "Dad, is this irreparable? Have they given her a prognosis?"

"They previously focused on the usual treatments which she took amazingly well and until recently, they had detected no growth in the number of cancer cells. But recently, they found additional tumors. We meet with them tomorrow and perhaps we'll learn more, but I am asking if you can plan to be here next week. I can wire you funds."

"Dad, I have money and God yes, I'll be there. I will finish up a few things here and then head to you straight away. Can I talk to her?"

"Of course, she is right here and eager to talk to you, but please be kind my special girl. This is all about her, yes?"

"Of course, Dad, I'm switching to FaceTime. I need to see her. Hold on." She clicked and her dad appeared briefly as he gave the phone to Annini. Her mom looked amazing as always, and it was difficult at first for Sara to take the diagnosis seriously, as she thought she might see it. They spoke for twenty-five minutes despite frozen video and an occasional drop in words,... all on the sidewalk of Essex Street: laughing, crying, and occasionally yelling as Italians do. Her mom was tiring, so they said their tearful goodbyes, and she handed the phone back to her dad, who did the same. When Sara finally pressed end to the call, she literally fell to her knees. Oblivious to those around her who might wonder what was happening, she slowly got up and went back to her house. Today, MIT would have to wait.

When Sara woke after a restless sleep, she had missed a call from Dr. Zimbrean, which she returned. He was not there, but Maggie, his assistant, asked if Sara could meet him at 9:00 a.m. the following morning and she agreed. The next morning came quickly, and still sluggish, she headed to his office; hurt, angry, and unsure of what to do. It was getting cold now and as she walked over the bridge, the chilly wind off the river with its frozen edges reminded her she had dressed poorly and was nearly freezing.

She walked up the stairs to Dr. Zimbrean's office and waited a few minutes until he concluded a call and invited her in. It was warm in his office and on seeing her, he immediately stood and motioned for her to sit and did so himself. "Sara, words cannot express our sympathies to you and your mother. I know little of such complex medical therapies and cannot make you feel better about her prognosis but as your chair, I feel compelled to offer some advice. It has been quite a journey for you this last month, given the ease of your coursework, but this is the most demanding phase of your program; a difficult time to have added stress."

"Dr. Zimbrean, I'm not going to fall apart," Sara said sharply.

"And I'm not implying that, Sara. Please, just listen to my words. Do not react to them. I am trying to tell you to use this trip away from MIT as a chance to reconnect to your doctorial journey. Take weeks, or even months, if that provides more clarity, and we will wait for you within generous reason. As I have spoken before; something might have to shake up that perfectly packaged image you have of yourself to reveal your true worth as a physicist and your revised thesis. Please travel safely."

Sara wasn't sure what to say, but thought she understood the message. He stood, and she thanked him for everything as she turned and left. In the foyer, Maggie was holding a tissue to her eyes and smiled as she nodded when Sara walked by, but said nothing.

8
Milan, Italy

The next two days passed slowly, and Sara had made no progress on her revised thesis, so she stopped trying. She packed, gave Lisa's cat a scratch, and an hour later was in an Uber bound for Boston Logan airport. Just before boarding, she sent a text to her dad saying she was about to leave, that she would see him soon and to give Mom her love. Restless most of the flight, she landed in Milan Malpensa airport the following morning. As she went downstairs to customs, she noted she had no cell reception but once she got to the taxi queue; she saw her dad had texted her: *"Pls call once you land."* She called immediately. "Hi Dad, I'm on my way to you."

A very despondent voice replied in almost a whisper, "Please tell the driver to come directly to the European Institute of Oncology on via Giuseppe Ripamoti. He'll know it. Come straight to room 6112." The call ended suddenly, which gave her cause for alarm.

Sara told the driver, who understood, and said they would be there in just a few minutes. Sara had not considered that her mom was in a hospital, but perhaps her father had called from there when they first spoke, although she hadn't heard the sounds of a hospital. But what did it matter? This was serious.

She paid the driver, who sensed her pain, and exited the taxi. She lifted her hobo bag on to her shoulder and pulled her small suitcase behind her. Inside the hospital, she stopped at the front desk to get her ID and went to room 6112. As she walked in, the room was empty; the bed undone with sheets ruffled, and her dad was sitting in a small and uncomfortable chair off to the right of the bed. He looked as if he had aged ten years since she had seen him just seven months before. She immediately stopped, rushed to him, and bent down to give him a hug. He stayed seated but held onto her for dear life.

Staying down at eye level to him, she asked, "Dad, where have they taken Mom?"

He looked up with eyes red and sullen from tears. "She is with our lord," he replied in barely a whisper, his eyes now returning to the ground.

Suddenly, the words registered. *Oh my God, Mom is gone.*

I never got to see her.

I never got to hug her.

We never got to say goodbye.

Sara collapsed on the floor to the background sound of her father yelling and a nurse rushing from the station across the hall.

9

Terrace Flat, Milan, Italy

Sitting with her dad in their modest terrace flat she had called home for so many years, she took in the wonderful city views and the cool breeze that was always present but rarely strong. In the late afternoon, the wind carried the smell of Italian cuisine, and with the sounds of the city beneath them, Sara felt very much at home.

She had little recollection of the hospital, her fainting, or the journey back to the house, but her watch said that seven hours had passed. Sitting in her trademark yoga pants with a long sweatshirt from her closet, she and her dad were not really talking. Just having a glass of wine together in silent grief.

The nurse had brought her back after she fainted, and Sara immediately had tried to argue about her mom dying. She now she realized this was just her attempt to relieve her overwhelming guilt. Deep down, she knew her parents, so proud and concerned for her, had simply waited too long to tell her. They thought they had time, but they didn't.

Sara also knew her father was troubled. He and his beloved Annini had been sweethearts since university, and lovers to the very end. Sara was still upset they had not told her but would not question him now. She was about to ask if he was okay when he said, "Sara, I don't wish to make you upset with me, but I realize we waited too long to tell you."

Used to the fact that they often shared thoughts, Sara replied, "Dad, you had no idea, and both of you assumed you had more time. You're a proud and protecting father and wonderful husband. I'm just so angry at myself for fumbling about on my thesis when I could have just come home hours after our call. We'll get through this, I promise you."

"I'll require some help for perhaps a week or two. Then you can return to your studies. I'll be fine." He said sadly.

"Dad, that's just it. I'm not sure I'm going back! My thesis was disproven, and this quest has cost me a memory I can never make right. Even if I restart, I would rather be here with you, in my proper home." Giovanni didn't reply, but his facial expression was obvious; he clearly did not like the answer.

She let it go and got up to refill their wine. In a sudden ironic moment, she thought, *wow, compared to this, I really drink crappy wine.*

When she sat back down, he asked. "Sara, you and your mom talked every day since our first call and yes, we honestly had no idea. But I can promise you, Annini was not showing any sign that would leave me to believe we had days or hours when we were thinking months, perhaps even years. She loved to hear your voice and while perhaps not a physical goodbye, she was at peace hearing and seeing you. I heard those conversations, and they were about life, about the past, about the future, and nothing about university or doctoral themes. You and your mom had the exact moments she needed at the time she needed them. Please do not blame yourself." Sara listened and liked his tone. He was going to be okay.

The week passed quickly, with plans for the funeral and getting reacquainted with friends and family. The service itself was simple and thoughtful, although too religious for Sara's taste, but that was the custom here. It became very clear that her mom and dad had not only duped her, but literally everyone. All were shocked at her passing, and most knew nothing of her cancer or her treatments over the last few months. The hours went by, and soon they were alone again on the terrace.

Sara put on some light jazz and her dad opened a bottle of wine and brought out a small antipasti platter. They said nothing for some time when he spoke. "In your prior research your mother and I always wondered to what extent you came across your great-great-grandfather, Gilberti."

"Early on I found significant reference to him," Sara replied between bites of salad, "Although until we spoke, what was that, like three years ago, I did not equate his name to mine. I just assumed he was yet another Ricci from the Vento area where so many have our surname. Once I knew we were related, I tried to understand him as a scientist, but couldn't find much. Not even from the University of Padua."

Sara took a small sip of wine and continued. "At one time I even corresponded directly with a professor there, who had been a first-year student under him the year of his death, but nothing came from it. I could only gather bits and pieces. It was believed he was killed by the Nazi command and his later work, said to be advanced for its time, was lost, or taken by those who killed him. Sad, it's like an entire career erased. Why do you ask?"

"Much of him is a mystery and perhaps even a conspiracy and I too know very little about him or his life, just that his son, Bortolo, said it was one of tragedy. But the end, according to him, differed from the scripted narrative created on his death."

"I'm not following."

"Gilberti was not killed, Sara. He took his own life, leaving his lovely wife and son behind."

"What! Why would this just come out now, Dad? I'm twenty-six fucking years old."

"Sara, your mouth, please. I know you like this vulgar American word, but it is not for you. Anyway, we didn't want you to be affected by the past because we really don't know why he killed himself. Was he a victim? Was he evil?"

"Well, I appreciate the concern and I'm saddened by this new information, but it means little now. It was 75 years ago."

He sat still and with an odd look of pride and fear said, "What if I told you I had his research papers?"

"Why would you have his papers?" Sara asked in disbelief.

"My father received them a year before Bortolo passed, and I received them when my father passed. Bortolo was a literary scholar, and my father was a pension administrator like me. We had no idea what any of this meant, so they have simply stayed hidden. You, however, might understand and shed light on Gilberti's troubling decision. It might also offer ideas to help you."

"Dad, I would love to look at his material, but to be honest, much from that time has been proven and disproved by space travel."

"Perhaps that is all I can ask. I just would like to understand why these papers were worth his life," he replied calmly.

10

Terrace Flat, Milan, Italy

The next day, Sara sat across from a large wooden crate the building maintenance man had brought up from the basement. It smelled of old wood and even older oils and though she couldn't place the smell; it was as if the crate had once held machinery. Removing the top with a screwdriver, she assumed the original nails were long gone. Inside were stacks of papers, several thousand, arranged in a classical method of research and to the left, a small wooden box. She went to grab it.

"Sara, please let that be," her dad said, alarmed. "Those are Gilberti's personal effects that the University Rector removed and gave to his wife Sonia, and I presume found their way to Bortolo on her death. When I received the crate, I opened the box out of curiosity. It contains several personal effects, but also a gun. I thought nothing of it at first, but realized that perhaps this was, you know, *the gun*. I think it is best to leave this alone and concentrate on the papers."

Sara nodded, put down the unopened box, and removed the papers.

Over the next few weeks, Sara alternated her time between Gilberti's papers and helping her dad with the administration of her mom's death. They reviewed accounts, contracts, and met with Annini's attorney, regarding her various trademarks and copyrights.

Eventually, Sara had gone through every page in the crate, but this was not a stack of research papers dedicated to a single project. It was actually a series of important research papers surrounded by worthless papers of unrelated items. Sara assumed this was a ploy to throw off someone, should they get this material illicitly. In order to find the needle in the haystack, she was forced to organize each page and sort it out by the type of science and type of research.

The information itself was fascinating considering the knowledge of physics during Gilbert's time. His work followed the theorem of classical physics, but in some drawings and math, he was suggesting perhaps an additional unnamed force and she thought back to his time. Of course, he would have studied linear equations that followed the Maxwellian knowledge of the time. But nonlinear dynamics, where the change of the output is not proportional to the change of the input, was not really yet known until Enrico Fermi uncovered it in the 1950s. That alone made this all very intriguing.

As she went through the important papers, there were several drawings of atmospheric energies, including the aurora borealis and magnetic field lines, also known as Birkland currents. Several more showed what was now called the Van Allen Belt, a zone of energetic charged particles originating from the sun captured by and held around the planet by Earth's own magnetic field. The greatest concentration of material, however, were drawings that depicted thunderclouds, lightning, and what appeared to be a relationship between lightning and these Birkland currents. The math suggested two things that derived from these sources: high energy gamma rays and positrons, a type of antimatter.

She took a break and met her dad in the kitchen.

"I see she emerges yet again," he said causally.

As she grabbed a Pellegrino, she replied. "Yes, there are many topics I would not have expected, but the theme is energy from space, but it's surrounded by unrelated papers should this have fallen into the wrong hands."

"Do you have a sense of the secret itself, the reason for such deception?" he asked excitedly.

"I see a pattern and it's related to highly energetic particles that might be connected to lightning, but it's too early to speculate."

"Well, I appreciate you trying. I'm sure you'll figure it out. Has this helped reignite the scientist in you?"

Sara laughed, "Dad, I'm still a scientist and always will be. What I question is being in America, and the consequences of that decision as my life moves forward. Think about it, I've never even had a boyfriend, or a dog," she added, smiling but serious.

"Ah, yes, this is the problem. Go out then and get a dog and a boyfriend and then we can continue this conversation. But first, sit. Let us have some risotto. You're getting skinny again."

Maximillian Drummond sat listening to the rambling of his DARPA contact who was speaking far too loudly on a speaker phone as if the distance between them had somehow impaired his hearing. He absorbed the update on various topics, including the absence of the young scientist, Sara Ricci from MIT. The call ended and Maximillian turned to view the ocean.

He understood his interest in her research, but the other DARPA department, the Microsystems group led by Ralf Müller was operating independently. Was it just a coincidence that they, too, saw something of interest in her work, or was there something else?

He decided to ask Grant Aiken, his head of security, and rang for him. As Grant headed up the stairs to the residence, his sister, Bridget, was walking down. Grant, besides running security for all of MDE Enterprises, also handled Maximillian's private security detail. A compact, muscular man, he was about the same height as Bridget, five foot ten, so when he turned facing her, his eyes went directly into hers. When communicating with someone, he immediately put his entire self into the process. There was never a casual meeting with him.

"Bridget. All is well with Maximillian?"

"Yes, he seems in one of his moods." She continued to walk back down towards her office while Grant continued upward.

Bridget, intimidated by no one, always kept Grant under observation. Not that she didn't trust him. Far from it. She knew; however, he was a one master dog, and she wasn't the master. Regardless, Bridget and Grant were the only ones that Maximillian allowed to get close, and they formed the entirety of his inner circle. But Maximillian was hard to read, and she was never really sure where she stood with him.

On the darker side, Bridget was reasonably sure that Maximillian was involved somehow in Blaney's death, although she had never confronted him. He wasn't a violent person but was so logical and pragmatic she wasn't sure if he really knew right from wrong. However, she wasn't about to complain. She had over a billion reasons to be happy!

Grant stopped in front of the large glass door and waited to be allowed in. A buzz was followed by the sound of a mechanical withdrawal and as the large, frosted glass door slid to one side, he entered. Like Bridget, he too had a fob that allowed immediate access, but only Bridget used hers. Grant always waited for Maximillian to let him in.

He walked in and asked, "Sir, what can I do for you?"

Maximillian motioned for Grant to sit and as he did, he said, "I have a concern about timing. Please work with Angus and consider if this Ralf Müller, an Assistant Director at DARPA is feeding information to my contact to get to me. This is as if to say, the hack simply revealed a planted theme meant to be located."

Grant was used to Maximillian's paranoid reactions, but they had also kept them both alive and prospering, so he didn't dismiss them. "If I understand the sequence of events, a liaison from DARPA hears of the research topic on campus and informs his boss, Ralf Müller, unaware that your contact has overheard this exchange. Angus randomly starts the hack and locates her limited work. That all makes sense, but if this Müller knew your contact was listening, that would suggest a possibility that she, or her research, could be a plant. Although they couldn't have known that Angus would try to observe it. We'll monitor the situation and test for signs of covert activity."

"Just make sure I am not walking into a trap." Maximillian asserted.

Sara finished packing her clothes and glanced at the larger suitcase her dad had just purchased for her. Her five-week stay had included some shopping, and she had hundreds of copies of Gilberti's work that required more in-depth study. Her dad had spoiled her over the last few weeks, which was nice, but he had also persuaded her to return to MIT.

He understood academia and made Sara realize she had a rare and gifted mentor in Dr. Zimbrean and possibly a new thesis given what she found in Gilberti's archive. She herself thought more and more of Zimbrean's suggestion that an emotional crisis would be necessary for her to see. Perhaps that was why she felt so different now.

After a light breakfast, they took everything down to the car. Giovanni had Gilberti's crate taken back to the basement storage, and together they left in his vintage Alfa Romeo for Milan Malpensa airport. After arriving and parking in the short-term area, they approached the ticketing area and waited together until she had her documentation was ready to pass to the departure gates.

Looking at him now, knowing he would be alone, almost made her grab him and run back to the car. But he looked comfortable, and she knew returning to MIT would make him happy, so she ignored the thought. They talked for an additional twenty minutes before they shared a tearful hug. Heading towards security, she waved as he waved, before turning and walking away, alone.

As she waited for the call to board, she texted Lisa to say she was on her way home and thought about her checked suitcase and its contents. It was going to be an interesting next couple of weeks and one thing she would have to resolve was who could she trust to go over Gilberti's work. Her skills were just not there and while she needed help, she couldn't lose control of the information.

Sara finally arrived at their house close to 7:15 p.m., several hours after she intended. The reason was a delayed flight, hellish trip through customs, and a long wait for an Uber back to the house in the freezing cold. And, of course, Sara had not dressed properly.

Happy Lisa was home, even the cat acknowledged her initially, but then played it cool. After a much-needed shower, she changed into warm clothes and came back downstairs, where she caught Lisa up on all that happened in Milan. Lisa then gave her the goings on of Boston and MIT.

After a restful sleep, Sara awoke with apprehension as she was forced to readjust to where she was. It amazed her that her brief time back in Milan had been like a comfy blanket, familiar, but here in Boston, she felt she was starting over all again. It just wasn't home.

The cold weather had officially started, and Sara bundled up before she walked over to meet Nathan at the Mud Room. When she arrived, he was already inside and as soon as he saw her; he rushed over and gave her a strong and needed hug. She could tell he was at a loss for words and spoke instead. "Thanks for the texts of encouragement and for listening to my occasional rants. This has been hard for me, but I'm okay and dad is doing well, considering."

The Mud Room was quite small and there was always a queue to order, but at least she was inside, as several were now waiting out in the cold. Once at the barista, she ordered an expresso and Nathen a hot herbal tea, and they found a small corner with two chairs that had just been vacated. They caught each other up before Sara told him about her discovery. "So, I read some research from a relative who was also a physicist, and it has expanded my thinking, but I'm told this information has a secret past. Given the hack, I need to design a data security protocol that has nothing to do with the MIT primary servers."

"Sara, you can't just go rogue," Nathen said matter-of-factly.

"Yes, I know, which is why only discrete information will live on the MIT side. I need to control my thoughts and the analysis data. I don't have this worked out, but that is our job today."

"Okay, no problem. We can put something together. Actually, it's great timing. My dad is in town and would love to meet you. If I hadn't mentioned it, he runs a security company called Fortitude that provides private and personal security to high wealth and high-risk clients. Although data security is not the focus of his business, he gets involved in data and fine art security often and can help us. How about meeting him for dinner tonight?"

"That would be great. The sooner we can do this the more secure I'll feel."

"Great, I'll call my dad and set it up. How about 5:30?" Sara nodded affirmatively as Nathen gave a thumbs up and headed for his class. He was happy to have Sara back and even happier she seemed herself again.

The weather declined that evening as they left to meet Richard "Rottweiler" Chase, Nathen's dad. Nathen was an old hand at winter driving, and with no concern, he drove them to a seafood restaurant in Cambridge and pulled into the parking lot. Nathen didn't much care for this restaurant, but his dad liked it. As they entered, it was exactly as Nathen always remembered, busy and exceptionally loud, but there was Dad, standing stick straight next to the hostess, his back to them.

Without words, he turned and smiled, "Nate, my boy," and gave him a brief man-hug. When they parted, Nathen introduced Sara. "Dad, this is Sara Ricci. Sara, this is my dad, Richard Chase."

Richard responded. "Ms. Ricci, I have heard much about you, and I wanted to say I am sincerely sorry for your loss. I hope our company tonight can make you think of happier thoughts." He reached out to grab hold of her hand.

Sara nodded and smiled as she shook his firm, highly calloused hand, saying, "Please Mr. Chase, call me Sara."

"Very well, and please call me Richard," he replied.

Her first impression of him was a cross between an older Nathen and Jason Sykes; ruggedly handsome, clearly a soldier and, at first glance, someone you did not want to mess with. He just had that look and posture. The hostess took them to a booth by the window and they had a typical American dinner, very good, but way too much food. During and after dinner, the conversation was a mixture of Fortitude Security, Nathen's journey to MIT, and security threats before they settled on Sara's concern.

"So, if I understand, MIT had a hack," Richard said. "Just the fact it occurred at MIT means the hackers are professionals looking for something specific and whatever you had on the server, it contained the field heading or keywords of that very interest."

"From the limited information given to me by a liaison from DARPA, that is precisely the case, but they don't know who or why," Sara answered.

"So, you're under a grant with DARPA?"

"No."

"Then why is DARPA involved?" Richard asked, surprised.

"Well, it's things just like that which give me concern. Since my mom's passing, I've had a change regarding my thesis, but it holds family secrets from the past. It is for this reason I am no longer comfortable using the MIT servers unless I have to, as some information must be located there." She pulled out her tablet and showed him the sketch Nathen and she had devised.

He looked at the tablet with a nod and said, "Sara, this is fine, but I suggest a more robust server location and a tighter protocol. Let's consider a server at my home, using the firewall from Fortitude Security; it's quite safe. You will have access to a physical person within the company and a digital key. When you want to access or download, then and only then will that server be connected to the internet, which would then allow you access. Immediately after the access or download, it will close the connection and go back offline. Nothing in, nothing out unless you and your key are cleared by me, or my employee. Thoughts?"

"I like this plan. Please let me know how much it costs so I can arrange this."

"Sara, we have lots of stuff sitting around just for such an occurrence and do this often. There is no charge, and I'll brief you both once it is up and running. Once more thing, though."

Richard had lowered his voice now and said, "Sara, DARPA is up to something, and somehow it involves you. They'll probably soon want to arrange security for your data themselves. My advice is, don't agree unless they have offered, and you have accepted, a grant from them."

"Why do you think DARPA has any interest in giving me a grant?" Sara said, surprised.

"Because without one, you and your research belong to the university. Be careful and call me if you suspect something funny. That goes for you too, Nate!"

"Do you know of this Jason Sykes from DARPA?" Sara asked.

"No, but I know his dad and lots of ex-military like him. That's one reason I'm telling you to be careful. They do exactly as they're told, and someone is telling this liaison, Jason, what to do."

12

MIT Campus, Boston

Sara was reading in the Barker library when Jason entered, saw her, and walked directly toward her. She was not interested in socializing, but his face looked determined and unfortunately, the surrounding seats were empty.

"Hi Sara. I was just checking to see if you needed help to set up a more robust data storage."

"No, thank you, Jason. I have already arranged for private data security." She put down her tablet and turned to him. "I still find it odd that anyone would be interested in my work since I haven't even defined what my work is. While I must admit that I know little of DARPA, it is troubling to me that your organization has a liaison so concerned for my well-being. Is this all some roundabout way of trying to ask me out?"

"Interested?"

She blushed. "Well, no, not really... Perhaps. But what about the question? Why is DARPA and you, by extension, paying any attention to me at all? I don't feel I should have any conversations with you if you can't tell me what is going on!"

"Sara, I am seriously not trying to ask you out, and even if I were, DARPA wouldn't allow it. As for the interest, I honestly don't know, but my boss has asked me to monitor you."

"Has he ever mentioned why? Anything at all? Even my committee doesn't know my thesis yet. Is it my research he is interested in, or is it me?"

"I shouldn't say this, but the answer would be yes to both questions. On one hand, he is interested in beamed energy, but I have also heard him say that you are a unique student with a past that warrants learning more about you."

"Is he referring to my great-great-grandfather, perhaps?"

"I have no idea. Those were as close to the original words as I recall, but I cannot put them in a different context. Who is your great-great-grandfather?"

"It is not important, but thank you. I am sure we'll meet again." With that, Sara went back to reading her tablet.

Jason realized he had been dismissed and walked out of the library. As he did, Nadia, who was sitting with an engineering student, watched him leave. As Nadia moved her eyes from Jason and then back to Sara, she wondered, *is she now involved with DARPA?* She would find out, but first had to get back on Sara's good side. Her article on the Chinese researchers had clearly pissed her off.

Later that afternoon, Sara told Nathen of the visit with Jason, but left out the part about Gilberti, and they went their separate ways. As he left, Nathen called his dad, "Hey Dad, Nate. Any new intel on the DARPA angle to Sara?"

"No. What's up," Richard asked.

"The DARPA guy, Jason Sykes met with Sara again and she confronted him about their interest in her. He mentioned his boss, a guy named Ralf Müller, was interested in her research, but he also said something about her past that made her special. Sara was trying to understand what that meant."

"Nate, I have a few people I can call, but have hesitated because those calls might tip the hat above them. Of course, if it does, at least we'll know for sure that something is up. That said, perhaps I should also run a quick check on her through a source I have in Interpol to see what, if anything this past might be?"

"I trust you, Dad. Let me know."

Angus Adair watched his group go about setting up the second attempt into MIT servers. Maximillian had asked for an update and while Angus thought not enough time had passed to provide information that could offset the risk of trying to get in, he did as he was told. The multi-phased effort might be detectable but not traceable and after a few hours, they were in, but nothing was there. All folders or files related to the scientist were gone.

Angus picked up the phone and called the boss, "Sir, regarding MIT, we got in and out, but all folders or files related to her have been removed. Her data is being protected outside of MIT or she has taken herself off the network."

"To what end? She hasn't even done anything to our knowledge," said Maximillian.

"Well, not to our knowledge," answered Angus as Maximillian disconnected the call, pondering those last few words.

Maximillian texted Grant to come up to his office, and he arrived a few minutes later. Maximillian buzzed him in. Grant pulled an Irn Bru, a Scottish soda from the bar fridge, and motioned the bottle to Maximillian as if to say, *want one?* Maximillian waved his hand as a no and Grant sat down across from him. "What can I do for you?"

"Angus did a second pass at MIT, and, as I suspected, the files are now gone, as is anything related to our young scientist. Angus suspects she is being protected, but it elevates my concern. We have been led to believe that her research is new, and not well established, but what if her research is more advanced, or is that simply what something someone wants us to think?"

"As we have done nothing, it is of no consequence."

"Yes, but have a team go into her office and see what they can uncover. Have them look at everything but leave no trace that anyone has been there. I require no physical evidence, just confirmation of where she might be in her research."

"On it," Grant said as he rose with his empty bottle and left.

Grant chose a team of two, both ex-military. One had a rudimentary knowledge of physics and could understand the outcome requirements of the sweep. They had done work like this for Grant before and had firsthand knowledge of MIT and the area where her office was located.

Early morning two days later, having watched Sara to understand her habits and timing, they pulled a small van into an access way off Albany in front of the lab. They put out cones on the traffic side of the van, leaving the emergency flashers on. The side of the van was adorned with the name and logo of a fictitious heating and air conditioning repair company and they both had on insulated uniforms with a matching logo. With piping and duct work visible in the van, they entered the main hall and located Sara's office. Once in the room, they used special LED infrared penlights in the early morning dawn and systematically went through her office and all areas where she might have left unfinished work or clues. Nothing was locked, everything was accessible, but there was extraordinarily little to see. They found ideas for lessons to be taught and physics concepts, but as for an extensive research project, if she was working on something, it wasn't being done here.

They retraced their steps and placed everything back into the van. As they were pulling out, they called Grant and gave him the update. Grant thanked them, thinking *perhaps Maximillian was right. Could this be a setup?*

Sara arrived at her office several hours later and entered the office cold and a tad bitchy. She really didn't care for this weather, as she turned on her second monitor and casually looked at the desk for a folder she knew was there.

Sara was not OCD, but she had quirks. One of the biggest was that she needed materials to always present themselves perpendicular to her. As she faced her computer monitors, the folders to the right of the monitor were normally askew so as she saw them, they would be perpendicular to her. Weird perhaps, but now, everything on that side of the desk was straight. She immediately looked around the room, but nothing else seemed off.

Her immediate reaction was someone had been in her office, so she searched and found Jason's business card and called him explaining her concern and he asked her not to touch anything else; he would be right over.

Arriving quickly, Jason asked Sara to describe the surfaces she used most often and took out a small handheld black light to scan those surfaces as he clicked off the lights above. After several minutes of doing this on drawers and all items she touched regularly, he said, "Well I would love to say otherwise, but you were right, someone was here. Almost all surfaces have been wiped clean, so your prints, which should be there, are not." He turned the lights back on before calling security.

"Could this simply be the cleaning staff?" Sara asked hopefully.

"Maybe, but I doubt it. I have watched them. They aren't detailed enough to clean all these surfaces, but I'll check it out. Maybe that's all it is. We'll also review the hall camera, but there does not appear to be one in this exact direction."

"Okay, let me know. I hope it's just cleaners and nothing more. This kind of crap shouldn't be happening to me," Sara said, confused.

As Jason walked away, he had a bad feeling about all this. Sara knew something and someone was going to great lengths to understand what that was. He needed to keep a closer eye on her for her own safety.

13

MIT Campus, Boston

Sara spent the rest of the day teaching a lab class, and afterwards tried again to review Gilberti's papers with little success. She was sure certain equations meant something significant, but the math did not resonate with her. After a few hours without success, she called Dr. Zimbrean to see if he knew someone trustworthy to review them.

"Hi Maggie, Sara here. Is Dr. Zimbrean in? I wanted to ask him if he knows anybody who can review some dated research. I'm just not sure who to trust anymore."

"Oh, love, I doubt anything is as sinister as all that, but he's out at the moment. I'll let him know you stopped by."

"Thanks, Maggie."

Just after 2:20 pm, her cell rang, and it was Zimbrean. "Sara, I understand you may have had visitors. Strange and, no doubt, concerning. Please stop by if you can. Perhaps we can talk about this help in private."

"Yes, that would be great. I can be there in thirty minutes if that works?"

"It does, and please just come in. Maggie is running errands."

Sara entered the foyer and knocked lightly on his door when Zimbrean said, "Please come in." She shut the door and removed a stack of papers from the only available chair and set them down on the coffee table. Sitting facing him on the small couch where he sat, he was surrounded by even more papers.

"Thanks for the time," she said.

"No problem at all. What is this about needing assistance?"

"I have come across some old research papers, and I want to better understand some of the math. But its advanced, and I wondered if you knew of a colleague who could look at this with me. Considering the hack and break-in, I am becoming concerned, and frankly you are one of the few people I trust to even ask."

"Does this involve Gilberti Ricci?" he asked casually.

Sara stared at him. "What? You know of my great-great-grandfather?"

Startled, Zimbrean replied, "Sara, everyone in classical physics knows of him and while few might realize you are related, some of us know this as well. It is frankly the reason we consider you special and more capable. Can I infer that you have located his missing papers?"

Sara shut down for a moment. *What was happening? Was Dr. Zimbrean involved in all this? Was the whole university in on this?*

"Sara, please don't be so melodramatic. You realize that most of the emeritus branch of academia in classical physics worldwide are aware of the mysterious circumstances in which Gilbert's career was silenced. While he never created lasting theories in his own name, he was the person who allowed many to do so, and it was long rumored that he himself was on to something. The cover-up by the University of Padua is the stuff of conspiracy theories, so it is a fair question. Yes?"

Sara sighed and for a second, almost cried. "I'm sorry. It's just so many things are changing. I'm intrigued by this diversion, but have a sense I'm sharing this journey with some terrible people."

"Your concern is understandable, and the reason I asked you here privately is that I am also concerned. Sara, perhaps only you and I should review this information and then decide next steps. Your thoughts?"

Sara smiled. "That's the best idea I've heard and thank you." Sara paused and then added, "Dr. Zimbrean do you think that all this sudden interest in me is linked to Gilberti?"

"It would explain these strange goings on when you have not yet yourself accomplished much of anything. No offense, but clearly someone thinks you have."

In Kalispell, Montana, Richard Chase hung up the phone for the third time in an hour. He had called two acquaintances from his past, one still in the CIA and one retired from a company called MITRE. That company was once connected to MIT and for the last sixty years had been providing the United States government with outlandish tools to solve clandestine problems. Much as the Q-Branch did for fictitious James Bond of MI6 fame. Both inquiries would likely create a second and possibly third call before, Richard assumed, he would get word to stand down. That was the confirmation he was looking for as much as any direct information. His last call was to a former member of the French DST, now an agent of Interpol. Richard called him for a simple dossier on an Italian national, Sara Ricci.

As he was leaving the office, his assistant motioned to him he had a call. Without returning to his office, he merely took her phone and said, "Richard Chase, Fortitude Security."

"Mr. Chase, my name is Jason Sykes, and I work for DARPA."

"A fine organization. Is DARPA interested in a special security assignment Mr. Sykes?"

"No, sir, and neither do I believe you actually assumed that. I am calling you regarding a young doctoral student, Ms. Sara Ricci. I am formally asking you to discontinue your efforts to engage in her work. Neither she nor your son are in any danger, but this is a controlled project."

"Young man, you were shitting mustard when I started working on controlled projects. As neither my son nor this researcher is under a grant with DARPA, I can and will do whatever the hell I want. And thank you for letting me know DARPA has flagged her and has something they want to stay hidden. You have a great night."

He hung up, smiled, and walked out. Back in Boston, Jason also hung up, realizing he had likely just screwed up.

14

Cambridge, Massachusetts

Sara arrived at Dr. Zimbrean's house on Soden Street in Cambridge just before 6:30 p.m., as they had planned, and walked down his narrow driveway to the side door and knocked. Nothing. She knocked again, saying loudly, "Dr. Zimbrean, it's Sara." Still nothing. Going to toward the rear of the house, she headed for his small sunroom, which, as one might expect, was a small room with windows on all sides and a steep glass roof. It was like a greenhouse, but for people. She approached the fogged windows and cupped her hands to peer into the frozen glass, and there he was, unmoving on an oversized chair. With everything going on, she immediately became concerned and knocked on the door loudly.

He was actually asleep and woke with a start. He sat up, rubbed his eyes before looking over at the door and, seeing Sara, rose to let her in. Slightly embarrassed, he said, "At my age, one simply drifts off when the mind is not occupied. Please, let me make some coffee."

At the kitchen table, Sara had laid out small stacks from the hundreds of pages she had copied from the old crate in Milan as he started the coffee and came over to the table. "So I imagine you have gone through all this several times. What have you have found and what areas concern you?"

"Sure." She picked up a small stack of papers and handed them to him. "The early part of his research shows he was looking into the energized particles from Van Allen's Belt. All signs suggest he was interested in the source of the polar auroras and he even theorized that the electrons were possibly moving in what we would now call Alfvén waves. Notes say he believed these energized particles had significant energy potential, and much of this is trying to determine how to convert these particles into power. After much consideration, however, he concludes the area is too vast to harvest and moves his research to thunderclouds and lightning events."

"Yes, I see many sketches of clouds and concepts of electrification."

"With lightning, he correctly theorized that powerful electric storms, especially those near the earth's field lines can create a burst of gamma rays."

"Ah, so he is trying to detect antimatter?" he asked with a smile.

Sara picked up a small stack of drawings and held them like a deck of playing cards. "If you take these pages and arrange them in a manner like an old cartoon, as you flip through them, you can see his depiction of electricity changing within a mature thunderstorm cell. On very rare occasions, as the lightning occurs, he depicts what can only be an early version of a relativistic runaway electron avalanche that would predate its actual discovery by some forty years. This upward acceleration creates what we now call a terrestrial gamma ray flash or TGF. Proven to exist in 1994, these TGFs create gamma rays and, sometimes, highly energetic electrons and positrons. So, no, he is not trying to detect antimatter because he has already concluded it is there. He is, however, trying to determine how to convert this into usable power."

"Given the times, do you suspect the purpose was to make a weapon?"

Sara considered the question. "Well, no, not that I could see. Mostly, he is simply trying to locate and quantify the energy. There are some obvious application theories, but none are well defined, but that is the area where I could use some help." She grabbed a small stack of papers and handed them to him. "I'm not sure of these equations."

Dr. Zimbrean slowly and methodically went through each page for several minutes before answering, "I suspect he considered using the power from the gammas and annihilation energy to create thrust."

"Thrust? Like in a spaceship?" Sara asked.

"That is how it appears and there seem to be several iterations. Perhaps this was the influence of the Germans and as a scientist, curiosity got the better of him. These examples are dated very close to his death." He pulled out one drawing and held it up. "Here he uses a parabolic dish to centralize the energy and then send it to a nozzle." He put that drawing down and grabbed another. "In this one, he is using a similar dish to convert the interaction energies of the gamma rays to power magnets. Using argon gas as a plasma, he creates Lorentz Force propulsion not unlike the theories of today's magnetoplasmadynamic drive concepts." He smiled proudly, shaking his head. "In this one, he has designed a deep parabolic dish to capture and convert the gamma ray interactions as they collide with the dish. Sara, it is such a loss that he did not publish any of this work."

Sara reached for the page Dr. Zimbrean had just mentioned. "You say he is trying to convert gamma radiation, but that simply isn't possible. Gamma rays are photons that will pass through any form of natural matter trying to stop them. Even though the parabolic dish is made of lead, and he has some with some type of coating on it, it still makes no sense." She handed the drawing to Dr. Zimbrean.

He looked at it again, then back up at Sara. "You of all people know that just because it has not happened, does not mean that it cannot. That is the beauty of physics, but to your point, this is just a theory. I see no solid evidence to suggest that he figured it out."

Sara tried to take all this in. It was a lot to absorb, but it also made sense why the Germans would be so interested. Still amazed by the concepts, Sara said quietly as she looked down. "The Nazis did not physically kill Gilberti. He took his own life, and it would appear he did so rather than be forced to weaponize his work."

Dr. Zimbrean absorbed the words and removed his glasses before rubbing the bridge of his nose. He replied sincerely, "Then you are of noble stock, Sara. There have been many conspiracy theories about his death, but I must admit, this provides a more realistic alternative. I thank you for sharing and I will, of course, keep this to myself, but someday, the world must know his story, and you must tell them; for him. No one has any idea how advanced his mind was."

Days later, Sara called her dad and told him of the revelations regarding Gilberti and his work, his theory, and the likelihood that this was what led to his death. Her dad was thankful and relieved to have the actual story and fully agreed that someday they needed to get this message out.

He was also saddened by the news. "Poor Bortolo never knew the truth. His father wasn't weak. He was a hero."

15

Milan, Italy

Alitalia flight 3536 got Sara into Milan after lunch the twenty-third of December for her Christmas Holiday Break. She was happy to get home and see her dad. Of course, Christmas Eve was difficult without her mom, but they made the best of it and even attended mass at the Duomo di Milano, a spectacular cathedral any time, but exceptional at Christmas.

Giovanni himself was doing well and surprised Sara when he told her he had kept up Annini's monthly meetings at the terrace flat. Her mom's early books were based on snippets of actual events involving Sara. Eventually, her mom added new characters, new messages, and she used a five-person group of men and women as inspiration to generate those ideas. They had been meeting for almost a decade and, although final stories were always chosen by her mom, the group brainstormed and made collective input to the premise, artwork, and message. In fact, whoever created the original thought was given a set amount of the royalties.

Sara asked her dad about this. "How does that work? Without Mom, who picks the stories? You?"

"Good heavens no. I have little creative talent, so our attorney has created a separate copyright. This next book, and all that will follow will not be under my beloved Annini Boscolo Ricci, but a new entity which is *'Amici di Annini'*, Friends of Annini. It was the idea of the group, and I couldn't be more pleased. It aids her foundation and keeps her legacy alive all of which gives me great hope and joy."

As she hugged him, she said, "Dad, mom is shining down on you right now; I can feel it."

Back in the fierce Boston cold eight days later, Sara was in the foyer of Dr. Zimbrean's office, waiting for him to end a call. She had not bothered him over the holiday, but needed his help in completing her research question.

Several minutes passed when his assistant Maggie motioned for her to go in and Dr. Zimbrean greeted her fondly, apologizing for the delay.

"Sara, I hope your holiday was pleasant. All is well, yes?"

"Yes, I had a great time with my dad and I'm back and eager to go."

"Excellent."

"Dr. Zimbrean, I want to continue Gilberti's theory of atmospheric energy as an energy source," she said with confidence.

He had expected this. "Well, it involves atmospheric energies as did your original thesis, but the material we went through was exceedingly broad. You will need to narrow it down to the type of atmospheric source and also the type of radiation you are trying to capture."

"Yes, I already have. Sorry. I'm most interested in gammas from terrestrial gamma ray flashes."

If he had any emotional reaction, his expression offered no clue, but he calmly replied, "I think your committee would likely accept this."

"So, you're okay with this line of research?"

"Sara, this is your journey, not mine. Although these concepts are hard to replicate in labs, my primary concern is not so much what you choose, but how long it will take. You must be able to complete your PhD effort in the time allotted to you. Extensions have been granted, but they are exceedingly rare."

He looked up at her and asked, "Sara, might I ask how your fund-raising efforts are coming along? As you lock in this research question, you must also lock in funding."

"The change in my thesis set me back considerably. On the plane, I have made a list of companies that can benefit relative to applications, as well as companies involved in gamma research and detection. The prospectus is drafted and I could start sending these out as early as next week."

"Yes, well, you are significantly late in this quest, so please make this a priority."

Maximillian's security head, Grant Aiken and sister, Bridget, sat around a small table talking of the issues of the day. They were relaxing now and sipping a wonderful eighteen-year-old peat infused single malt scotch whiskey. It had a subtle cherry finish that hailed from Tobermory, a distillery over two-hundred years old, south from them on the Isle of Mull.

The topic had moved to updates on various viable research projects, including Sara Ricci, DARPA's interest, and the sudden disappearance of her data.

Bridget said, "I would feel better if we had direct information from her."

"So, you suggest we kidnap and interrogate her?" Maximillian chuckled as he took a sip and savored the rich consistency.

Bridget replied coldly, "Yes, in less than forty-eight hours we would have answers on exactly why DARPA is interested in her, and what she is really doing."

Grant looked up with a grin. "How would you like to see this done?"

"Grant we do not!" Maximillian huffed. "My sister has absolutely no patience and such action would effectively kill the goose that might lay a golden egg."

Grant could see the storm clouds forming over Bridget's head and left before all hell broke loose. "You two can talk. I can accomplish whatever you require," and left the room.

Bridget thought about trying to sway her brother, but knowing full well that was not possible, she took her leave as well. As she walked out, Maximillian realized at some point, he would have to tell them that Sara Ricci would soon to be working for them without ever knowing it but left it alone for now.

Bridget, confident she was right, however, went to Grant's office with a smile and popped her head inside. "Well, that was difficult. You know how stubborn he can be, but it's a go. We need a professional team to grab her, drug her, and get her to a safe house. We'll use a scrambled voice box and with only her in the room, and a secure video link to ask her questions. She needs to be drugged, but able to communicate."

Grant, who was looking right at her, saw the excitement and said, "Okay, I'll set it up."

16

Packard's Corner, Boston

At the end of the week, Sara reviewed the single sheet of paper for the umpteenth time. In the background, her small speaker released the powerful orchestral version of *Out in the Real World*, by the Dutch band, Stream of Passion. This simple paragraph was the culmination of her experience to date, and it seemed silly that something so small could create so much anguish. Sara laughed at her physics joke and read it again:

> *"Quantify the rate of terrestrial gamma ray flashes*
> *and the energies within, then consider methods to*
> *convert this into usable power."*

Satisfied, she called Fortitude to open a download window and sent her tablet information to the server before closing the connection. Following acceptance by her committee on her revised thesis and research question a week later, Sara mailed off her professionally printed grant prospectus folders, looking to acquire a grant of one-hundred-seventy-five thousand dollars.

She knew upfront this would be difficult as pure research was a tough sell, but based on realistic applications, these initial companies could all benefit if her research was successful.

Sitting now at the Mud Room two weeks later, she stared at her half-empty cup, concerned. She had not received a single acknowledgement and knew in her heart, Zimbrean had been right, she should have started this much earlier.

Boris Turgenev, Managing Director for MDE Commodities was at his office in Madagascar reviewing sales and production reports from the previous week. This job was demanding as it required him to shuffle between the island of Madagascar where they had a small boutique mine, and an inhospitable island off the coast of Antarctica in the Southern Ocean. There, he spent six to eight weeks.

Heard Island was little more than a rugged, barren volcanic rock, unknown until the 19th century, primarily because of its remote location and lack of a natural harbor. It was largely used as a research location and restricted to just a handful of researchers annually.

That had changed in late 2008 when, at the height of the financial crisis, Maximillian Drummond got a limited land lease. It was tightly worded, allowing him to mine a specific and tiny area of the island for exotic rare earth elements under very strict controls. Despite their name, rare earth elements, those with an atomic numbers of fifty-seven to seventy-one, are actually not rare at all, but they have to be extracted from common ore, a laborious process.

Boris looked at his watch, which signaled it was time for his video call with the CEO of MDE Enterprises. As he logged in, the video call engaged and Maximillian Drummond appeared, stoic and impeccably dressed as always. "Boris, an update please."

"Yes sir. We are on track to increase sales by eighteen percent this quarter, primarily due to increased individual orders and more activity from MDE Defense. We have also seen a small uptick in orders from universities and scientists worldwide. As you know, this side of the business is one of many minuscule sales but at the highest margins."

"Excellent," Maximillian replied. "As far as the small orders, do you still support our decision to go direct rather than through brokers?"

"Yes sir," Boris added carefully, "Without a middleman, these transactions allow twice the profit margin. Besides our strong and loyal customer base, we are getting increasing requests from researchers who then come back for more orders. As an example, last week I received a first order from an MIT researcher for samarium and lutetium and I know she will purchase from us again."

Maximillian's ears perked up. "MIT you said. Who is the scientist?"

Surprised by the interest and the question, Boris reached for the prospectus he had received a week before. "Let me see. Her name is Sara Ricci. Besides the order, she also sent a grant request."

Maximillian cocked his head slightly. "Sara Ricci from MIT in America? Amazing."

"Sir, do you know her?" he asked, now intrigued.

"Yes, although she does not know me, and it is important she does not. I have an interest in her field of study. Tell me, has her order shipped?"

"No, sir."

"Contact her today if possible and explain that you have received her proposal but require more information. As a show of good faith, send her the metals gratis if she will share information regarding her application."

"I understand and will call as soon as I hang up." Boris smiled very glad he brought it up.

Sara was walking to the magnetics lab when her cell rang. She looked at the international number but did not recognize it, so she let it go straight to voicemail. She was late for her undergrad class and trusted that whoever the caller was would leave a message.

Hours later, Sara and Nathen were in her office as they mapped out a crude research budget. As Nathen was writing on the board, Sara noticed the voicemail and listened. With a thick Russian accent, the caller said, "Ms. Ricci, my name is Boris Turgenev, Managing Director for MDE Commodities, and I am calling you from my office in Madagascar, which is eight hours ahead of you. I have received your order, as well as your grant prospectus, and I'm interested, but more information is required. Please call me back at your convenience, so we might arrange a meeting and for many reasons, please keep this inquiry confidential. Thank you."

Sara turned to Nathen who had heard bits and pieces of the conversation saying, "MDE Commodities was a long shot, so I'm surprised that of all the companies, they would call. They are quite disconnected from my research."

"Well, at some point, call him back. You have nothing to lose." Nathen responded as he continued to noodle with numbers.

A short while later, Sara looked at her phone again and hit the callback button, knowing it was late there. Boris answered, and she addressed him in Russian, saying she had received his call and apologized for not calling sooner. He was surprised she knew Russian and thought her British/Italian accent was intoxicating.

They reverted to English and although he was a geologist; he seemed to understand what she was attempting. He mentioned being part of a larger organization, MDE Enterprises. While his interest was new applications for the mined materials, his colleagues would be equally interested in energy conversion of gammas if that was even possible. Meanwhile, he asked about her order.

"So, I take it from your order, you seek materials with high density and high atomic values."

"Yes, that is correct. My experiments will include several composite materials."

Boris got as far as, "Ms. Ricci…" before Sara cut him off, saying, "Boris, please it is just Sara."

"Very well. Sara, our rare earth metals from the mine in the Southern Ocean are extremely pure, but here in Madagascar, we have a small boutique mine where we have located an unknown element. It is like lanthanide series, which contains the rare earth elements like samarium and lutetium, but it also has characteristics of higher atomic elements found in the actinide series and is closely related to thorium. Are you familiar with this?"

"No. I was led to these from prior research."

"Well, unlike most actinide metals which are synthetically produced, this natural unnamed blend, while difficult to isolate, has a much higher atomic value and density than lutetium."

"But wouldn't it then be radioactive?" Sara queried, recalling her knowledge of the periodic elements table.

"Well, yes, all actinide series elements are, but the half-life of this material is billions of years, so it is extremely safe to handle, although care must be taken if processing or grinding. The reason I bring this up is we have received little commercial interest. Given your needs, this might work much better for you."

"Boris, let me check with my team. On a per pound basis, what are the differences? We still do not have a design specification, and I have very limited funds." She left out that she had zero funds and was buying this with her own money.

"Sara, if you help me understand the application for possible marketing ideas , I will not only work something out for any major purchase but will give you these a hundred gram samples gratis. As to retail prices, samarium is just over three-thousand dollars per pound and this unnamed material is approximately forty-eight thousand dollars per pound. How much do you suspect will be needed by your compounder?"

"I actually have no idea, as we have yet to locate a source, but let me get back to the team and get you some answers." Sara replied, and then in Russian, she said, "Thank you for the information and support." As she hung up, she knew she needed to run this by Lisa Payne, her geologist roommate.

Sara finally connected with Lisa that evening when she got home. "Lisa, just before you left on your trip, I ordered a one-hundred grams of samarium and lutetium from that company you mentioned, MDE Commodities. Yesterday I spoke to the Managing Director, Boris Turgenev, who was really helpful, and he mentioned they have a metal that is not thorium but very similar. What are your thoughts?" Sara asked.

"Considering what you are trying to do, it is a much better choice, but it's insanely expensive."

"He said the retail cost was forty-eight thousand dollars per pound, but would give me the 100 grams free if I helped him understand the application."

"Oh, my God. Take it. That is amazing," Lisa said, shaking her head before smiling. "Maybe you can get me a gram of two for future experiments?"

"I'll see what I can do!" Sara said with a smile.

17

MIT Campus, Boston

It was mid-morning and Sara was in her office when there was a knock at the door. Assuming it was an undergraduate student, she causally said, "The door is open," and turned around.

In walked a man she'd never seen before, an older man, distinguished with a touch of gray in his hair, dressed in a tailored suit with an impeccable camel colored cashmere over coat.

"Ms. Sara Ricci?" he spoke.

"Yes, and you are?"

"We have not met. My name is Dr. Bernard Cummings, and I am the Associate Director of Tactical Strategic Technology for DARPA."

"Ah, you are Jason's boss?" Sara proclaimed with a smile.

"No," he said almost offended, "Jason actually works for another associate director under Microsystems Technology."

"Then I do not understand."

"I work on Tactical Technology, while my counterpart works on Microsystems Technology."

"Okay. what can I do for you, Mr. Cummings?"

"Doctor Cummings, if you please."

109

She tried not to laugh at his pretentiousness.

"Ms. Ricci…" he said before Sara cut him off. "Please, it is just Sara."

"All right, Sara, what do you know of DARPA?" he asked.

"Very little, but nothing positive. Several things have happened to me over the past two months regarding security. I suspect DARPA must be involved, since they have been trying to attach themselves to my research, even though I am only right now deciding what that is. Yet somehow, you seem to know all about it."

He sat down. "Sara, I am aware of your security issues and assure you that DARPA has no reason to spy on you, and I suspect our liaison has actually been trying to protect you."

"Protect me from what?" Sara piped up.

"It is premature to have that conversation, but perhaps I should explain why I am here."

"Yes, perhaps," she said coldly.

He pulled out a folder and laid it on the desk, facing her. "Sara, this is a two-hundred-fifty thousand dollar grant from the Tactical Strategic Technology program of DARPA." He took pleasure in watching Sara's face go from mild anger to utter disbelief. "We are aware of your field of study and would like to offer you this grant, hoping to gain knowledge of how to collect and store energy from space. Our goal is to power a satellite based non-nuclear electromagnetic pulse (EMP) weapon."

"A weapon! Wait. How do you know anything about my revised field of study? This information is not public."

"Sara, we track smart people on the campuses of all major American universities. You intend to work on this anyway, and this is an incentive to assist in a manner that helps us both. We are not asking you to build the weapon, only provide its power."

Dr. Cummings sat silent when Sara reached for her phone, saying, "I am calling security. If you know what I am working on, then you or your organization are behind the recent attempts to steal my research."

He stood up. "Go right ahead, Sara. I can be almost anywhere on this campus, including places you cannot, and likely never will be. I've heard that you're brilliant and suggest you give this more serious thought. Windfalls like this rarely happen to unaccomplished scientists." He let that comment linger and then got up and walked out, leaving the proposal on the desk.

Furious, Sara picked up her cell and called Jason, explaining what had just happened.

"Bernard Cummings was just in your office?" Jason asked in shock.

"Yes, I just told you that," she yelled.

"And he offered you a grant to make a weapon?"

"No, he offered me a grant to locate the energy to power a weapon. It's all right here, he left the proposal here."

"Sara, this makes no sense at all. I need to see that proposal." Jason said sternly.

"You and your DARPA need to leave me the hell alone and stay out of my research and my life," she screamed and hung up.

Totally confused, Jason called Ralf, and explained everything that Sara had said had happened. Müller listened and responded tersely, "Sykes, I have no idea what is going on, but hold tight while I try to figure this out."

Müller hung up and started to call the Director of DARPA, Dr. Levin Bechtel, but decided against it. Instead, he called Dr. Cummings on his cell phone, but after several minutes of arguing, the call ended without providing clarity.

Ralf sat holding the phone as he tried to understand Bernard's actions and wondering how he ever received approval to issue the grant in the first place. This researcher was an Italian national without a United States security clearance. If that wasn't weird enough, he walks out, leaving the unsigned grant with her.

Something was very wrong.

Sara met with Nathen that afternoon and told him of the entire sequence of events. He was dumbfounded. "Holly crap, I work with you for less than a month and your research has changed. You now work for DARPA and have all of your funding."

"Nathen, I have not accepted the grant, but I'm still concerned about how they knew of my plans. God, I hope Dr. Zimbrean is not involved."

Shocked by the accusation, Nathen replied, "What the hell, Sara, you can't possibly think that!"

"Nathan, until yesterday only four people knew my revised thesis and I'm confident that neither my dad nor either of us spoke to DARPA, so who else is left?"

"Jason?" he said cautiously.

Troubled by the thought, Sara replied, "I thought of that, but he honestly seemed as surprised and angry as I was. Besides, I never told him."

"You know, there is another possibility," he said calmly.

"Like what?"

"That your great-great-grandfather's past is known within US intelligence, and DARPA simply put two and two together."

"So, this isn't about me, it's about Gilberti Ricci? Is that what your dad thinks?" she asked excitedly.

"Well, I know he quickly discovered you were related to him. As he tried to understand more, he was asked to stand down by, guess who?… DARPA. He says there is something they're trying to cover up."

"That actually makes sense, but I wonder. Is that why I was accepted at MIT?" Sara said sadly.

Sara awoke days later thinking of the DARPA grant and realized she really wasn't sure how a non-nuclear electromagnetic pulse weapon worked or how much power it actually required. She understood electromagnetic pulses derived from nature could melt transistors and many types of modern electronics by overwhelming them. Like a solar flare from the sun did in 1989, taking down the entire power grid in Quebec for nine hours. She also knew that a manmade pulse could do the same thing: destroy unshielded electronics.

After an earlier than normal coffee and some breakfast, Sara researched how a non-nuclear electromagnetic pulse could be created and the general requirements of such a device. Avoiding everyone for much of the day, she quickly learned the basic requirements needed to make the pulse itself. It could be done by a variety of sources, although the conventional method was a flux compression generator.

Hours later, she had learned that a flux compression generator was just a magnetic coil made of wire. Once electrically charged, at peak, an explosion is triggered. This causes the coil to short circuit, which compresses the magnetic field, generating an intense electromagnetic burst.

She noted however, that a flux compression generator creates just one burst.

If the EMP weapon was going to be reusable, as one would expect with a satellite-based weapon, then a piston or rotary disk type generator would be needed to create the pulse. But this reusable device needed far more initial power. Armed with a rudimentary knowledge of what she might get into, she closed the file and called Fortitude to save her many EMP weapon sketches, crude designs, and analysis.

The next morning Sara had returned to her PhD research to understand Fulminology, the science of lightning. After several days, she sat rubbing her tired eyes. Just as she turned off her computer, Nathen walked into her small office.

"Hey what are you working on? I have an hour between classes and thought I would say hi."

Sara smiled with weary eyes. "Nothing right now. I think I've hurt my brain!"

Nathen glanced at the plethora of literature on her now crowded desk and, reading upside down, said, "Fulminology, the science of lightning. Learn anything new?"

"Well, yes, and no. I get that there is a water cycle on earth. You know, the sun heats the ocean, the ocean water evaporates into the air, this water vapor cools into droplets which form clouds, creating rain which returns the moisture to the earth. The tricky part is the electrification of clouds. Not all rain clouds produce lightning, and not all lightning clouds produce rain."

Nathen added, "But electrification of a cloud occurs when the rapidly moving warm air is being pulled upward into the cloud and the higher it goes, the colder it gets. As that occurs, the moisture in the air forms larger water droplets and ice crystals, right?"

"Yes, and it also produces a type of hail called graupels. The lighter ice crystals continue upward at a high rate of speed where they become positively charged, while the heavier graupels remain negatively charged as they suspend or fall. For simplicity, the top of the cloud takes on a positive electric charge, and the bottom nearest earth has a negative electric charge."

Nathen nodded. "And that makes lightning possible?"

"No, it simply creates the electrical charges," Sara answered. "There is scientifically debated, but what I understand is this. At some point, that negative charge in the cloud's bottom nearest earth becomes so strong that the naturally occurring negative electrons on the ground are repelled deep into the earth. This creates a strong positive charge at the surface right under the cloud."

"Okay. So, that makes sense. Lightning itself is simply the electrostatic discharge when two electrically charged objects equalize themselves. Here, the negative charge in the cloud's bottom and the now positive charge of the earth directly under it. Opposites attract. But how does that even work? Air is not conductive. It can't carry an electrical charge." Nathen asked.

"Well, that is an unknown as well. Most scientists believe that the high-speed electrons moving up into the cloud are moving so fast, this can sometimes ionize the air. It is there that the initial lightning leader is formed."

Nathen understood. "So, as the lightning leader forms and approaches the ground, the air gap between the two charges is bridged. That causes resistance to drop and the electrons speed back up the leader network at a fraction of the speed of light. That creates the luminous lightning discharge we see."

Sara smiled and added, "That's right. And don't forget the heat generated from that return stroke raises the temperature of the surrounding air so fast, the air has no time to expand. The result is a shock wave of compressed particles in every direction, which we call thunder."

Thankfully, ever since Benjamin Franklin proved lightning was actually electricity in 1752, and Alexander Popov created the first lightning detector in 1894, most developed countries have since created nationwide lightning detection grids. They map lightning events around the world and on average, there forty-four per second or just under four-million strikes each day.

Nathen glanced at his watch, and realizing the time, walked to the door. "Hey, cool stuff. I have to get to my next class. Good Luck."

18

Packard's Corner, Boston

It was just after 7:00 p.m. when Sara left campus and she was looking forward to a quiet night, since Lisa had left on her geology field trip to Arizona. Turning onto Reedsdale Street, she finally found a place to park several houses down from her house. She pulled in behind a large truck, turned off the car, and gathered her things.

In the shadows two houses down, a young man watched her with intent. He and two others had made sure that parking spaces nearest her house were taken to force her to this dark side of the street. There, several streetlights didn't work and the light from those that did couldn't penetrate well the mature trees that had grown around them.

A second man was standing on the opposite sidewalk under a bright lamp and his job was to make sure she stayed side of the street.

Completely unaware, Sara gathered her things and started to walk across the street when she stopped. A big guy was standing there one house up in the middle of her sidewalk, waving his hands and talking to no one animatedly. She cautiously stayed on the side of the street she was on, although it was really dark. Even though she had replaced her flats with her snow boots at school, she was still having trouble keeping her balance on the patches of ice and snow.

Oblivious to Sara or the trio watching her, Jason was now just three houses behind her, having just walked through a small alley after being forced to park one street over on Linden. Usually, he wouldn't have bothered with a social visit, but knew Sara was mad about the DARPA grant. Thinking they could talk it over, he brought her a peace offering, which, in this case, was a bottle of wine. Turning onto her street, he noticed a weird guy on the sidewalk and wondered what his deal was. Looking forward, he also thought he saw Sara and sped up.

Sara heard Jason coming but not knowing it was him, grew concerned. In a sudden move, she went off the sidewalk into the street, trying to get to the better lighting about twenty feet past the guy talking to himself, who was now staring right at her.

At that same moment, a silent shadow jumped out from behind a snow-covered hedge that she would have passed. Jason saw the shape and movement of attack and yelled "Sara, watch out!"

Sara heard his voice and took off in a run just as the hand of the attacker, arched above his head, came flying down, narrowly missing her right shoulder as she hurried across the street.

As she did so, the attacker fell forward just as Jason brought down the wine bottle with all his strength. Although he was aiming for the attacker's head, as he dropped, the impact was on the back of his shoulder. It was a good hit, shattering the bottle. The assailant, clearing dazed, righted himself and kicked out as he pivoted toward Jason.

Jason turned just as fast, deflecting most of the impact. He immediately jammed his right hand forward directly into the guy's windpipe, momentarily incapacitating him as he went down, clutching his throat, with his other hand limp at his side.

Sara was almost at her door when the crazy guy on the sidewalk started running toward Jason. She yelled back, "Jason, look out!" He spun as he withdrew his Glock 32 and leveled it at the guy's face, stopping his movement instantly. Jason moved back three large steps to get both assailants into his direct view. With quick deliberate movements from one guy to the next, he held them at check, but could hear a vehicle in the background, wheels spinning, knowing it was coming down the street towards him.

Jason who was now in the center of the street, glanced over his left shoulder and saw the van aimed right for him. At the last minute, he forcefully rolled to the right to avoid getting hit, but immediately jumped up. As he tried to sight them, both guys went around the front of the van toward the driver's side sliding door, which was open. Jason fired two shots, taking out the passenger side window and damaging the front windshield, as the van tore off down the street and around the corner.

Adrenaline pumping, Jason holstered the Glock and did a quick visual sweep of the street and surrounding area. Lights were coming on and window curtains opened as he ran to Sara's, knocked, and said loudly, "Sara, it's me, they're gone."

Her face, full of panic stared out of the side window and on seeing him, she immediately opened the door, pulled him in and closed it, locking both locks. His shoulder and face were covered in dirty snow.

"Are you okay?" she shrieked. "What the hell was that?"

Monetarily ignoring her question, he asked, "Are you OK?"

"Yes, but what just happened?"

"Give me just a few minutes," Jason said firmly. "I need to call Metro PD and report this."

When he hung up, he went back and sat down next to her. "I have no idea what just happened. I came over with a bottle of wine to apologize about Dr. Cummings. Once I saw you run, I tried to stop the guys, but they jumped into a van. I got off two shots, but don't think any hit them, although I damaged the van. The police might be able to trace that."

"You have a gun?"

"Yes. Remember, I protect the scientists."

"Well, thanks for that. I ran to the street because I heard someone behind me and thought I was going to get mugged or something. I guess that was you."

"Well, thank God for instincts. Had you stayed on the sidewalk he would have gotten you, although I still would have gotten him." He half smiled.

Over the next hour and a half, the normally quiet street was bathed in erratic blue light as several police cars filled the area right outside the house. They had taken statements and talked to neighbors, although no one had seen or heard anything except a few who had heard the two shots from Jason's gun.

With police coming and going, a petite woman with jet black hair in a black jacket and an FBI cap came through the door and entered the small house. When she saw Jason, they warmly shook hands and Jason said to Sara, "Sara, this is one of my friends, Special Agent Raven Maddock. Raven, this is Sara Ricci." He added, "The FBI helps me occasionally."

Sara said, "So, this happens a lot?"

Special Agent Maddock replied, "No, and we're not sure exactly what this is, but we'll find out. How are you holding up?"

"I'm okay, thanks to Jason, but this is all getting out of hand."

"What is all this?" Special Agent Maddock asked skeptically.

"Jason can fill you in, but someone wants something from me, although I'm not sure what that is. In six weeks, I have been exposed to hacks, an office break in, and now I guess someone trying to kill me. I'm scared and don't know what to do."

"I'm sure it seems out of hand now, but we'll understand all this in time. It rarely turns out as you imagined."

She turned to Jason. "Whoever they are, they are professionals who have done this before. Outside is clean, but they left a damaged syringe in the street." She turned toward Sara. "Ms. Ricci, my guess is nobody was trying to harm you but incapacitate you. We'll get confirmation on the drug, but given the staged setup that Jason described, I'm certain this was an attempted grab. Somebody wants information and they want to hear it directly from you. I'll be in touch, and it's okay to act paranoid for a while." She shook Sara's hand and then Jason's before she turned to leave.

At the end of the street, Nadia pulled her car to a stop and got out. She had heard that something big happened on Sara's Street from a friend who owned a police scanner. She didn't want Sara to see her, but if this wasn't proof that she was up to no good, nothing was. Police, FBI, what the hell was going on? She sauntered down the street towards Sara and Lisa's house. Two police officers were out front with an FBI agent. Nadia approached one of the Metro policemen, asking, "Hey I live next block over. What's going on? Should I be afraid?"

"It's nothing miss. Just go on home," said the older officer.

"The hell it is, Metro PD, the FBI? Is this a drug house? Is there human trafficking going on here?" Nadia said loudly.

The younger police officer, who was smitten by the attractive grad student said softly, "It was nothing. Possible attempted grab, nothing to worry about. The victim is some kind of famous scientist, but they failed."

"Jefferson, quiet!" the older cop said quickly. He turned to Nadia, "Miss, please just go home. You are safe and there is nothing to worry about." Nadia had what she wanted, so she turned and went back to her car thinking, *somebody tried to kidnap Sara. Why? Maybe Nathen knows? Famous scientist, you must be joking!*

19

East Somerville, Massachusetts

Twenty minutes later the damaged van pulled into the drive on Arlington off Alford in East Somerville next to an industrial outbuilding and into a garage. The driver parked, and they all went into the building, closing the garage door. Inside, they spoke for a few minutes, one of them still unable to talk and favoring his left shoulder.

The van driver reached in and grabbed a beer from a small mini fridge and told the other two to leave. He sat down and dialed an international number on his cell phone. It was late there, but he would have to report this. *No one had told him she had protection, so this was on them, they damn near got killed.*

The phone rang and head of security, Grant Aiken picked it up and said before any other words were spoken, "Hold for a minute." He allowed himself to awaken completely and returned to the conversation. "You are late on this call. Let me complete arrangements on my end, and I'll call you back on the video."

The van driver twitched his head from side to side and said quickly, "Yeah, that will not be possible. The target had private security. Somehow, she made us, and her security guy foiled the attempt. Bastard almost killed one of my guys. The police were en route, but we were long gone. We left the scene clean. Perhaps this scientist is more than you think she is."

Grant shook his head, fuming. "Did any of the drug enter her body?"

"No, it was a miss altogether."

"And you have the unused drug?" Grant asked.

There was a pause before he replied, "Ah...I'm not sure about that. Let me get back to you." He realized he had no idea where the syringe was, but had to assume it had been dropped during the attempt.

Without hesitation, Grant answered, "This is your definition of clean? The police will certainly know this was an abduction."

"No way," the van driver barked. "Don't fucking worry about it. You said nothing about her having protection."

"Apparently, you can't properly assess a situation, and since when does it take three people to attack a PhD student, you idiot? Our business is concluded." Grant hung up angrily, knowing he would have to give the bad news to Maximillian.

He palmed the phone, noted the time, and walked upstairs. Maximillian slept little. He paused at the dual glass doors, sucked it up and pressed the buzzer. The door clicked, and he walked in.

"Grant, that is a rarefied look for you. You seem shaken." Maximillian said with concern.

"Sir, I realize it is late, but my team failed in Boston. Apparently, the scientist had outside protection, and they didn't get her, but..."

Maximillian jumped up from the desk with such force the chair slammed into the wall with a loud crash, toppling and leaving a sizable dent in the patterned aluminum skin on the wall. "What the hell did you do?" he screamed. "I made it clear there was to be no such attempt." His shock at the betrayal was clear in his expression.

Grant stood, realizing he had been duped, and would kill that bitch, but first he had to avoid being killed by Maximillian. He said quietly to defuse the situation, "Sir, please, I..."

Maximillian raised his hand as if to say *shut up*, which Grant did, and their eyes locked. Seeing the look of bewilderment on Grant's face, Maximillian then understood. Grant had left Bridget and Maximillian to sort it out and when she left, she no doubt told him it was a go. She had disobeyed him!

Neither said a word until Maximillian said calmly, perhaps too calmly, "I now understand what has transpired and I will deal with Bridget. Make sure we have no open issues in the United States." With no words, he motioned to the door and Grant left.

Although he had been warned, this was personal, and Grant headed straight for Bridget's office despite the late hour. With no formality, he walked into her office and toward her desk. She was on the phone her back turned to him as she held up her hand as if to say, "Quiet" to whomever might bother her. Coming alongside the desk, Grant disconnected the call with his left index finger, and with his right hand grabbed her neck, squeezed, and lifted her several inches off her chair. Her eyes turned to him in horror.

Staring straight into her enormous eyes, he said in a monotone voice, "If you ever do that to me again, I will kill you."

He let go, and she dropped into the chair still holding the silent phone, gasping for air as he walked out of the room. For the rest of the evening, Grant and Bridget were left alone with their own thoughts.

The next morning at 8 a.m., both were asked independently to join Maximillian for breakfast. Not speaking, they walked apart from one another toward the doors into the residence. Wearing a turtleneck sweater to hide the bruising on her neck, even Bridget pressed the buzzer rather than just enter.

Maximillian sat at the table with a cup of coffee and motioned for them to sit. They did so silently, and he looked at each, then back to his cup. "Organizational strength cannot exist without hierarchy, respect, and a little touch of fear. Bridget, you made a significant error in judgment and Grant, you forgot who feeds you. The reason I was adamant not to approach the scientist was because I have someone inside DARPA working for me. That person recently presented Sara Ricci with a sizable grant, which is tantamount to her working for me without knowing it. To assure that does not fail, Boris Turgenev at MDE

129

Commodities has approached her to assist her efforts with our own metals tying us to her inventions. Soon I would have known everything she knows, and all I had to do was wait for her to do the work."

He stopped for a moment, took a sip of the coffee, and said, "An excellent plan, now in jeopardy because of your actions." He again paused, reflecting on what had been said, and added, "You have both violated my trust, but given who you are to me, I will forgive you this one and only time. But I caution you. Neither of you is outside of my considerable reach." Breakfast never came.

Although Sara had not yet accepted the DARPA grant, she continued to do research on the power that might be required for the EMP weapon. To answer the unknowns, she reluctantly called Dr. Cummings to better understand the requirements before she decided. To her surprise, he knew very little about the final EMP weapon design. Apparently, it had not been invented as yet, and such a design was waiting on how much power could be generated. After the call, Sara saved all she had on the EMP weapon on the Fortitude server and went back to her original research.

20

After teaching an undergraduate class, Sara headed back to her office to put the final touch on her research plan document she owed her committee at the end of the week.

The first phase of research would involve all literature about Fulminology, or lightning, and of particular interest, how electrification occurred. She assumed she could cite much of the literature but allocated ten thousand dollars to this phase just in case she had to recreate any experiments or purchase papers.

In the second phase, she would review all literature and known data regarding terrestrial gamma ray flashes (TGFs). While it was possible that all lightning events produced some gammas, unlike Gilberti, Sara had real data from modern detection sources that were recording lightening event that encountered. She would allocate twenty-five-thousand to this phase, but suspected she might not need that much.

Tied closely to the second, the third phase of research the unknow. Unlike lightning, TGFs only moved upward and presently were only being detected low earth orbit (LEO), a maximum of twelve-hundred miles above sea level. The question she needed to answer was, were there lesser energy TGFs occurring at lower altitudes, undetected from space? That is where Sara believed she needed sensors within thunderclouds that could detect gamma rays. This would require the most money, which she estimated at least one-hundred-fifty thousand for sensors and plane rentals.

The last phase, which might not be included in her final dissertation, was how the energy from the TGFs could be converted into useable power. This entire phase depended on finding enough energy and second, having enough money to pursue this. The budget she had just created showed there could be as much as sixty-five thousand remaining, but she would worry about that later. Satisfied, she called Fortitude and saved the file.

The next morning at the Mud Room, Sara reviewed the DARPA grant and concluded Nathan was probably correct that DARPA was influenced by Gilberti's work. Despite how that sounded, it wasn't all bad for Sara. After all, DARPA was tied to the military and could work seamlessly with MIT. It also included Jason, exemplary lab security, and a guarantee of on-campus housing.

The more she thought of it, the more she was comforted, given all that had just transpired. Taking a sip of expresso, she decided to accept the grant and attempted to phone Dr. Cummings, but he didn't answer. His assistant took her message, and he called back two hours later. "Sara, do you have more questions regarding the grant?" he asked.

"Dr. Cummings, thank you for calling me back. I accept the grant but have one important question. If the energy is present and could be converted, it will probably require metals with high atomic values, which are very expensive. I have been working with a company called MDE Commodities and they are interested in giving me the metal outright if I will help them understand the application itself. Would DARPA allow this?"

Cummings was momentarily taken aback. Of course, a man like Maximillian would leave little to chance, but he never thought he would approach her directly. "Well first, congratulations and I have no issue, as long as you share any correspondence with me first, so I can review it with the authority to approve or deny. Is that acceptable?" He replied.

"Yes, that should be fine." Sara said honestly.

"Then it's settled. Please call Dr. Zimbrean who will work with MIT to get a formal acceptance. Thank you Sara." He hung up thinking, *well I have done my part.*

On the Isle of Skye, Maximillian summoned Grant up to his office several weeks later. As Grant entered, he said calmly, "I have been in contact with my DARPA contact, and the young scientist has accepted their grant. They will soon take over her data security, but for now, she is using a private source that nobody seems to know about. My immediate concern is that my contact may lose quick and informal access to the data. I still think something is off because I'm convinced that Gilberti Ricci's work was related to a weapon which would explain the Germans' interest. But it would also explain DARPA's interest on the systems side of things today. Based on that, how difficult would it be to locate her data before the transition to DARPA?"

"Locate or retrieve?"

"Both."

"At some point, she has to upload, which is the only way to determine the server's location. Her computer is the most obvious choice but I'm sure MIT sweeps it regularly, so it's probably best to monitor her outbound sends off campus. We have no idea if she does this from home, so we'll just have to monitor to find out."

"Okay, but you head this up. We have given up too much using others who have failed."

"I'll do it personally with only my team."

Grant and five members of his private security team waited for their SUV to be brought forward, having just flown to the United States on a leased Dassault Falcon private jet. They were now inside the warmth of the Flight Support center at Logan Airport.

The day before, Bill Aiken, one of the two who had searched Sara's office had posed as a cable repairman and installed a device on the telephone pole at the back of Sara's neighbor's house. The device had been placed between her house modem and the coaxial cable junction box on the utility pole. Soon, it would monitor outflows from the modem to determine where each outbound packet was sent and special software would research each IP address. From the safety of their hotel, Grant could analyze them.

After three days, they had followed several dozen outgoing requests, but all were being received by commercial DNS servers. Their first thought was that she might only send data from her MIT office, but was six hours later they got a valid hit. The software had registered the IP address to a company called Fortitude Security.

Less than ten minutes later, they verified the server was in Kalispell, Montana. They also discovered that Fortitude Security was owned by Richard Chase, father of Nathan Chase, the research assistant to Sara Ricci. They had it.

21

Kalispell, Montana

Grant and his team were met at the plane in Boston before they took off by Aiken, who supplied each of them a large black canvas bag. Inside were tactical gear and weapons as they boarded the private jet. Destination, the Glacier Park airport in Kalispell, Montana.

Once there, the team went to the hotel and Grant and one of his men left to do surveillance. Pulling off the highway as they approached Fortitude Security, Grant used a scope to survey the area. He could see a large barn-like structure with several windows, and assumed that was the company itself. The land around it spread out for what appeared to be twenty acres with high ground on the far side. Closest to him was a small lake and clustered trees, the only other structure was a modest log cabin to the right. There was no outward sign of security personnel, but probably electronic surveillance. Troubling was the single driveway that went from the main highway up and around to the barn about half a kilometer long. There was no way in without immediate detection.

Grant put the SUV back into gear and they continued past the property, thinking through their initial assessment and plan. While the team could hit both locations, they would not have much time to locate the servers. What he really needed was to determine if the server they had flagged was in the house or in the large barn structure. The problem was he couldn't get close enough to use the device he brought to detect that.

Driving back to the hotel, he asked the likelihood that both buildings were using the same firewall to his partner.

"Given the complexity of the business firewall, I doubt he would then go to a local ISP for the house."

"I would agree. What about the servers themselves?"

"The business is the safest place, but given the relationship of the son to the researcher, I think this is just a favor, meaning she is not a paid client. It would seem unlikely that a business guy would risk his paid client's security, so I'm saying the server we are after is in the house."

"Are you willing to bet your life on it?" Grant answered, smiling, but serious.

Shorty before midnight, the security team boarded a leased helicopter armed with AS Val's, an older model Russian fully suppressed assault rifle. Favored by their special forces, the Spetsnaz, they weren't known for range but were highly effective and silent.

As the helicopter raced towards the grass in front of the house, the clock struck one o'clock in the morning and Grant used a heat signature device to scope the barn and surrounding area. Other than two dogs, there was no one in the large structure. As they came in over the house to the landing point, a lone occupant, likely Richard Chase, was already up and coming for them. This would have to be fast.

All six men were out and on the ground before the helicopter skids hit the grass. As they jumped off, three immediately fired their silenced weapons at the front of the house to pin Chase down. The other three went to each of the sides and rear of the house, doing the same.

In the dark, the suppressed bullets immediately forced Chase to the floor near the front door where he had originally headed. Although he was well trained, he couldn't move as it appeared all sides had been immediately covered. Grant and two others came toward the front door as they continued to fire while Chase, still pinned to the right of the door moved to the other side, thinking *what the hell is this?*

At that exact moment, the front door burst open, and three men entered, fanning to the right and left. They were firing, but so did Chase, hitting one attacker before he was immediately hit in the shoulder and leg. Before he could react, they quickly disarmed him and zip tied his hands. After they blindfolded him, he was forced into a sitting position against the wall.

By the sound of their movements, Chase sensed five or six guys were all in the house now, but he had not heard a sound other than their movements; they had yet to utter a single word. It seemed like just seconds when they exited as the helicopter increased rotor speed, lifted, and then retreated off into the distance, heading south. Chase suspected it had been less than four or five minutes since they touched down.

Trying to move his bound hands up to the wall, his wounded shoulder wouldn't allow it, so Chase pushed his back against the wall. Using his good leg, he used his core strength and powerful leg to slowly push himself up the wall into a standing position. Shaking off the blindfold, he surveyed the damage but could not see any sigh of the guy he shot, so he must have been wearing body armor.

Smoke was everywhere and Chase assumed the open door and broken windows had disrupted the fireplace, but it was then he noticed the rear of the house was actually on fire. He sighed and hobbled to the kitchen. Still bound with his hands behind him, he accessed his home tablet with his voice, calling the fire department and the local sheriff. As he shuffled back to the front, away from the flames in the back, he could already hear the sirens. Somebody was going to fucking regret this.

As the fire department tended to the small fire, the sheriff arrived minutes later. He rushed to Chase who was sitting up on a gurney outside the door of the paramedic's van.

Neither of them paid attention to the sound of a business jet taking off in a steep climb before banking right and heading toward London.

The day after, Chase was released from the hospital as both wounds were through and through, hitting no bones or arteries, and he had no infection or fever. The Sheriff picked him up, and they drove back to the house. He and Richard had known each other for almost twenty years and often hung out together, helped each other solve crimes, and occasionally prevent them.

Over a beer, he asked, "Well, Richard, you're the damn expert. What the hell do you think this was?"

Standing up with his crutches supporting him, he said, "These guys were fast, fearless, and never said a single word. They all used suppressed fire, operated in the dark without night vision headgear and wore black armor head to toe. Given that they used all that capability to only disable me until I can look around a bit more, I would have to say they were out to warn me. But I have no idea why."

Well, we checked, "They only hit the house, they never went into Fortitude itself. Anything worth taking?"

"Burglars don't fly helicopters and shoot Russian AS-Val's!"

The sheriff chuckled and asked, "What was in the closet?"

"What?" replied Chase, surprised at the question.

"The hall closet, where all the wires are?"

"Those are servers I use for special projects. Why?"

"There are only wires there now. Christ almighty, they did all this to get access to your servers!"

"Oh, shit!" yelled Chase, his expression one of fear. One server belonged to Sara, but there were two others that were his!

22

Isle of Skye, Scotland

Angus Adair sat at a large but comfortable table in a meeting area outside of Maximillian's study with four others. They had been reviewing the information from the three data servers taken from Montana and were preparing to explain what they uncovered to him.

Inside his study, Maximillian sat comfortably on the sofa while Bridget was preparing a glass of Rombauer Sauvignon Blanc from a small bar to the left of a small conference table. This was the only room in the residence that was decidedly not modern, nor minimalist. Here he had created a space of warmth that one might find in a large European villa. The only difference was the massive windows overlooking the ocean. The calm of the room was disrupted when his scientist, Dr. Berniece requested entrance and, along with Grant, was buzzed in.

"Sir, we have a summary of two of the three servers," Berniece began. "One is clearly that of the young scientist and the other seems to be historical financials possibly related to the Fortitude Security business. The third server is encrypted, and Angus has yet to decipher the code key. We are certain there is a

protection device to scramble the data if it meets the incorrect code after so many attempts, so for now, we don't know if this is related to the scientist."

Maximillian said, "Can Angus break the encryption?"

Grant replied, "Because of the type of encryption, not likely, but I suspect this server may contain Gilberti Ricci's lost work papers. When you and I discussed the DARPA timeline, I noticed her interest in energy from thunderstorms occurred only after her return from Italy. It is possible that the physical files of his papers are actually in Milan, and these might be images of those files."

"Interesting. If we cannot break the encryption, then perhaps we should search the family home. Let's see what Angus can find first. Dr. Berniece, proceed with the contents of the scientist's server."

Grant nodded in acknowledgement as Dr. Berniece began. "Most of the information concerns atmospheric energy, and especially lightning events. Data files are focused on how clouds are formed and how they get their electrical charge and how lightning is created. It should be noted that there are several historical images, so we know she has access to Gilbert's papers."

Continuing, he said, "Based on her research, when the electric field within the cloud is strong enough, the lightning can cause a terrestrial gamma ray flash (TGF). This creates an upward burst of gamma rays, as well as energetic electrons and positrons, or antimatter. Her notes suggest concern because the only gamma ray detection monitors are in low earth orbit. Evidently, she believes there could be tens of thousands of occurrences daily at lower altitudes, and energies from TGFs have been recorded as high as a hundred million electronvolts."

"That sounds impressive. Is it?" Maximillian asked.

"Singularly, no. It takes something like six quintillion electron volts to make just one watt of power, but this phenomenon produces trillions of electrons and positrons. Presumably, if you could encounter them and convert some portion to say thermal energy, it might in total add up to something useable, although perhaps not worthwhile."

Maximillian pondered this and asked, "Does she imply what she wants to do with this energy?"

Dr. Berniece replied, "Her thesis is only looking to see if energies are there and if so, could it be converted into useable power, but that doesn't mean she hasn't thought about applications. There are several drawings and pages of equations related to using the energy as thrust for spacecraft propulsion and also as a power source to a magnetoplasmadynamic thruster also for spacecraft. Most of the files, however, are related to a satellite based non-nuclear electromagnetic pulse weapon. There are several iterations, including reusable ones and one-shot versions, all of which are quite sophisticated."

"And this young researcher is designing these weapons?"

"No sir. The EMP weapon appears to be related to the DARPA grant, and I think she is trying to understand the power requirements of these various designs."

"How interesting. As I suspected, there is a weapon, but not from the past but rather, DARPA's current thinking. What of these propulsion ideas?"

"Well, if the energy were present in sufficient amount, and if it could be converted to power, it could, in fact, be used in the vacuum of space as described. Some of these ideas could be related to Gilberti Ricci."

Maximillian stood but said nothing for several seconds before he looked up and said to the room, "This young scientist appears genuine. DARPA is clearly interested in Gilberti's research to locate and collect atmospheric energy to power an EMP weapon or to convert naturally produced gamma rays into a power source to propel a spacecraft."

"That is essentially what was on the server," replied Berniece, unsure if Maximillian was excited or furious as he rose to leave.

Berniece left the room and Bridget followed him but paused at the door when Grant, who remained seated, noted the look on Maximillian's face and asked, "Sir, you have something on your mind?"

"I knew of the DARPA grant, so it is not surprising she is looking into atmospheric energy, including antimatter or beamed energy, but a power source for an EMP weapon? As a propulsion device or a power source for a magnetoplasmadynamic engine in a spacecraft? Such things never came up."

"Is there anything I can do now?"

"No, but give some thought as to getting Gilberti's original papers if we can't get more information from my DARPA contact."

23

MIT Campus, Boston

When Sara formally accepted the grant, several legal details had to be concluded before her research could start. As a result, DARPA had arranged a meeting to discuss the confidentiality of the grant itself and sign various documents. In a small conference room on campus, Sara sat with Special Agent Maddock, Dr. Cummings from DARPA, Dr. Zimbrean, and a man she did not know.

Special Agent Maddock was speaking. "Sara, the FBI is not officially involved, as this is outside our purview. I have been assigned to assist DARPA, however, because of the abduction attempt. Starting back with the first hack into MIT, we now see an escalating threat that culminated with the sophisticated raid on the location of your data in Montana. We know you and your research are the target, and we're working with other intelligence agencies to understand who might be after you and your research. Allow me to introduce Director Jeremy Hicks with Homeland Security."

Without a pause, Director Hicks said, "Ms. Ricci, you have been given a limited security clearance to perform your research

147

here at MIT on behalf of this DARPA grant, and this includes your assistant, Nathen Chase. It also allows you to hear the following words, words that cannot otherwise leave this room."

He paused and took a sip of water, and they all nodded in confirmation. "As you may have suspected, American Intelligence is aware of Gilberti Ricci, and that knowledge brought you to our attention. What you do not know, very few people left on earth do, is that Gilberti Ricci at one time was working with the Americans. He was most distraught by the racial laws of the fascist party and the CIA recruited him in 1941. To their surprise, he refused to move from Italy and as a result, the CIA received little information related to his work on atmospheric energy and space propulsion systems. When your application was received at MIT, interest was reignited and that is the reason we are here now. The problem is we apparently are not the only ones with this knowledge."

Pausing for effect, he added, "Ms. Ricci, we believe you are being targeted because someone thinks you have access to Gilberti's research and are following in his footsteps. We suspect an organization from the UK in behind this."

On hearing this, Bernard held his composure. Special Agent Maddock had been looking at him through a reflection on a glass monitor and noticed a slight but perceptible reaction.

Hicks saw it as well. "The CIA and DHS have been monitoring the situation, occasionally sharing information with UK intelligences agencies as necessary."

Sara was stunned, but relieved to better understand why these things were happening. She saddened, however, when she looked back toward Director Hicks. "So, it really is true. I was only accepted to MIT because of Gilberti Ricci."

"Not to my knowledge. I only said we knew who you were and watched you. There is nothing to show that any United States agency guided you to this path or that this knowledge influenced MIT."

"Perhaps that is the right perspective, Director Hicks, but it might take me a while to get there. What I don't understand is if you have an idea who this is, why the hell don't you just stop them? Why do I have to always keep one eye open, wondering what will happen next?"

"Ms. Ricci, we can only act on the information and evidence we have, and to be honest, we have very little. The DARPA grant does, however, offer protections, and we will do everything we can to assure your safety. That will include increased security, transfer to campus housing, secure lab access and NSA backed data storage. Additionally, the DARPA liaison, Jason Sykes will monitor you," responded Director Hicks, and Sara smiled at the thought.

It was then Cummings spoke for the first time. "Ms. Ricci, can we be assured that any data lost in Montana did not contain any information regarding the purpose of the grant request?"

"What!" said Sara abruptly.

"It is not a difficult question. The grant prospectus needed to be treated with respect. Now that research has been stolen, it is fair to ask if your actions compromised DARPA secrets."

Sara jumped out of her chair. "Are you kidding me? I had to create my own data security protocol because I was hacked at MIT, and if I understand this, you apparently knew what could happen, and even who might do it. And now you're asking if *I compromised your fucking project?*"

"Well, did you?" he said smugly.

It took everything Sara had to contain herself as she sat seething, but said nothing more. Director Hicks chuckled at the exchange but wanted to stop the briefing and did so by saying only that he would be in touch if any new information was learned.

Dr. Zimbrean tried to defuse the tension further and reiterated Jason would help her with data security and would facilitate her and Nathen's access to the secured labs. MIT administration would facilitate her relocation onto campus. The meeting adjourned with quick goodbyes.

Later that day, Sara went to meet Nathen in the high clearance building within the Plasma Science and Fusion Center. They waited for Jason who would help them set up their security profiles and biometric data. Nathen was outside the lab as Sara walked up.

"How is your dad?" she said.

"Good, he was up and out of the hospital in a day and there has been no infection or problems."

"What about the cabin? I saw pictures from Special Agent Maddock, and it looked pretty beat up."

Nathen shook his head. "Yeah, he's still pretty hot about that. You know, he and I built that house from the ground up, and it means a lot to him, but he'll fix it. I'm glad you decided on the grant and was pleasantly surprised they worked so fast to get me clearance as well."

"Yes, it's perfect. We can continue with little disruption. Ah, there's Jason."

Nathen watched him walk towards them. He knew a little of him from Sara, but had only met him once.

As Jason approached, he said, "Morning Sara... Nathen. Follow me." He went directly to the door, and it clicked loudly as he approached. They all entered the foyer and, once inside, a woman came out, shook Jason's hand, and said to Sara and Nathen, "You are Sara Ricci and Nathen Chase?"

"Yes," both said at the same time.

"Very good. My name is Ingrid Vassar. I will assist your security setup today. May I please see your student IDs?"

She scanned each with a small tablet device and handed them back. She then pulled out two cards and handed one to each of them. "Here is a Cardkey/fob, and they are coded for you and only you. Consider it one of your most valuable possessions and it is best to always keep it around your neck, under your clothing. Never in a pocket, wallet, backpack, car, or purse."

As she said that, both Sara and Nathen placed the lanyard around their necks and looked at each other, excited and a little nervous.

"The card is dual purpose; it is used as an electronic fob for most doors and also as an access card. As a fob, it does not require any effort, just proximity to the lock. As you enter any of the secure facilities, all doors have at least one, and up to four levels of security. The first is the fob which unlocks the door. If there is a second level, insert the card itself. The third level is your left thumb print and if required, the fourth is your right eye scan. As each level is required, the access point will light up blue. Questions?"

"No," they both added independently.

"If you look at the top right and bottom left, you will see two small tabs on the card itself. Should you ever think the card is in danger, place your index finger and thumb from both hands on the upper and lower tab. Squeeze and hold simultaneously for three to five seconds and the card will deactivate. Once the card is deactivated, you must contact security to reactivate, which is subject to a review of the incident. Questions?" Impressed, they both nodded no.

Ingrid then asked Sara to approach the scanner and use her card for the first time as she went through the process to set up her thumb and eye scan. Afterwards, Nathen did the same. When they were done, Ingrid stated, "The system has now linked your card and biometric information to the information on file when your security clearance was processed. When inside a building, only locks that you are cleared to enter will accept your credentials, so if you encounter a door and cannot enter, it is because you are not authorized to do so. Questions?"

Nathen asked, "Is there a map to know which doors we can and can't enter?"

"No. Dr. Zimbrean has determined the labs required and I will show you each. There is little need to explore other spaces and should you decide to be curious, after an unspecified number of attempts to enter unauthorized areas, the card will deactivate. You would then have to call security to leave the building and they would only allow that after you are interrogated to determine your intent." With no additional questions, she opened the door with her card and all three of them followed her to Sara's new office and then to three other lab facilities.

When they were dismissed, Sara headed back to her old office to transition for the move, and Nathen headed to his car. He was almost there when he saw Nadia coming toward him. He stopped and waved, and she continued straight for him saying boldly, "Nathen, want to go out for drinks and dinner?"

"Your asking me out?" he said with a chuckle.

"Well, a girl can't wait for you, can she?"

He smiled. "Sure, when and where?"

"Tomorrow at seven at Catalyst in Technology Square on Main and Albany."

"Can I afford that?" Nathen asked as a joke, but Nadia simply smiled and walked away.

A few days later, Lisa helped Sara move her things from the house to her car and they said their goodbyes. After everything was in the car, Sara gave Lisa a hug and the cat a scratch before heading over to her new home at Ashdown House.

Washington D.C.

Following the MIT Briefing, Director Hicks boarded a small DHS Learjet and returned to his office at the Nebraska Avenue Complex in Washington, D. C.

Arriving at the near empty building, he went to his office, locked the door, and poured himself a small glass of Courvoisier. He was not much of a drinker, but he liked this spirit and it relaxed him. Despite Hollywood depictions, he did not have an elaborate bar behind a hidden wall, just a nice bottle and two glasses he kept in a place normally reserved for file folders.

As he sipped the rich amber fluid, he gave thought to the events of the last few months. The brilliant Maximillian Drummond thought he had recruited a high-level source into DARPA, but he didn't realize the CIA allowed that to happen. Maximillian had not yet surmised that the DHS had orchestrated a direct conduit to him.

It was a strange marriage of combined interests. Maximillian wanted secrets; DARPA wanted access to Gilberti Ricci's research; the CIA and DHS wanted Maximillian; and Bernard wanted money. These interests, however, were far from linear.

MIT Campus, Boston

As Sara walked toward her office, she ended a call with Jason Sykes. She was pleased with all the increased security, but in the back of her mind, whoever had been trying to get to her was still out there. The call to Jason had been to determine if he could help her figure out who it might be.

As he walked in, they exchanged pleasantries when she asked, "Jason, Director Hicks mentioned during my briefing that a UK based company was possibly behind my issues. He wouldn't have said that if there wasn't reason, and I was wondering if it was possible to help me determine who this is?"

"Well, I agree he likely has reason, but DARPA is not an intelligence agency and as a field guy, I have limited connections to that type of information. I have heard nothing about this."

"What about your boss, Mr. Müller, or perhaps Dr. Cummings?"

"Sara, I want to help, but information at DARPA is highly compartmentalized and if information is not readily provided, the assumption is you don't need to know it. Asking can bring suspicions."

"Okay, I understand. I don't want to get you in trouble, but you must have some acquaintances who do this sort of thing. Let me tell you what I have. Maybe you can help me understand who I can work with."

"Fine, but I'm still not sure I can help."

Sara paused for a moment. "Over this last week, I made a list of metadata, you know, keywords, that sum up my research. Yesterday, I met with Myeong Yoon in MIT cyber security, and she fed those words into a more detailed search engine she has access to. Refining the search to only UK companies, she gave me the names of two companies that matched much of the metadata. One was a company called Roland Controls out of Ireland, and the other was MDE Enterprises in London. MDE Enterprises is the corporation that owns MDE Commodities, the source of my specialty metals, and they have offered it to me for free for application information."

"Okay, so given you are working with them already and they have been helpful, it doesn't sound like they need to harm you. Have you found anything about this Roland Controls?"

Sara turned her monitor towards Jason. "Well, they are a small company that makes medical detection systems, primary X-Ray, microwave, and ultrasound alarms. They are privately owned and run by a thirty-something engineer. They appear to be smaller than fifteen million euros in annual sales, which seems way too small to finance the things that have happened."

"Makes sense. Type in MDE Enterprises."

Sara did, and the screen populated with thousands of search hits. She clicked on a few as Jason looked on. "So, this is a public company. Click on the investor page," Jason asked. She did and then he asked, "Click on the Officer's tab." She did and thirteen names came up with Maximillian Drummond being first, followed by Bridget Drummond. They owned the most shares.

"Have you ever heard of these names?"

"No, but I guess I could ask Boris Turgenev, the guy helping me from MDE Commodities."

"Sara, I think you need to be careful here. It is highly probable this means nothing. But if they are involved, inquiry could be dangerous."

"So, what do I do? Nothing?"

"Let me give this some thought and we'll talk again."

"Okay, Let me know."

Richard Chase sat with a few friends who were standing members of a team at Fortitude Security used for projects that could not follow normal channels or methods. They were in a secure conference room at Fortitude, following leads on who raided Richard's house.

Without difficulty, they investigated general aviation flights in or out of the three airports near Kalispell and got a lead at Glacier Airport. A Dassault Falcon private jet had landed and stayed less than forty-eight hours, leaving just two hours after the raid. The tail number was from France, and they also located the motel where the occupants had stayed near Somers, Montana, some twenty miles away. No one got a good look at them, but there were several men with no luggage. All arrangements were made by a local jet services company, and they were paid by a wire transfer from a corporation no longer in existence. No names, no credit cards, not even cash.

Richard pulled up an online tool on his computer to look up the tail number and typed it in. It accepted the number but would not refresh the screen. Assuming the number was valid, but not public, he tried a few other variants which worked, but not this one. It was then he called a former colleague who now worked in security at the Federal Aviation Administration (FAA).

After a brief hello, he asked, "I need some help to look up a tail number Foxtrot, Whiskey, Foxtrot, Bravo, X-ray (FWFBX). I can pull it up online, but the screen will not refresh. Can you help?"

"Sure, hold on let me change computers. Okay, that was Foxtrot, Whiskey, Foxtrot, Bravo, X-ray." A few seconds went by when he said, "Oh Shit! I gotta go! The tail you are looking for is flagged by DHS, and we are both going to feel some heat within the hour. I'll call you later."

It took less than twenty minutes for his phone to ring, and he picked up "FAA Security."

"This is Director Jeremy Hicks from DHS. What is your interest in a general aviation aircraft from France?"

"Nothing sir, I received a call from a friend who was interested."

"I can likely guess, but who is this friend?"

"He works in security. That is all I can or will say."

"Okay, we'll play it your way, but I hold the cards here, not you. If you want to remain employed, you will not pursue this further. Is there anything about this conversation you do not understand?"

"No sir," and the call abruptly ended. He hung up the phone thinking, *why does everything Chase touches turn to shit?*

In Montana, Chase sat back in his office thinking about the call from his friend in FAA Security, which again confirmed a cover up. What troubled him were the other servers taken. The FBI and DHS had assumed all three servers were Sara's, and he didn't say differently. But one server was an immense problem, and he couldn't help but wonder if it was an equally valid target for the raid. Meaning, this could be about him and have nothing to do with Sara.

At the Catalyst restaurant, Nathen waited for Nadia. The location was just a few miles west of his dorm, so he had walked over but was regretting his decision, given the cold and expected snow. When Nadia came through the door, he rose, gave her a hug, and helped remove her heavy outer coat. Her perfume was nothing short of exotic and he continued to smell it as he took their coats to the coat check. Taking the check stub, he motioned to the hostess that they were ready and they were seated a few minutes later.

Nathen had never been there, but Nadia had, so she walked him through the menu. Once the server arrived, Nathen ordered for them and as they waited for their main course, Nadia asked, "So how is your master's effort going?"

"Good, I've accomplished a lot, and the thesis is coming along. And you, how about your efforts?"

Nadia, who was in her first year with a master's in journalism, answered, "About the same. I'm also balancing classes with work and some freelance stuff to pay the bills."

"My apology, but where is your accent from?" Nathen asked.

"Morocco. My parents are still there along with much of my family, but I stay with my cousins in Brookline while I go to school."

"Did you do your undergraduate at MIT?"

"No. I went to Harvard for my undergraduate, my father's alma mater. I came to MIT for my master's degree because I focused on scientific journalism. My father pays, but will never forgive me for leaving Harvard," she laughed, but with serious eyes.

During their dinner, Nadia asked, "So what is your thesis on?"

"As of this moment, it's measuring space weather signals in geomagnetic observations on the ground."

"Wow, that's a mouth full. And this is related to the work you do with Sara?"

"Not really, but her work expands mine and it might intersect in the future."

"What does Sara work on? She never says."

"Conceptually, she is looking for ways to harness atmospheric energy."

"But you work with her almost daily; certainly, you know more than that?"

"I actually don't and regardless, my NDA prevents any discussion about it."

"An NDA? So, it's secret? Is she working with the military? I notice she is often heading toward the secure labs, and that someone tried to abduct her. Even the FBI was involved," she said rapidly, smiling now with a wicked grin.

"Nadia, to be honest, I'm not sure why we are spending so much time talking about her. Did you ask me out because you're interested in me or just to learn more about her?"

"Well, both, actually. I do like you, but there is something about Sara and her actions of late that smack of a good story. Considering the abduction attempt, it is no longer just a hunch, but I'll stand down while we have dinner. I can see you're protective," she replied with a smirk.

26

Packard's Corner, Boston

Sara spent the day going over the second wave of research, the study of gamma rays, and how this whole connection to lightning and antimatter had been discovered. She looked at the clock and noted it was almost six as she gathered her things to head over to her old house where Lisa stilled lived. They tried to meet once a week now that Sara lived on campus. As she walked in, Lisa was making popcorn. "Hey you, how is your research coming?"

"Slow and a bit mind numbing, but I'm onto the second phase, which is gamma rays." Sara said as she plopped on the sofa, and the cat immediately jumped on her lap.

"Gamma rays are the ones that are deadly to humans, right? I always get confused between waves and rays," Lisa replied from the kitchen.

"Well, technically, any discussion of light should be called a 'ray' because that is the correct usage of the noun. The term stuck with x-rays and gamma-rays, however, because they behave more like a point particle. Are you familiar with the electromagnetic spectrum?"

"Kind of. I know of radio waves, microwaves, x-rays and gamma rays. The spectrum is the range of wavelengths or frequencies, right?"

"Close. It is actually the range over which electromagnetic radiation extends and it reveals left to right, the seven known forms of radiation. Those you mentioned, plus infrared light, visible light, and ultraviolet rays. Humans can only see visible light without enhancement."

"So why are gamma rays so dangerous to humans?"

"Unlike other forms of radiation, gamma rays are photons. The thing is, they move so fast and have so much energy, they are *ionizing*, meaning they can alter an atom when they encounter it. That makes them deadly to our organs and tissues. They pass right through us, altering the atoms and molecules of what's there as they go."

"Wow, scary stuff. And this is what you work on? Seriously?" She scooped popcorn into bowls, handing one to Sara.

"Yes, but my research doesn't really place me anywhere near them." Sara answered without pause.

"Holly crap, robot girl. Better you than me," Lisa joked as she sat down on the couch.

The following morning, Sara was back in her office reading when Nathen walked in. He put down his backpack and some research papers before saying, "Hi, how's it going?"

"Good. I feel like we're making progress."

"So, you mentioned we need data?"

"Yes. To determine baseline data regarding TGFs, we need the actual raw data from the most relevant satellites that have been launched to detect them. I made a list here of the ones with the most data, Fermi, AGILE, and the ASIM. Once we have the raw data, we need to organize it into one dataset, and then try to correlate the altitude, latitude, and energy of each detected TGF."

"Sounds good. I'll check the MIT database first, since some of this may already be here." Nathen left to study.

27

Isle of Skye, Scotland

W eather on the Isle of Skye was overcast and windy. A large storm was expected to take hold of the island late that afternoon and most of the staff had called off. Maximillian, on the other hand, found the environment down right pleasant. He liked dark surroundings the best.

His brain was very active now, and he was thinking about the EMP weapon idea as Grant came in and joined him. Grant walked to the sofa facing the rugged coast and sat, turning to Maximillian before he asked, "What can I do for you?"

Maximillian was still in thought but responded after a silent minute. "I have been thinking of the information from Montana. I am intrigued by the concept of this TGF induced energy, but that is perhaps years away. As I understand it, DARPA wants to use this energy to power a space-based EMP weapon. Within the defense apparatus of the United States, perhaps a space-based endeavor is a worthwhile pursuit, but it made me wonder. What if a small one-shot EMP weapon could disrupt the normal state? My newest company, MDE Trust could benefit handsomely from such fears, given they are in the business of shielding electronics from just such events. I suspect building the devices is quite easy and we could repurpose commercial drones to launch them, but I believe it would require a partner to carry out the task. Any ideas?"

Grant paused before he answered. "I'm not aware of anyone I trust, but given the logistics involved, my advice is this. If you really want this, own it and make it happen through a shell company that we create and control."

Maximillian took a minute to think this through. "I'll get the team together to start the design and test phase. Meanwhile, look at how we could do this. Ideally, it would be nice for the shell company to act and behave as a terrorist organization for the sake of public image. And to maximize our profits, I am looking for a continuous series of attacks that take place over time to keep the panic going, so to speak."

With that, Grant excused himself and rose before heading out the door and downstairs to his office. With Maximillian, you just never knew what kind of day you may have.

The dark blue Eurocopter AS365 Dauphin with the MDE Enterprises logo banked left. Slowing forward movement, it hovered downward to the heliport atop the joint headquarters of

MDE Aerospace and MDE Defense, touching down in a light rain and foggy skies.

Maximillian exited and was met inside the sliding doors of a protective rooftop structure by his assistant, an attractive woman in her mid-forties who had been with Maximillian for almost a decade. Much like his sister Bridget, she was fearless and protected him as much as she assisted him. Although he was quite fond of her, Maximillian never associated with women related to his companies for good reason. He got the greatest pleasure from pursuits of the mind, so to the extent women were involved romantically, it was always as a challenge, not a relationship.

Walking with her, they headed to a small room where they would soon meet with a group of scientists. He planned to discuss the concept for an EMP weapon and had created a fictitious story to tell the team why they were doing this. The room and the route they took to arrive there were part of a secret area of the company. So much so, few even knew it existed, and those carefully selected to join him became part of his personal team. When summoned, they were dedicated only to his pursuit and whatever jobs they had within MDE companies previously were on hold, causing havoc for their bewildered managers.

When Maximillian entered, all the chosen team members were seated and rose on his arrival. A maroon folder placed in front of them remained untouched as Maximillian sat and began to orate his premeditated story.

"Team, good day. We have an opportunity with a branch of a United States counterterrorism organization to develop a small compact, single use Electromagnetic Pulse (EMP) weapon. As I understand this, they are interested in designing a more portable, less expensive version but with MALE (Medium Altitude Long Endurance) drone launch capability."

He stood and continued the charade. "The conceptual idea is to pack two EMP weapons on a single drone and, because of US congressional requirements, they will use the Javelin 400 drone by our competitor, Galant Industries. The EMP design specification is in the packet in front of you with some drawings that were created with them. That said, I refused any of their actual material because I see a market for this weapon outside the United States."

What he had not said were that these were actually Sara's concepts taken during the Montana raid. All hands reached forward, and they perused the ten-page document in excitement. Ten minutes later he added, "I need this team to design and build a full-scale prototype in forty-five days. The clock starts now."

Faces drained of their euphoria at the seriousness of the deadline before Maximillian added, "There is a fifty-thousand euro bonus to each of you if we meet the exact specification and deadline."

Some smiles returned to the engineers' faces, and they gathered their folders to go to a lab where they would likely be sequestered for the next month.

A little more than a week later, the secret team had moved quickly to determine the initial design and a crude prototype had been developed. Maximillian stood with the two team leaders, an engineer and physicist who both worked for MDE Defense.

Noting the similarity of this design to one of Sara's sketches, Maximillian asked, "Any sense of how effective it will be?"

The engineer answered, "With this small prototype, we estimate it will knock out thirty percent of unprotected electronics in its path."

At ground level of the test facility, they had wired up several types of electrical systems into a nine-meter square area to test the electromagnetic damage from the pulse. In that space was a variety of electronic components and third party peripherals that, in theory, they would hope to incapacitate. In actual use, the pulse would occur much higher in altitude, so the lethal radius of the affected area would be much larger.

Soon, the countdown sounded. "Three, two, one, sequence," but nothing happened. All stared at the prototype when suddenly, the muted sound of a blast suddenly occurred. Unlike a conventional bomb, the area in the room was completely undisturbed. No smoke and nothing blown across the room.

The engineer looked at his monitor. "So, it would seem there is a longer delay than expected, but we've had a successful test. These are early numbers, but today provided a single shot of fifty-seven kilovolts of output energy at five-point-four gigahertz. We'll have to determine the kill ratio of the solid-state peripheral devices made with commercial hardware."

Happy to see it worked, Maximillian asked, "What output do you envision from the final design?"

"Still unknown, but we are targeting at least forty percent more output with the same frequency and duration. We estimate damage of up to forty-rive percent of electronics in the affected area."

Maximillian took but a second to understand and responded, "Excellent. Let's proceed to the full-scale model," and rose to leave the room to the smiles of the team.

Angus walked back to his office, having just had a conversation with one of his technicians. The information he possessed had to be shared with Maximillian, and he called to arrange a few minutes but his schedule was full, so he asked Angus to update him on the phone.

"Sir, it could be nothing, but I have a program that runs in the background twenty-four-seven looking at those who might look at us. Grant often supplies me with names and when the program sees them, I get alerts. In the last week, the researcher at MIT, Sara Ricci, looked at the MDE Enterprises webpage, followed by the DARPA Liaison Jason Sykes and an hour ago, an FBI agent, Raven Maddock."

Alarmed, Maximillian replied, "What do you make of this?"

"If it were just the researcher, I would think nothing as she is working with MDE Commodities and might inquire about the parent company. But the DARPA guy and now an FBI agent? It seems too coincidental."

"Please explain this to Grant and tell him I would like his input." He hung up, disturbed.

28

Ashdown House, MIT Campus, Boston

Sara awoke in her room to bright sunshine and while it was bitterly cold outside, she was warm under the covers from the radiant heat coming through the windows. Sufficiently awake to consider movement, she rose out of bed, used the toilet, and shuffled to the kitchenette. There she started a large cup of expresso from her new machine, a gift from her dad. The outcome was a strong expresso complete with frothing, and as she took the first sip, it almost made her forget her beloved Mud Room.

After her second cup, her mind drifted back to science, and she decided to work from the dorm for a few hours. Sitting at her small, crowded desk, she dug back into material related to TGFs.

In the office, Nathen had gathered data from the detection satellites and was slowly aligning the fields of information from the different formats to create one extensive file.

After several hours, he alerted Sara who came down from her dorm. Opening a software program which allowed raw data to be analyzed in various scientific methods and formats, Nathan worked with Sara to define the parameters of their design of experiment before running the MiniTab program.

After it ran, it suggested there were approximately five hundred TGFs occurring each day. As Sara contemplated the data, she was surprised, having expected much more. Was this all a colossal waste of effort? Would she have to reconsider her thesis yet again?

Jason met with Sara days later and explained that he had called in a favor with Special Agent Maddock. While the FBI was focused on domestic issues, they had access to a great deal of resources.

"Sara, Maddock didn't do a thorough analysis, but the CEO of MDE Enterprises, Maximillian Drummond, is flagged by several US intelligence agencies. He has never been convicted or even seriously considered for crimes, but the fact he is flagged says these agencies are looking at him for a reason."

"It just makes little sense. Why would he harm me if his own companies are already working with me?"

"No idea, but a guy that far up might not understand that they are even working with you. That said, I agree this makes little sense and just because his company matched your keywords, doesn't tie him or the company to you."

"Okay. Thanks just the same. Let me know if anything comes up."

29

Woodmont, Virginia

Ralf Müller, Jason's boss at DARPA, sat in an aluminum patio chair in his backyard, which would be perfectly normal if it weren't early March. The patio and surrounding yard were still covered in six inches of compacted snow and here he was, bundled in several layers of clothes to ward off the cold. At that moment, it was hovering at nineteen degrees Fahrenheit. No one was home to question why he'd gone in the backyard, removed the snow from the chair and sat down with a healthy gin & tonic and a Partagas black label cigar.

He had been with DARPA for almost fourteen years after two tours in the Air Force. Starting as a program manager, he became an assistant director six years before when his boss stepped down because of colon cancer, regrettably dying months later. Ralf knew he was in good standing, but also knew some thought he lacked the political savvy to make the jump to Section Director, the job he coveted.

Based on the events of the last few months, it might seem as though Bernard Cummings was his concern, but Ralf didn't really care about him. What got to him was the grant to Sara Ricci.

Why would DARPA, in austere times, offer two-hundred-fifty thousand dollars to an unproven scientist for an initial concept grant to get energy from space to deploy a space-based EMP weapon that didn't even exist? And it wasn't as if Bernard could have done this on his own. He would have needed the approval of the section director and possibly the Director of DARPA himself, Levin Bechtel.

As he took a sip of the now slushy gin and tonic followed by a powerful pull from the fine cigar, a thought struck him. Did DARPA simply want the secrets of the past from Sara Ricci? He had not previously known of her or Gilberti Ricci, but it actually made sense, although it didn't explain the involvement of Director Hicks from DHS, who had never been involved in DARPA projects. Was the DHS using DARPA? He would have to consider his next moves carefully, as part of him thought others were watching to see what he might do.

30

The Thirsty Ear Pub, MIT Campus, Boston

Sara toyed with her glass as Nathen surveyed the room as they enjoyed a week ending beer at the Thirsty Ear Pub. They were out of Peroni, Sara's go-to beer, and in a weak moment, Nathen convinced her to try an India Pale Ale (IPA) from Goose Island out of Chicago. She drank it, but her face clearly implied each sip was a struggle.

"I take it hoppy beers are not for you," Nathen said with a chuckle.

She laughed. "I was raised on wine, so beer is an acquired taste, and compared to the beer I'm used to, this is not beer."

"Fun fact. That's because you're used to lagers and pilsners which use mild bottom fermenting hops at low temperatures. IPAs supposedly were created to prevent spoilage on long sea voyages and use very strong top fermenting hops at higher temperatures. That gives it the unique smell and higher alcohol content," Nathen replied, proud of his knowledge, having occasionally made his own brew in small batches.

Sara laughed, and after a few minutes of small talk, she recapped their progress. "Well, we knew TGFs were rare and now have confirmation. With about three-point-eight million lightning events daily, only one-third of one percent will become a TGF. The bigger problem is that a satellite will only encounter between zero and two of them mathematically. My current reaction is that if we cannot locate a significant amount of lower altitude TGF events, this is not a viable energy source."

Alarmed, Nathen asked, "I thought you said a TGF is producing trillions of gamma rays and energetic positrons. How can that not be real energy?"

Sara smiled. "Nathen, think of your studies. As you know, physics can make things sound big, but please recall we are dealing with photons, electrons, and positrons all of which are point particles. With photons, a trillion of them could likely fit on the end of a small nail and they are traveling in wave-packets at nearly the speed of light. Second, please recall the first law of thermodynamics: energy can neither be created nor destroyed. Energy can only be transferred or changed from one form to another. Even if it is there, we have to encounter it, an enormous challenge. Then we have to convert it, which is perhaps an impossible challenge."

She took a sip of the beer, winced, then added. "Let me put this into perspective. When the TGF occurs, let's say it produces one trillion particles, and our theoretical collector encounters one percent of all TGFs in its path over a twenty-four-hour period. Let's further assert that we can convert ten percent of this potential energy to thermal heat, which we will use to create electricity. In an entire day, that will yield about eighty watts. The equivalent power of about twenty AA size batteries. It's absolutely nothing."

Amazed at how fast she could get from here to there, Nathen was now being defensive and said, "But if you knew this why even bother?"

"Nathen, we are just getting started. If this is what we have learned in a month, just imagine what we will know in a year. Yes, I knew that space-based observations were limited, although perhaps not this limited. But I rest my hopes on finding tens of thousands of lower altitude events."

She took a drink of water and finished. "Bottom line, what makes this so exciting is that our research has three key variables: the number of events, the number we can encounter, and the amount of energy we can convert. Each is its own research project?"

"Okay, that actually makes sense. So where do we go from here?" Nathen shrugged, feeling a little better.

"Well, we have the TGF data from space. We now need to determine if there are TGFs occurring at lower altitudes. The only reasonable way to prove this is to design an inexpensive gamma-ray detector we can place into thunder clouds. Any ideas?" she asked with confidence.

Nathen shrugged and said, "We'll have to research this. Perhaps I can discuss this with Jason. His work and contacts in nanotechnology could help."

"That sounds great and many of the satellite detectors in space use manmade crystals to detect the gammas. Maybe we can too," Sara answered sounding upbeat.

The next day, Nathen and Jason had agreed to meet in the lab to discuss the sensor challenge. As they sat, Jason said, "Hey, thanks for asking me to help. What I do with DARPA is a job, but this is my passion," he said, beaming. He then asked for a review of the design parameters before adding, "How far away is the receiver?"

"Presumably, the sensors will get caught in the updraft, so based on the data we have, it could be forty thousand feet, or about eight miles."

"It will be tricky to get enough power in something that small to send a signal that far."

Jason grabbed Nathen's pen and pad and drew a crude design, which he and Nathan revised several times. Twenty minutes later they thought they had a solid design.

"Okay, I think we have something. I need to talk to some old friends in Seattle and see if we got it right and also see if they can help us." He took a picture of each page with his phone.

A few days later, Jason called his old college roommate, who was now President of Versilant Nanotechnologies, a company he had started eight years before. Using the pictures Jason had taken, they completed the design and ordered the components, but had them shipped to Jason's house in Virginia where he would build the prototypes.

Jason then took a moment to explain the design to Sara. She nodded in agreement as he added, "Once a gamma is detected, the sensor will send three signals, one that the gamma ray was detected, the strength of the charge, and the GPS location. The finished sensor will be encased in a heat resistant epoxy shell about one-eighth an inch in diameter. Have you given thought to how many sensors you'll need?"

Sara nodded. "Our computer simulation model concluded we need at least one-hundred-eighty sensors for each thunderhead under test. I want to test six clouds in six locations so that would be sixty-five hundred sensors. Any idea at this point what that would cost?"

"Well, I don't have an exact price, but an educated guess is around twenty dollars."

Dejected, Sara said, "Well thank you for this work. It is amazing to have such a resource. Beyond that, wow, that is significantly more than I thought, Much more than my entire budget. For now, see if you can get a quoted price so I can figure out what is possible. We may have to do significantly fewer tests, or I'll need access to more money."

"Okay, will do."

Sara nodded in agreement, and they both left to get some rest.

The following morning, Sara was thinking beyond the sensors. How in the hell could you actually stop a gamma ray? Her mind went back to the papers of Gilberti and his theory of a parabolic shield. Looking at these equations, she needed to talk to Lisa to get more expertise on the geology of minerals in Gilberti's working papers and modern equivalents. They agreed to meet the next day.

At the geology lab, Sara asked Lisa, "So, I still have a couple of questions." She pulled out some of Gilberti's original papers and laid them flat. "When we last spoke, you said that the composite mixture that lined the lead dish was like a crystal, right?"

"As far as I can tell, the minerals are a composite. Once mixed and cured, I imagine they would probably look like a sea of diamonds under magnification."

"Okay. So, I have been researching this and think that is entirely by design. The energy absorption of gamma rays depends on the energy of the photons themselves. Besides these older materials, modern researchers have made significant achievements with artificial materials that have a mass forty to two hundred times higher. I theorize that the shape of the crystal can influence the gamma interactions with the atoms in these different materials."

"Sara, that may be true, but seriously, this drawing shows a dish ten meters in diameter. I don't believe it's even possible to get that much material, let alone afford it. This could be tens of millions of dollars."

Undeterred, Sara said, "Forget the size depicted. I'm not trying to make a commercial invention; I'm only trying to determine if it can be converted. My tests will be with small panels, just a one foot square."

"Ah, got it. There is significant research on gamma ray attenuation rates, so chances are, papers already exist documenting such experiments, but pay attention to the energy used in the experiments. You have much higher incoming energy."

Sara shook her head, trying to imagine where to go with this, and looked at Lisa. "Thanks. I'll load up on published research and see what I can uncover."

Weeks later, Jason had been staring into a high-power magnification lens for several hours at his actual home in Virginia. Using a small machine with robotic arms, he attached the multitude of miniature circuits in the two prototype sensor units he was building for Sara. If they worked, he would send them to Versilant Nanotechnologies in Seattle for a formal quote. Satisfied, he pulled himself back from the unit and rubbed his eyes before putting everything away and sat down with a cold beer.

Returning to Boston the next day, he met Sara at the lab and showed her the sensor. She used the only magnifier she had, a swing arm lamp with a magnification lens, to see it. Although the magnification was not enough, she was still amazed how Jason could have possibly put it together.

With two engineering grad students and a safety officer the following day, Sara and Nathen had set up the X-Ray room to mimic a low energy gamma ray. They did this by using the X-ray machine at higher voltage. This test was to determine if the power on the sensor came on and whether it signaled the crude receiver Nathen and Jason had made the week before. They started the test and happily the sensor came to life, which showed it had successfully sensed the output as a gamma ray. It then sent the energy equivalent and altitude data to the receiver.

Excited that it worked, Jason overnighted the two prototypes to Versilant Nanotechnologies and the within that same week, they quoted just over nine dollars per unit. Likely their material cost, no doubt as a favor to Jason. Although Sara was still concerned about money, she approved the purchase of five systems, or fifty-four hundred sensors.

31
Maracaibo, Venezuela

Over the next month, several things happened quickly. Sara had updated her committee, the sensors arrived, and she began work to organize the various research teams around the world needed to complete the TGF tests. To save money, she had asked DARPA to allow her to give these various universities the raw data in exchange for performing the tests, and DARPA agreed. Although Sara had wanted to supervise the data collections herself, she just didn't have the funding to travel to the locations.

For the low altitude tests, Sara used data from National Oceanic and Atmospheric Administration (NOAA) to locate the five locations with the highest concentration of lightning flashes.

Using MIT as a host, she had contacted and chosen fellow PhD candidates at five universities in Maracaibo, Venezuela; Teresina, Brazil; Tampa, Florida; Pinar del Rio, Cuba; and Selangor, Malaysia. There, these lead researchers would perform the tests and send the data back to Sara. Once verified, Sara would send a copy back to them.

At the University of Zulia, in Maracaibo, Venezuela, a month later, Sara's lead researcher, Mauricio Perez, had just sent a team of three by boat across Lake Maracaibo. Their destination was a campground near the outlet of the Catatumbo River. This location was one of the few places in the world that observed a lightning storm almost every single night of the year. All because the frigid high mountain air surrounding Lake Maracaibo met the warm air from the Caribbean and had done so for perhaps thousands of years.

At about the time his team settled into the campground, Perez himself had arrived at the Aeropuerto de la Chinita and boarded a WP-P3 Orion plane, specially designed for weather experimentation. The cost of hiring the plane and pilots was the most expensive part of the experiment, but thankfully on all but one site, the university was providing the flight. After he changed into a special flight suit and completed the required special safety training, the plane took off. Flying at fifteen thousand feet to the first GPS target, the skilled pilot brought the plane directly into the thunderhead and conditions in the plane immediately went from bad to worse. Extreme weather buffeted the aircraft from all directions, as Perez tried with all his might to not to get sick.

Sara had chosen a series of locations within each cloud with data supplied by the researchers. They knew the area best. In most cases, there were six drops at each location. As the plane approached the first GPS target, the copilot signaled, and Perez immediately pulled up the handle, which opened an unseen outer door beneath him. The sensors flew out before he quickly pushed the lever back down to close it. The safety light on the sidewall of the plane went from red to green and he opened the inner door and quickly refilled it with the next one-hundred-eighty sensors before closing it again. Moments later, the copilot signaled again, and he released the handle once again.

They repeated this process four more times before the plane headed into the last GPS location. In less than 15 hectic minutes, all the sensors had been released and the plane promptly headed back to the airport as Perez, green to the gills, prayed for smoother air.

On the ground in the small, wet campground, the three researchers hunched in their waterproof tents. Using laptops, they waited for the software designed by Nathan to receive data from any active sensors. The sensor would only work if it encountered a gamma ray, and each researcher was monitoring two different clouds. Within minutes, small detections began to populate their screens, and this continued until the sensors eventually lost power.

In the MIT lab weeks later, Sara said to Nathen, "These field teams were just outstanding. I assumed the worst, but all sites did really well. Have you seen any of the data?"

"Not yet. We have four of the five sites uploaded, but I needed to ask what you wanted me to do with the individual sensor recordings. We originally thought that each sensor only had enough power for one recording, but many sensors triggered more than once, some up to ten times. Do you want all data points or just the first detection?"

"Any idea why some sensors gave multiple signals and others didn't?"

"It appears the closer the sensor was to the receiver, the more readings it could take."

"Okay, so altitude based. Since we know which sensor was in each cloud, we can determine the number of TGFs, but let's use all data points to maximize the number of altitude readings. Let's also wait for the last upload."

Florida, the last of the five locations, reported a few weeks later. Armed with all the data, it showed that of the thirty thunderheads they monitored, four storms had recorded a TGF event. Thanks to the multiple readings they ended up with a thousand data points with detections from as low as eight-thousand feet and as high as thirty-nine thousand feet.

Sara and Nathen then took the satellite data and combined that with the low altitude sensor data. Adjusting for seasonality Nathen re-ran the software program which revealed, a TGF of varying strength was occurring approximately sixty-six hundred times per day, significantly more than they had assumed from satellite data alone.

Using the same quick math as before, Sara quickly concluded that would be about one thousand watts of converted power each day, but frowned. Solar power on existing satellites already made ten times that much. This was not good.

32

Kalispell, Montana

Richard Chase sat in his office with a few of his team discussing the raid on his house when one of them asked, "Any more thoughts on the helicopter? It had to have been leased from within a hundred-mile radius of here."

Chase shrugged. "I've racked my brain over this, but just can't seem to picture it. It was a commercial helicopter big enough to hold six large men, that I know."

"So try this. Close your eyes and describe the event for me from the minute you woke up."

"Let me think for a second." He looked toward a blank wall and closed his eyes thinking of the moment he heard the helicopter. Recalling the scene, he said, "I awoke to the sound of a low-flying helicopter, too low, and immediately jumped out of bed, grabbing my sidearm and looked out the window. It had come in over Fortitude, banked quickly and was coming in fast, so I headed straight to the front of the house; it's the only flat area to land. The helicopter had turned on its landing lights and aimed the nose at the front door, so all I saw was bright light. Immediately, shadows jumped from the open doors to the ground and started firing silenced weapons. I was forced back to the shear wall next to the door and took a quick look when the spotlights on the helicopter went out."

Chase opened his eyes and quickly closed them, picturing the lower foot windows and nose shape, and his eyes suddenly blinked open. "Holly shit. Good call guys, not sure why I couldn't see it before, but I think it was an old Bell helicopter, maybe a 407. It was white or light blue with red on the bottom and maybe the top. There was a logo on the door."

He immediately brought up a search engine and typed: "Bell Helicopter for lease, Montana." As the images came up, he turned the monitor toward the guys. He clicked them one by one, but none matched his description. He then changed the search typing in: "Bell Helicopter, Montana." Several popped up and again he went through them one by one.

On the sixth one, Chase stopped and said, "That's the one." Sure enough, it was a 1997 Bell 407 helicopter owned by Polson Photo Adventures in Polson, Montana. "That's about forty driving miles from here. Let's call the guys. We're going to need a show of force to approach since we have no idea if this is a friend of the raid team or a simple business transaction."

The team of six men, including Chase, met Saturday morning as planned. They were all dressed in matching tactical gear and arrived at the Polson Photo Adventure building at the end of Irvine Flats Road forty-five minutes later. They were in a large Mercedes Sprinter van, black with no emblems or noticeable markings, and as they parked, all men got out and three followed Chase while two stood outside the van.

As they approached the building, one of the three stayed out front facing out to the road and the other two went through a side gate marked "Employees Only." They walked around to the back and stood facing the hanger where the helicopter sat on a dolly used to pull it in and out of the hangar. The two employees working on the helicopter stopped what they were doing and one asked, "Hey guys, can I help you? You really can't be back here for insurance reasons."

One of them said sternly, "We are with a client who is conversing with your owner. We won't bother you if you don't bother us. Please stay within our line of sight and continue your work." Whether it was the inference or the tone, they shrugged and went back to work.

Inside the small office, the alarmed receptionist saw Chase and looked at her husband. The owner and pilot also noticed the attire and his holstered sidearm as he looked out to the men in front. "What the heck is all this?"

Chase came forward. "Are you Blake Edmonds?"

"Yes, and this is my wife, Bentley."

Coming closer still, they both took a step back when Chase asked, "Forty-three days ago, you leased your helicopter to six men. I need the records of that transaction."

"Sir, I don't know you, but that information is not something we just hand out. It would be bad for business."

"And by business, you mean aiding and abetting a terrorist cell who used your helicopter to raid a private residence, shoot the owner, and then stole secret government information?"

"No, no, that can't be. The guy was a pilot with a valid license and was using the helicopter to check on land his wealthy boss might buy."

"Mr. Edmonds, I am here on government business and either you assist me, or you will be arrested. When you and your business are subsequently linked to this terrorist group, which I will make happen, there will be no business left to worry about."

Blake looked at his wife, back to Chase, and sighed. "Come over here. You can photocopy the limited file we have." Bentley went to a small file cabinet and pulled out the folder, which Chase took and looked through. He handed the folder back to Bentley and asked, "Please make two copies of each of these documents."

Blake turned to look into the hanger and saw the two large men standing still and facing the hanger thinking, *who are these guys?*

He recovered and said, "I'm not sure it will help, but I have security cameras here and always keep footage of the aircraft leaving and arriving for insurance. Do you want to see it?"

Trying to conceal his smile, Chase said, "Yes, pull it up."

Blake went to the computer behind Bentley and doubled clicked a file. "The first video is when they arrived." He clicked again, and the timestamp was 11:21 p.m. The video showed a large man, dressed in black, enter a key code into the gate lock. With his face down, he held open the gate as five equally large guys walked past, looking down carrying black bags. The guy back at the gate closed it and walked toward the helicopter, where he entered a code to open the helicopter door and then climbed in, starting his pre-check.

As the pilot closed his door, one man moved forward, waved the men into the helicopter, and climbed in last, his face again barely showing in profile, but clearly this was the leader. Last in, first out. The main rotor started and at 11:41 p.m. the helicopter rose as the video ended.

Blake looking ill, brought up the other file. "This is the return." The area in front of the camera was immediately brightened by the landing lights and the timestamp was 1:36 a.m. as the helicopter came in fairly hot. The pilot was skilled enough to set it down with little force and immediately the side door opened, and the men jumped out carrying black weapon bags and headed towards the gate. One of them returned and removed the three servers they had taken from the closet, and a few minutes later, the pilot exited. The video ended at 1:44 a.m.

Chase handed Blake two thumb drives. "Copy both files onto each of these and then insert them and from each, play the files to assure they were copied."

Blake snapped his eyes at Chase, and you could tell he had something to say, but Chase stopped him. "Do not underestimate me or the trouble you are in. Copy the files," he barked.

Blake did as he was told and verified both files on each disk. He handed them to Chase and asked, "So, what happens now?"

"How much did you get to betray your country?"

"Now wait a goddamn minute, I...."

"You what?" Chase yelled for effect. "Six men, who all look like special forces, board your helicopter, the livelihood of your business, at close to midnight, and you tell me they are looking at land for a wealthy buyer? Bullshit! How much?"

His tone worked. Softly and barely audible, Bentley replied, "Fifty thousand dollars. We vetted the pilot, and Blake even flew with him earlier that day. When we watched the video, we realized the story was a lie. We just... we just were trying to earn more money to get a newer helicopter."

Blake was looking down. Bentley was now crying softly as he put his hand on her shoulder and said, "We honestly did not know what happened. You have to believe that."

Chase looked at him directly in the eye and said, "I do. Depending on what happens with the apprehension of these men, you're either in the clear or you're not. I will do what I can to help you as you have helped me, but there are many in this fight, and I can't speak for all of them. Go back to your business, but do not leave this country."

Chase turned and walked out the door, wondering what he would do with this new information.

33

Isle of Skye, Scotland

Angus went into the area next to his office, looking over the shoulder of a young analyst. He and others had been trying to crack the 256-bit encryption on the third Montana server for over six weeks. They had tried a dictionary attack first, where a separate computer uses a database of billions of words and phrases until it finds the right one, but it didn't work. Angus then got access to a crude quantum computer, and it was trying now to decode what they assumed was a long and complex password. It had been running for weeks when it suddenly beeped.

The tech looked back at Angus who shrugged his shoulder and said, "Go ahead." The tech entered the code. Both he and Angus expected the cursor to return to the input field, but it stayed and suddenly the screen changed. They looked at each other and both smiled simultaneously. They had gotten in.

Angus quickly thanked the tech, but asked him to leave. He had no idea what was there, but the fewer who knew the better. Twenty minutes later he sat back perplexed. The server data was not related to the young scientist at all but a series of files that appeared to be jobs completed around the world by security firm

Fortitude. Several of the files were related to agencies within the United States government, including some he had never heard of. Angus was not a soldier but thought that perhaps Fortitude Security might do things the government couldn't do. Grant was going to love this.

He pulled a flash drive from the drawer and placed it in the USB port on the server to get a backup of the files when the screen went black.

His first thought was the monitor had lost power but as he tried to get a response from the server, he suddenly yelled, "Bloody Hell. Shit! Shit! Shit!" He knew then there had been another failsafe, which activated when he started the copy. He had it and lost it. He picked up the phone and called Maximillian.

"Sir, we were able to break the encryption on the server from Montana, but a third security protocol activated when I tried to make a backup to the files. All data has been scrambled and rendered useless."

"Unfortunate. Did you determine what the information was?"

"Yes sir, I reviewed several of the files, and they are not related to the young scientist. The files contained quasi-military operations in many places around the world by the company, Fortitude. Many are for various security agencies of the United States, and I think they were doing things that the Government cannot or will not do."

"That is much more interesting. Excellent work."

"But sir, we lost the data."

"Angus, please discuss this with Grant. He'll immediately understand. We might not have the actual data, but what we know is enough proof that we have seen it and presumably still have it. As these same agencies continue to interfere in my life, now I have something to challenge them back. You have done well."

Outside of London at the secret works within MDE Defense, the heads of the design team stood facing the steel platform that held the full scale EMP weapon just finished that afternoon. On the digital display next to them was a reading of fifty-six kilograms, a last reminder that the prototype was slightly overweight.

Frustrated and tired, the engineer said softly, "I just don't see any easy options to save two kilograms without adversely affecting performance."

The physicist nodded. "I suggest we test and assure the results are positive before sharing this failure."

After several minutes of thought, both agreed. The team prepared for the test, and most were nervous because while they mentally enjoyed working on Maximillian's projects, the real prize was the bonus. They all needed it, and some had likely already spent it. As the various checklist items were marked off and completed, the team started the countdown.

The blast itself was noticeably stronger than the first and they had corrected the delay issue. Both looked at the computer readout with a frantic mind and immediately relaxed. The screen showed they had exceeded expectations.

"Complete the verification and validation sequence, but it looks like we nailed it and have room to play if weight really is the biggest factor," the physicist said happily.

The next morning, both faced a computer screen for a video call with Maximillian. "Gentlemen, an update."

"Yes sir. Yesterday, we tested the full-scale model, and it produced eighty-eight kilovolts of output at a frequency of six-point-two gigahertz for fifty-nine microseconds."

"And the circuitry failures?"

"Using the same setup as previous, the blast effectively killed forty-one percent of the solid-state devices in the lab and fifty-three percent of the peripheral devices made with commercial hardware."

"Final weight?"

The engineer cringed slightly but firmly stated, "The final weight came in at fifty-six kilograms. As we exceeded the output handsomely and remain well within the drone's payload, I would suggest we stay with the higher output. Sir, we can likely remove the weight, but we'll lose up to five percent of the performance."

"I would agree, please freeze the design, and instruct the team to build a third device for real world testing." Maximillian had moved toward disconnecting the call when the engineer asked, "Sir, can we inform the team that they were successful in meeting the challenge?"

"Your definition of success lacks merit, as the device is overweight to a clearly specified goal. But I appreciate the effort and higher output and will award twenty-five thousand euros to each team member in consideration."

Relieved at least there was something, he replied, "Thank you, sir." As the line went dead, the video went black. As always, there was no gray area with Maximillian Drummond.

Sara and Nathen worked for several weeks on a technical paper of their TGF findings and referenced the many who had helped from each institution. The draft copy was sent to Dr. Zimbrean, the committee, and DARPA had been well received.

Sara spent the rest of the week reviewing the paper for publication and poring over literature related to gamma ray absorption. Of particular concern was the simple fact that gamma interactions with the atoms in the crystalline coatings were still very difficult to capture. Once the interaction occurred, some would not interact at all and just bounce off. Others would actually pass right through while others still would interact, but once they did, they would blast all over the damn place. Like the old Pong game, but at a million times the speed.

She knew Gilberti's parabolic dish was designed deeper than normal, likely to hold the interactions low enough in the dish that they could be absorbed by the walls as they bounced all about. But before she could consider that, she had to see if any of these coatings even worked.

They planned four tests on four different panels. For each experiment, they would use a sintered tungsten carbide panel, and each would be coated with one of the four crystalline versions to test the attenuation and penetration rates of each design. The panels had been ordered and received, but they could only find companies to coat two of the variants.

Jason recalled that Versilant Nanotechnologies had done some work like this a few years back and with Sara on speaker, Jason called the president and his old college roommate, Dann De Veers. When he answered, Sara explained the two variants they needed. Dann replied, "Ms. Ricci, we have done some of this here, but we lack the sophistication to do this in any volume. I would suggest a company near us called Cerium Scientific Compounds. I have a financial interest in the company, and this is practically their entire business. Allow me to call them and see what they require, and I'll get back to you or Jason."

"Thank you, Mr. De Veers." And Sara disconnected.

Several hours later, Dann called Jason, who returned to Sara's office and reiterated the conversation. "So great news. Cerium Scientific Compounds have done this several times and they see no issue with these mixtures. I had them send me a contract and NDA, which I just emailed to you."

"Jason, this is fantastic. I was starting to worry." Sara said happily. Over the next few hours, Sara and Jason created the purchase order and then shipped the panels to them along with the samarium, lutetium, and thorium like metals from MDE Commodities.

Four weeks later, Sara was with Nathen in the MIT Plasma Science and Fusion Center, working with other grad students to test the small panels. Using an x-ray machine at higher voltage, they again mimicked a gamma ray and tested the panels with four different incoming currents. The Thorium-like metal from MDE Commodities had no comparison. They had found their composite material.

35

Bridget sat in the main conference room at the residence as she prepared to meet with a young analyst and review a list of potential targets. While he thought these were going to be used as sales leads for MDE Trust, they were, in fact, the actual targets to deploy Maximillian's EMP Weapons.

Once the attacks started, vulnerable companies would want to protect themselves from these terrorist attacks. Bridget was, of course, there to assure that MDE Trust was poised to call on them and protect them from such attacks, thus creating a nice revenue stream for at least a while.

Bridget signaled for the nervous young man to start.

"Ms. Drummond, as you know, we took targets from the previous lists created from last year's sales effort and ranked them on the likelihood the target is already protected; the ease of getting to that target; the lethality of an EMP attack based on the type of equipment most likely at the target; and the ability for the attack to create major disruption to clients or society."

He stopped for a moment to let her review the original data and then continued when she looked back up. "That original data was mathematically derived, so we chose to look at this from the eyes of the attacker and concluded the only relevant criteria were ease to the target and lethality. We sorted the targets accordingly and then considered the actual companies, including where they are located with names and numbers to contact. That is the updated list."

Bridget had not spoken, but agreed with the logic. She scanned the list and saw several obvious targets in many of the normal sectors they had used in the past. "If this is what the team considers complete, please forward it to me."

The analyst stammered for a second before responding, "Very well. Thank you."

Maximillian had summoned Grant and waited for him as he looked over the ocean. When Grant came in, he waved him over, asking, "Would you care for a small glass of Tobermory?"

"Thank you, that would be excellent. It has been a busy day."

"Anything pressing or urgent? Any new information from Angus regarding the DARPA and FBI inquiries?" Maximillian asked.

"Nothing urgent, just readying the logistics for the EMP weapon deployment. As far as the search results, Angus confirmed they only looked into who the company is, what they do, and who the officers are."

Maximillian gave Grant a glass with a healthy pour of the eighteen-year-old single malt, "So we have no idea why they are looking, but know that they now have my name, which is unfortunate."

"Yes, sir, although that is all public information. Based on the timing of the searches, I suspect the researcher heard of MDE Enterprises, told Sykes, who then told the FBI. There have been no new inquiries."

"Fine, monitor this. In other news, I'm told the drone and full-scale weapons will be complete on Wednesday. I would like you to take them to Madagascar using the boat."

Grant chuckled to himself as he listened. The *boat* was a ship that cost over two-hundred million euros. Sixty-six meters long with a beam of twelve meters, it took a crew of twelve just to leave its berth and cost over fifty million euros a year to maintain. "Will you be joining us?" Grant asked.

"No, it is too much time at sea for this time of year."

"Very well." Grant swirled the last of the whisky and left to get ready to sail.

A week later, *Princess Alana* named after Maximillian's mother, was cruising at twenty-one knots down the south Atlantic Ocean, staying clear of the Gulf of Guinea to avoid piracy from Nigeria and neighboring countries. The captain had continued in a straight line for South Africa, bringing them farther from land, but the danger was still there. Many pirates now used aging ships to bring crews out to the sea to wage their war from a floating base. Grant and his ten men were technically ready for just about anything, and there were three men on deck at all times.

The night was cloudy with rough seas. Rain was predicted for most of the night, although at that moment, it had not yet started. Bruce Morgan, one of Grant's men was on the stern watching the seas intently with his eyes and occasionally using night vision. The clouds had assured a very dark night.

He could not see them, but around 1:30 a.m., he heard one or more rigid hull inflatables or RIB's with fast outboards coming in and out of the wind. He alerted the teams at port and starboard and then the bridge. The First Mate woke the captain who then woke Grant as all went about manning defensive positions. Grant set his frequency and spoke to Bruce first via their private comm system.

"Visuals?"

"Negative, sounds like two boats, one on port and one on starboard."

"Team, if you have a direct kill shot with the rocket-propelled grenades (RPG) take them out away from the ship, but only if you can hit them both. If not, allow them to come alongside thinking they are safe." He turned now to the men on the bridge.

"Captain, no lights and no change in course or speed. We need them to think they have not been seen." Returning to his comm device, "Team II head to the stern. Team III to port and Team IV to starboard. Do not let anyone board this ship and do not let them leave if they try."

Grant's men were all dressed in black should any light come toward the ship. The sound of the outboards was coming closer, and Bruce radioed quietly from the stern, "Two boats, seven to eight men in each. They are holding just off the stern matching our speed but not trying to approach. Captain, be on the lookout for any craft ahead of us."

The captain had both radar and sonar active, and at least at that moment, there was no movement or any vessels. The only blips were small ones from the two RIB's and a large freighter fifteen nautical miles away. This was likely the pirate's flagship. He replied to the team, "All is clear in front of us."

Bruce spoke again, "Teams, both boats are coming forward. The front men are standing with grappling hooks. Team II spread out so that you fire forward. Team III and IV, finish anyone still standing with single shots. Captain, maintain this exact speed, but as soon as the shooting starts, have two deck hands prepare our RIB on the off chance they try to get away."

As the boats slowly came amidships, the pirate pilots slowed and moved in toward the *Princess Alana*. At once, the rubber coated grappling hooks were away and two were attached on each side. Hidden behind the rails, Grant's men waited for them to climb before silently jumping out and firing their full automatics at the men trying to board, cutting them down instantly. As they fell dead or wounded into the sea, those standing in the RIB's tried to return fire but were cut down and, as expected, both pilots disengaged and tried to pull away. Snipers from Team III and Team IV used their AK-12's in single shot mode to take out any remaining movement, including the dual outboards on each RIB. Both crafts stalled, and the night went silent.

The captain brought the *Princess Alana* to full stop. The deck hands had readied their own RIB in the water and four of Grant's men jumped in as the deckhands ran back to the bridge scared out of their minds. They approached the first pirate RIB fifty meters off port and boarded. Bodies and weapons were quickly tossed overboard, and they cut the inflated bladders and quickly scuttled the twenty-two foot vessel. They re-boarded their own and went around the stern to the second pirate vessel now 100 meters away, and repeated the process. Less than fifteen minutes later, they were back on board as the captain returned to full power, pushing twenty-six knots. Any sign of the attack was gone although half of the men remained on deck as a precaution. The rest went to have a coffee as if nothing had happened.

Back on the freighter *Athena* twenty nautical miles off their stern, a large man in a dirty uniform paced the bridge. He barked at the communications officer to hail the pilots again, but only static returned as it had for over twenty minutes, which was not a good sign. He had already brought the engines to power and ordered the anchor pulled as they began to sail toward the location of the hijack attempt. It was a large ocean but impossible to just disappear and he would find out what happened to his men and the prize that appeared to have gotten away.

36

Toamasina, Madagascar

Princess Alana arrived without further incident in the port of
Toamasina on the island of Madagascar, its usual berth four days
later. Grant immediately went about getting the drone, EMP
weapons, and flight system hardware off the ship undetected.
From there, a camper van would take the hardware to a location
in the forest near Antananarivo, the Capital city of Madagascar,
and await his word.

The command center was now operational, and the drone
was assembled, powered, armed, and ready. The camper van had
been made to look as though the husband-and-wife team of
technicians were actually camping. After dinner and a few hours
of sleep, Grant was back in the command center. As the time

drew closer, he gave word to the campers to start their countdown.

The Javelin 400 was a commercial drone built by a competitor to MDE Aerospace, Galant Industries in the United States, and had a range of one-hundred-fifty kilometers when loaded with the two EMP weapons. The shell company Grant had set up had purchased ten of these drones, all third party, and Maximillian's private team added the cradle to hold the weapons. Nothing would point back to MDE Enterprises.

As the clock ticked down, the drone fired and headed for the sky before turning up and out of the forest, heading to the Madarail substation. This live test had been labeled Phase Zero.

The first target was a nondescript building to the far left of the main rail passenger terminal. The drone flew parallel with the tracks steady at five-hundred meters as it began to course correct. Lowering as it came toward the building. At two-hundred meters, the screen from which Grant was watching flashed "Launch" in the upper left corner meaning separation of the weapon had occurred. Immediately to release, the drone increased altitude and abruptly changed course, heading for a similar target at the Ivato International Airport. The screen split as the feed from the weapon itself came into view and, following the glide angle, the target appeared. At seventy-five meters off the target, the screen flashed "Detonation", and the feed was lost. The EMP had been activated.

The video reverted to the drone as it hurried toward the airport. With more surveillance equipment there, the drone was taking an exceptionally long way around the airport to the target and would do the same on the route back to the forest. The drone approached the second target and again the screen flashed "Launch" in the upper left corner, showing separation. As before, the drone increased altitude and continued well past the airport before it changed course, heading back to the forest—a second successful detonation.

In the forest, the campers quickly brought the drone to the van from the clearing that acted as the takeoff and landing sight. They removed the two wings, placing all into lower hidden compartments in the van's rear. In less than twenty minutes, they were heading to a separate location to await instructions.

Grant awoke early and grabbed a cup of coffee from the galley and sat down in the main salon and clicked on a local news station, Television Malagasy (TVM), and the co-anchor was reporting. "Last night's storm, while light in terms of rainfall, produced lightning that caused major damage at the Madarail station in Antananarivo and separately at the Ivato International Airport. All trains into Antananarivo are canceled until repairs can be made to the switching command. Officials say that could take two to five days, a mess for freight and commuters. At the Ivato airport, there are no outbound flights, as all have been delayed. Officials say that lightning has damaged the main communications building, which affects the communication feed coming into the airport from outside sources, including pilots. A mobile backup system is already up and running to alert incoming flights and they will have landing priority...."

Of course, the damage had nothing to do with lightning or the storm. Phase Zero had been a success.

Grant clicked off the television and sent a secured note to Maximillian and Bridget that all had gone well. Once the campers returned and the drone was secured, the *Princess Alana* would travel to France to pick up Maximillian for a few days of holiday and Grant would take the plane home from Madagascar.

37

Crawley, West Sussex, England

Over the next several weeks, the secret team completed the build of all EMP weapons and readied them for shipment on the grounds of MDE Defense. They were then packaged and labeled and presented to customs as ocean-based sonar devices. On special pallets, they were placed into two containers for shipment to the Maritime Salvage Inc. in Boston, MA., a private group paid well for their discretion. This company was a front for the unnamed United States Counter Terrorism group Maximillian had used as a pretense with his defense team and in fact, all hardware was ultimately from the United States.

No sooner had the container left when workers disassembled all traces of the factory and test facility. This was not unexpected, as all their private projects ended this way.

As the date of the Phase I launch approached, Bridget worked with Candace Perez, the Managing Director of MDE Trust, to take advantage of the sales blitz on the targets. Candace knew nothing of the actual attacks.

Friday, late evening, as people were asleep with dreams of the weekend ahead of them, all field teams were getting set up to launch their drones into six targets in three countries. Some would launch from land and others from sea to lower the risk of detection.

The first and second drone left the launch ramp from a small freighter off the coast of Spain at exactly 1:00 a.m. In clear weather, the drones followed the test flight altitude, and within ten minutes, the same launches also occurred in Athens and Amsterdam. The first detonations were in Greece and at release, each drone climbed to assure it would not be affected by the electromagnetic burst before heading to the next target.

In the early morning, Maximillian, Bridget, and Grant were in the residence and had tuned to a local station, AT5 in Amsterdam. There it was reported that the North Gate Lock had lost communication, keeping incoming vessels out and not allowing outgoing vessels to leave the harbor. Officials close to the action said they had a severe electronic failure had occurred in automated controls, rendering them useless. There was also a major disruption east of the Amsterdam Central train station because of the loss of a switching station.

Bridget switched to Barcelona where Televisió De Catalunya, TV3, reported the loss of offloading systems, effectively shutting down the container loading and unloading operations at APM Terminals in the Port of Barcelona. At the same time, the main distribution warehouse for Tesco stopped operations as the control center lost power. Bridget then went to Athens where the co-anchor for SKAI TV reported that ferry traffic in the Port of Piraeus was down. This impacted all major carriers, Blue Star, Anek and Minoan, because of a power or systems failure.

Phase I had been a complete success.

MDE Trust was a service business that protected the electronic assets of major corporations and state and federal governments against threats of malware, power losses, naturally occurring EMP's. Although rarely used previously, these same skills had the capability to shield the critical infrastructure of companies from more sophisticated forms of electronic warfare, like EMP weapons.

Managing Director Candace Perez had been hand selected by Maximillian to head the startup company two years before and had grown the company's revenues to one-hundred-thirty million in that time. That success had recently brought MDE Trust out of Maximilian's private incubator companies and into the larger public company, MDE Enterprises.

Sitting with one of her top salespeople, Ramsey Denison over lunch, they were discussing their recent string of business success. Eating a decent but not exceptional plate of Haggis,

Candice asked, "One thing I don't understand is why the sales target list Bridget made is so controversial. Everyone in the company is talking about it. I mean really, we do this every year."

Ramsey eyed her carefully. "Well, this is the first year Bridget has led that effort, but more important, have you read about the recent EMP attacks?"

"The ones being pulled off by some terrorist group?" she asked. "Yes, I have. So?"

"Are you aware that of the targets they hit, every one of them is on our list?" Ramsey asked.

Candace stopped eating. "What? You're joking, right?"

"And that our business growth of late directly results from those EMP attacks?"

She stared at him, shocked. "What are you saying?"

He took a deep breath. "I guess I'm saying I don't think it's a coincidence."

Candace rolled her eyes. "Ramsey, my God, listen to you. That is exactly what this is and good homework on our part. Maximillian would never use a terrorist organization to blow things up just to increase revenues! He hardly needs the money."

"That's true," he admitted, and they dropped the subject and went back to a normal conversation.

Just a month later, the nighttime sky over Folkestone near Dover in the south UK was blanketed in a dense fog that would carry throughout the next morning. Once a booming port town, it was now a sleepy port town, but considered among the tourist class as a less populated gem.

Folkestone was also the terminus of the Channel Tunnel also known as the Eurotunnel or the Chunnel, one of the largest engineering feats of its time when it opened in 1994. It was here in Folkestone that the main system control was located, which controlled the three rail lines that passed underground in the limestone tunnels from the UK to France. Several hundred feet below the expanse of the English Channel above them. These rail systems included the Eurostar fast rail, the Eurotunnel Shuttle, the car ferry rail system, and the International Freight trains. The backup system was located on the French side of the tunnel in Calais.

Thirty minutes later, at 2:00 a.m., two drones left their sea-based launch platforms and were flying down the Strait of Dover under those same foggy skies. One was headed to Folkestone, the other to Calais. As each drone came within range of the main control building, they launched both weapons one after the other and then returned in the direction they had come. Within seconds, alarms went off throughout the rail systems and trains en route were temporarily halted until emergency systems could guide them out. Meanwhile, nothing else could get in.

Off the Isle of Sheppey to the east of London, a single drone had been launched, heading in a downward radius around central London. The riskiest of any launch so far, this drone was heading toward an outbuilding along the Piccadilly line. Part of the London Underground, or Tube, whose eleven separate lines were the twelfth busiest in the world, carrying close to five million passengers daily.

London, no stranger to terrorism, houses some of the most advanced counter-terrorism tools ever developed, and Grant had been concerned that these tools might detect the drone on the way in. Unsurprisingly, at that moment in the MI5 command center in Vauxhall, a weary technician was monitoring his screen and noticed a slight blip. It was thirty kilometers south of him, intermittingly coming and going. He thought little of it, as it was not in the city or aiming toward the city. He kept it in mind, but went to something else.

The drone had followed its curve to the outbuilding northwest of Acton Town Station when the pilot released both weapons and the drone continued in a clockwise circle back to sea. His screen showed release, followed a few seconds later by the second release. Both detonated as planned, impairing the Piccadilly line which served Heathrow, one of the busiest airports in the world.

As the pilot was tracking the drone's return, through a light patch of the fog, the captain noticed a Targa 31-foot fast boat. It was from the Marine Police Unit of the Metropolitan Police Service and was creeping forward on patrol. The pilot looked at the captain and they both nodded before he placed the laptop in a cubby as the captain started moving traps from one side to the other. When the fast boat motored a hundred meters off their port side, he glanced up waved. The Thames police officers on the deck waved back as the Targa slowing moved by. He waited until they could no longer hear the engine as the pilot returned to the cabin and removed the laptop that showed the drone would be to them in just ten minutes. Far too close, considering the fast boat was still close by.

The pilot called his expedition leader and explained the situation. "They are now a kilometer off our bow. Given their location, we cannot retrieve the drone without detection. I'm asking for permission to take it up to two-thousand meters and let it fly east until it runs out of power. I can see most vessels in the area on sonar and it will crash into the sea without notice." Reluctantly, the leader said, "Agreed," and ended the connection.

Although they would lose a million dollar drone, Phase II had been a success.

Candace Perez stared at the front page of the newspaper. All three of the most recent EMP weapon attacks had been targeted on the list Bridget had sent out. That meant that since the attacks began, all hits were not only on the MDE Trust sales target list, but all had ranked highest on ease of accessibility and the highest amount of perceived disruption.

Candace felt a panic set in. She wasn't sure what to do as she paced back and forth.

A buzz from her assistant startled her, and she hit the intercom button. "Yes?"

"Candace, I have Maximillian's assistant, Giselle, on the phone, and she wants to talk to you immediately."

Candace picked up the line from MDE Headquarters. "Yes, Giselle, how may I help you?"

"Candace, Mr. Drummond is en route to your location and will be there in ten minutes. I have no concise information as to way, but he is highly agitated and only said the subject had to be discussed in person. You will be available, yes?"

"Yes, of course. Thank you." Candace looked at her assistant, shrugged her shoulders and said nothing, but assumed she was getting fired. Drummond never came here.

But here he was. Maximillian arrived in a jet-black Range Rover minutes later and walked directly into Candace's office without comment, closing the door behind him.

"Candace, we have a serious situation. Last month, someone hacked into a server here at MDE Trust and I'm told whoever did this was quite sophisticated, as all precautions had been taken. My team could not trace the hack, but know the single file accessed. The list of potential targets for our sales campaign. Given this, the hackers may have had inside help." He stopped and looked at her.

Candace solemnly shook her head. "Mr. Drummond, I assure you I will do whatever it takes to find out what happened."

"Yes, of course. Unfortunately, that is not the bad news. While we initially assumed this was a case of espionage by a competitor, that the recent EMP attacks match our list precisely cannot be a coincidence. Please do everything possible to assure customers do not get a word of this. That we were hacked is a great embarrassment to me, and to our name—MDE Trust. You see the implications, correct?"

"Of course, sir, I understand completely."

"My senior analyst Angus Adair and head of security, Grant Aiken will determine how this happened, and to the extent, it may have involved an MDE employee. This is clearly bad news, but on the other hand, an opportunity for growth as we now know that anyone on that list really is a target, and we can help them."

"Thank you, sir. We have been enjoying a spectacular increase in business. I'll do my best to help in any way I can."

"I know you will, Candace. Good luck." He rose and walked out the door to the awaiting Range Rover.

38

Edinburgh, Scotland

Sharon Klein, Senior Sales Director at MDE Trust, the second most successful salesperson after Ramsey Denison, was troubled by what was going on. While Sharon didn't think Maximillian could be involved, she thought his sister, Bridget, was an absolute bitch, and very well could be.

The fact was, while this EMP scare was good for business, especially for her salary, it was too much of a coincidence that all attacks matched those on the potential client list? Conflicted, she thought she needed to tell someone, but who? She didn't trust Candace and wasn't in a position to call Maximillian himself. As she continued to clean her small kitchen, she came across a business card of an investigator from Police Scotland. Sharon had witnessed an accident several weeks before and Chief Inspector (CI) Timothy Hawkins had interviewed her.

She knew she was letting this get to her, but honestly thought this could not be a coincidence. Could Bridget, or Candace really be blowing things up to increase sales? Standing there with his card still in her hand, she thought, perhaps she should call him, but if she did, it was likely she would get sacked.

Even she knew that MDE, or rather Maximillian Drummond, demanded loyalty.

Two weeks later, CI Hawkins was seated in front of two large video monitors and on the far-right screen was the boyish face of CI Logan Stewart from the N-Division. On the left was Detective Chief Inspector (DCI) Nigel Hughes, of the Metropolitan Police, more famously known as New Scotland Yard.

Hawkins opened up the video chat. "Guys, I got a call recently from a salesperson at MDE Trust, which is part of MDE Enterprises. Since all of us at some time or another grapple with inquiries into Maximillian Drummond, this might just be another false lead, but it involves the recent string of EMP attacks. Apparently, MDE Trust made a list of companies that could be easy targets for such an attack, and the sales team was given this list to call on for potential new business. According to this woman, every one of the known EMP attacks has been a direct match to the list. This employee is concerned that either the terrorists have their list, or worse, her company is involved."

DSI Hughes replied, "Aye, there have been a few comments off the record that MDE builds drones, can make weapons, and owns a company that benefits from such attacks. But you can't even discuss such things without proof. The CEO is well connected."

"Right, well that's the reason for the call. Any thoughts on how to investigate this quietly? Have either of you heard anything that could be followed up?" Hawkins asked.

"Nothing on my end," Stewart said quickly. "As you know, Maximillian is beloved on the Isle of Skye, and any inquiry into him stops rather quickly. I have heard nothing, but I'll keep my ears open."

DCI Hughes weighed in. "Other than what I said, that is all I have, but I'll let you know if I hear anything related to these EMP weapons."

"Ah, okay, then. That is all I can ask. Thanks, guys. At some point, I would like to question the Managing Directors of MDE Trust and MDE Defense but need something more tangible than perhaps an upset employee," replied Hawkins, as he ended the call.

39

East River, New York

Off the coast of New York on the East River, a workboat was cruising into position far north of Rikers Island near Hunts Point. The captain had come through the Long Island Sound, heading past New Rochelle and then past Throgs Neck to their current location. The drones that would be used for Phase III were on the launch platform, still in a lowered position when they arrived and anchored just after 2:20 in the morning. They raised the platform to launch height, and the pilot had brought up the GPS coordinates, communications equipment on the roof of the New York Stock exchange. It would also target similar equipment on at the UN building.

The pilot was doing his last checks before launch when a flashing blue light became visible far across the water, headed their way. Watching the light, the captain quickly told the pilot to pull anchor, and he started the motors intending to head back toward Throgs Neck. Closing the computer lid, the drone pilot hid the computer before running out of the wheelhouse to lower the launch ramp. The flashing light had not changed course and as he lowered the ramp, he grabbed a tarpaulin and was about to cover the drones when the captain said, "No, over the side."

The pilot noted the flashing light was still coming right at them. Although an expensive decision, he ran around the four corners of the ramp, reluctantly pulling the lock pins that held it to the floor. Using the onboard crane, he lifted the ramp with drones attached up and over the side and released the hook.

The captain looked at the pilot, who nodded, and pushed full throttle, allowing the twin Caterpillar 3512HC engines to take flight before the crane was even back into position. The NYPD fast boat was now three nautical miles from their stern, and the workboat captain knew he had to create a significant diversion from the scuttled weapons. Both the captain and pilot had been trained for this mission, which included an edict. *You are being paid appropriately to take this risk. Do not get caught at any cost. If you are captured, it will become the least of your worries and if you put the edict first, your families will be taken care of for life.*

The workboat took off much faster than anyone could have imagined, and the NYPD fast boat was deciding what to do as the distance between them expanded. Earlier, a land-based detector had signaled explosives were aboard the workboat. Protocol was to call for backup and wait it out, as there was only one direction the workboat could leave. But when the NYPD skipper noticed the workboat suddenly jump in speed, he went after them while waiting for the backup unit to respond.

Holding some advantage, the NYPD boat was gaining on them as they neared the point at Throgs Neck almost fifteen minutes later. With still no response from the workboat or their backup, they continued after the suspects with both police officers now on deck armed and ready. They were within a half mile when the skipper hailed the vessel.

Despite revved engines, the quiet of the night allowed the message to drift across the water. "Vessel Wilmette, NYPD, stop your engines immediately and prepare to be boarded."

The captain of the workboat looked back and knew there was no way to outrun them, so he elected to widen the area they would ultimately have to search and perhaps try to sink them. He turned the wheel aggressively, heading into Little Neck Bay at full power. The NYPD boat, faster and more agile, easily followed and the NYPD skipper thought for a moment they would be cornered as there was no outlet here. Suddenly, the suspects turned sharply in an arc and then aimed right for their fast boat. He saw the maneuver coming and got out of the way as two officers on deck sprayed fully automatic fire towards the workboat. Too far away to do serious damage, the suspects turned again toward them without contact before heading again at full speed out of the bay towards open water. The NYPD skipper received word that backup was coming from lower Manhattan and continued to chase the suspects, now more aggressively.

Both vessels flew out of Little Neck Bay and past King's Point. The NYPD boat was gaining, but the workboat was at full power as they approached Port Washington North. It was then when the workboat captain looked one last time at the pilot, reached down, nodded to him with sunken eyes, and depressed a small red button. The blast shattered the night calm powerfully enough to disintegrate them and their vessel.

With no time to react, the NYPD fast boat was too close and took the concussion of the explosion and fragments at close range. Both police officers on deck were struck down with multiple hits from debris, and the wheelhouse offered little protection to the skipper.

Early morning two days later at One Police Plaza in Manhattan, close to the famed Financial District, a briefing had just gotten underway regarding the explosion in the East River. In the office of the Deputy Commissioner, was the Chief of Counterterrorism, and Chief of Special Operations Bureau. They were being briefed by Sergeant Waverly Degan and Inspector Ellis LaCour both from Harbor Patrol, and Waverly was standing and ready to present their preliminary investigation findings.

Sergeant Degan started on the signal from her boss. "We have confirmed the workboat was leased out of New Jersey for eight weeks by a company that was linked to several other entities before we lost the trail. We believe the explosion was a failsafe should they be detected, and the explosive has been analyzed as US military grade C-4 and appears to have been just aft of the wheelhouse."

She continued, "Divers scoured the suspect vessel, but found nothing. The hull was partially intact, but most everything else was gone. There were no contraband or weapons on or near the wreckage, and we have no idea what they were running from or running to."

Sensing no questions, Degan continued, "It was the explosives in the fail-safe that our land-based scanning device detected, which prompted the decision to follow. The backup patrol was still on a call when summoned, and the skipper waited for them. That is until we got a call twenty-two minutes later, saying the suspects were moving at high speed and he was going after them. The last correspondence said backup was en route, and they were narrowing the gap approximately forty-eight minutes later when the explosion occurred. Are there questions?"

The Deputy Commissioner went first, "So we have no idea what the suspects and their vessel were intending, but whatever it was, it was serious enough for them to blow themselves up."

"Yes sir. We suspect they were awaiting a pickup at sea or had something on their deck but scuttled it."

The Deputy Commissioner then asked, "So we can have a team search the area from the detection to the explosion?"

Degan, sensing concern, responded, "Sir, from the chemical detection sensor, the suspect vessel went all the way past Rikers Island into the bay in lower Manhattan. The explosion occurred back at Port Washington North twenty nautical miles away. Given the span of almost three hours from detection, they were on the East River channel for at least two hours before they could have seen the light of the NYPD fast boat. We have no idea how far inland they came, but based on that, it is a very large search area and we don't even know what we are looking for."

"Sir. Do you wish us to attempt a search?" Inspector LaCour asked.

"Yes. We have some intelligence from DHS that this may be related to a string of drone based EMP attacks in Europe. Your search should assume a launch ramp with one or two drones with EMP weapons attached. Any word on the DNA results of the terrorists themselves?"

"We believe we have some human remains related to the suspects, but it is unclear as yet if the DNA can be lifted. Using some bone fragments and tissue, ME is attempting an amplification process on the DNA called Polymerase Chain

Reaction, but no results as yet. The suspects were literally standing right behind the fail-safe," Degan responded.

"Degan, LaCour, good work and while I'm glad the land-based detectors did their job, I have yet to justify the serious injuries to our brave police officers and the almost total loss of their vessel. I expect another briefing to conclude what they dumped, and any known terrorist angle."

He then stared sternly at Degan. "I also want an explanation before day's end why your skipper abandoned protocol and went after a vessel without backup that he knew contained enough explosives to trigger the detection monitor."

40

Washington D.C.

Director Jeremy Hicks was in his office on his phone at the DHS headquarters and had just spoken to the NYPD regarding the explosion on the East River. While he suspected the incident might be related to the UK and EU events, the report provided no connection.

Over his last cup of coffee for the day, he pondered the concept of "proof" once again. This whole affair was getting to him. He was losing his objectivity and thinking perhaps it was simply time to move on. He had done all this almost as a favor to the CIA, but it was becoming a distraction. As he set down the now lukewarm cup, he thought of a potential source and picked up his personal cell phone. He searched for the contact, one he had not used in years, and hesitated over the phone number before hitting connection.

Richard "Rottweiler" Chase picked up on the second ring. "Jeremy Hicks, or should I say, Director Hicks. This is an unexpected call."

"Chase. It's been a while. What do you have on the team that raided your house?"

"Well, we identified the plane that brought them here, but you killed that inquiry, so we only know how they got here and a few of their actions once they landed."

"Trust me, the plane was a dead end. Anything on the raid team? Anything?"

"All I can tell you is there were six of them, moving like former special forces, and armed with silenced Russian weapons. They used no comms of any kind and were in and out in about four minutes."

"So that's all?"

"Hicks, Let me in just a bit, maybe I can help." Jeremy had fought alongside Chase many years before and considered him both a natural leader and one of the best soldiers he had stood aside. Positional authority had pulled them apart, but in his gut he knew Chase was the real deal, so he did the unthinkable. He told him what they were up to.

"So other than the raid on your house, the possible failed attack in New York, and this funny business with the researcher, Sara Ricci, all this is EU based. I have nothing to work with and the SIS won't touch this without a direct connection, so I called you to see if you had anything before I throw in the towel."

Richard thought for a moment and said, "Well, I may have something. We located the helicopter the raid team leased and approached the owners. They were not involved, but had a video of the raid team getting on and getting off the helicopter with my servers in hand. I have not yet identified any of them and none of them looked directly into the camera, likely knowing it was there. Perhaps you can apply better facial recognition tools?"

"This is a positive development. Send me a copy of the video. Maybe CIA resources or even SIS across the pond can pick up a name or two. Chase, thanks for the intel and I'll keep you informed."

"No problem, you should have the video files now in your safe account. I just sent them to you using the normal encryption. I'll stand down for now, but let me know what's going on. At some point, I want these guys." Hicks knew full well as he clicked end on the call. Chase was not one you wanted to cross.

Grant had called to update Maximillian on Phase III and waited to be buzzed in, saying as he did, "Sir, Phase III was a failure. I am still getting updates, but it would appear that a land-based detector located the fail-safe explosives, sending an NYPD fast boat after them. We know everything on deck was scuttled before the failsafe was detonated. What is unclear is whether the NYPD knows the cargo was scuttled, and how much distance was created between there and the explosion."

"I assume the NYPD is capable. Can they find the weapons?"

"The East River has a very dirty bottom and I understand there were over three hours between events, so unlikely, but not impossible."

"Well, let's hope they cannot locate them. Is it still our intent to upload the EMP weapon design to stimulate concern?"

"Yes sir. We'll upload soon."

"And is there any way to point these events to an actual terrorist organization?"

"Risky, but I'll look into it." Grant replied, wondering who they could target.

Maximillian was reading when the unique doors to his study slid open. Bridget, in the lead went straight to the bar area to get a glass of Rombauer Sauvignon Blanc and brought an Irn Bru soda for Grant. They all settled into the comfortable down-filled leather chairs in Maximillian's study.

Maximillian put down his e-reader and sat opposite Bridget before telling them both about the update from Sara Ricci's latest test. "The DARPA grant has kept her research under lock and key, but this young researcher appears to be doing actually exactly what she said she would. This idea of power at lower altitudes could be a major advancement in future years. I am told she has proven energy from these TGF events is there and has created an invention to capture it. According to my contact, the last test captured up to forty-four percent of the photons."

Bridget asked, "So, this is good, right?"

"Yes, but I was told clearly by my advisors that this would take over a year, if not more, and the opinion was that success was highly unlikely. I therefore never expected a tangible solution this quickly. The problem is DARPA owns her success and it may prove impossible to get them out of the picture. After all, this is DARPA."

Bridget spoke first. "Maximillian, there is no doubt this young woman is smart, but we don't really know how much of her success is her own thought and how much is the work of her great-great-grandfather, Gilberti. It would seem to me we get his research from Milan and have dear Angus hack into DARPA and get us her current work to kick start our own effort."

"Yes, that is possible, but it does not matter. She appears to have already done the work."

"Sir, there is another possibility," Grant suggested as both looked at him. "We are just weeks away from uploading the EMP weapon plans for the world to see in our effort to keep the threat alive. Although we have been talking about her thesis research, the fact is she more or less supplied the EMP weapon concept that we have actually designed. Her sketch is the one within the original grant package."

"I'm not sure I follow you," Maximillian replied.

"Sir, what if the design we release contained appropriate reference to DARPA to implicate and tie them to the EMP design and therefore a terrorist attack? Knowing the United States, this would become political overnight. Bernard Cummings would be implicated since it was his idea, and as you suspect, he appears to be working with the CIA or DHS. The young researcher would likely get caught up in the fallout, at least temporarily. But if this played out as I suggest, she might lose her loyalties to DARPA and MIT, allowing MDE Commodities to reappear as a white knight... there to save her when everyone else abandoned her."

Maximillian said nothing, but Bridget uncharacteristically added, "That is actually brilliant. Headstrong Sara, knowing she is innocent, would certainly lose all respect for DARPA and MIT. We could even help her get into an alternate university. Angus told me she was also accepted at Sapienza University in Rome."

Maximillian was pleasantly surprised at such a unique scenario. "I think this is an excellent idea."

Within a week, they had ironed out the plan. Maximillian had his private team make a set of detailed drawings of an EMP weapon from the original grant picture. Angus then altered those drawings with DARPA blueprint, letterhead, approvals, and an impression stamp for pages with critical information.

When complete and reviewed, the drawings were printed, and scanned to remove traces from the original print file, and sent to Angus, who would upload them on the dark web. He would also identify a relatively new terrorist organization, the United Brotherhood of Islam or (UBOI), as the organization responsible for the attacks.

Grant, however, had warned they shouldn't do this. He didn't know enough about the organization and thought they would enjoy the notoriety, but not the accusation. Maximillian disagreed and so it happened, but Grant's instincts told him this could be a problem.

41
Washington D.C.

Looking out of his window when the phone rang, Hicks picked up the phone. "Director, this is Ashley Jordon from Cyber Security. Sir, detailed plans of the EMP weapons have been put out onto the dark web and they imply the terrorist organization, United Brotherhood of Islam, is behind the EU based attacks. I am told the drawings are detailed enough for any competent person to build the weapon. The reason for the call, however, is that the design appears to have come from DARPA."

Unsure what he just heard, he asked, "DARPA? What are you saying Ms. Jordon?"

"The detailed drawings are photos of the original and show the DARPA seal and title blocks on most pages."

"Shit. Of course it does. Send me the file, I'll deal with it."

"Yes sir, it has been sent." Hicks hung up and went to his computer and double clicked the encrypted attachment. As he waded through the drawings, it took no imagination to see the connection. He picked up the phone and, without hesitation, called Admiral Richard Stockdale, Secretary of Defense. "Sir, I assume you are up to speed on the EMP attacks in the EU and possibly a failed effort in New York?"

"Yes, I am aware," the Secretary of Defense replied.

"Sir the reason for the call is that plans of the weapon were just leaked on the dark web by a young terrorist organization, the United Brotherhood of Islam or UBOI. The plans are detailed enough for anyone to build the device, which is troublesome. The reason for this call, however, is the design itself appears to be from DARPA."

"Was this part of what was taken in the Montana raid?"

"No sir. Shall I take the lead on this, or do you wish to involve the CIA?"

"Jeremy, you run with this as it was your idea to plant the design in the first place, but I must say, I'm a bit surprised you would provide that level of detail."

"Well, sir, that's the problem. We didn't. The design we released within the grant was a one-page drawing, just a cutaway of a viable concept. There was nothing that could be considered a build plan and certainly not for an airborne platform."

"Well, someone is going to a lot of trouble to prove you wrong. Deal with this, director!" hollered Stockdale.

After a few minutes of reflection, Hicks picked up the phone and called Dr. Levin Bechtel, the Director of DARPA, and reiterated the problem.

"Can you send me the design?" Bechtel asked in frustration.

"You should have them now."

"Hold on a second while I bring this up." Bechtel said nothing at first as he tried to absorb what he saw. "Director Hicks, I approved the grant, and it most certainly did not include this, but we are the only ones that know that. Shit, I don't need this."

Hicks replied, "I have already informed the Secretary of Defense Stockdale. Any thoughts on how to contain this? Are you absolutely sure this design isn't from DARPA archives?"

"Not that I am aware, but this is going to get ugly very fast. Given the stakes, we'll have to put Bernard and the researcher in the line of fire. Although we knew what he was doing, he provided the grant proposal to Sara Ricci before she had clearance and then left it with her. She then put everything at risk by placing it on the third-party server, which we knew about but didn't stop. That simply cannot become public."

"So, that is what would you recommend?" Hicks asked for clarity.

"Yes. I would implicate Dr. Cummings and let MIT determine what to do with Ms. Ricci. On my end, I'll order

Cummings to a congressional briefing next week, which will effectively end his career."

"Okay, explain all this to your team and MIT. Make sure this disappears quickly and quietly."

D r. Bernard Cummings was in his office when word got out that the UBOI had claimed responsibility for the EMP attacks and had simultaneously released the detailed plans. He was confused. His job had been to get the DARPA grant to the young researcher, Sara Ricci. It was the CIA, through DHS that inserted the idea of powering an EMP weapon. To the best of his limited knowledge, they only wanted to see if that information got back to Maximillian Drummond. And of course, it did. He was working for both sides and made sure Drummond got it.

He knew this was an enormous risk, but he was being very well paid. But with what just happened, he was now in real trouble. Possibly life-threatening trouble.

The UBOI design was a carbon copy of the cutaway in the DARPA grant. And it had DARPA all over it, but how? There was no such design. All he knew at that moment was he had just been set up to take the fall. If Drummond hadn't figured out that he was working for both sides, perhaps he could still pull this off.

Nervously, he left the office carrying a small duffle bag. After walking several blocks, hailed a cab to a used car lot where he purchased a late model car with cash, and drove all night to Columbus, Ohio. At a small roadside motel, he was now in his room, considering whether to call Maximillian Drummond for a lifeline.

Director Bechtel had made several advance calls when he rang his assistant and asked her to connect him to Bernard Cummings. She came back on the line saying he was not in his office and was not answering his cell phone. His reply was curt. "Trace his cell and call his home; this is urgent."

Five minutes later, she responded, "Sir, his wife says she hasn't heard from him and assumed he was on a trip related to DARPA. At present, his company cell is not active."

"Okay. Notify the security teams to locate him. Get his service provider and trace any personal cell phones he may have."

On the Isle of Skye, Maximillian handed his phone to Angus and asked, "This incoming cell number is from a contact in the United States. I expected nothing from him, but he has now called three times in under two hours, suggesting something is wrong. Can you first tell me where the calls are originating from?"

"Yes sir, just a moment." Angus accessed a program and entered the number and waited a few seconds for it to locate. "The phone is on, and recent calls came from the US in a location within the city limits of Columbus, Ohio."

"Okay, when that number calls again, answer it on speaker so I can assess if it is my contact. Initially, say nothing. If I nod no, disconnect immediately. If I nod yes, ask him why he is calling from a new location."

Twenty minutes later the call came in and Angus answered to Bernard Cummings, "Mr. Drummond, it's Bernard, I must talk to you." Angus looked at Maximillian who nodded affirmatively and then Angus replied sternly, "Why are you calling from a new location?"

Bernard paused at hearing the strange voice and then barked, "I'm running for my goddamn life. Where is Mr. Drummond? He has to help me."

Maximillian signaled for Angus to disconnect the call.

Angus did so. "I thought you said it was him."

"It was, but before I take the call, I need to think through what I intend to do. He is stressed and possibly unstable." Maximillian went back to his office and called for Grant, who arrived quickly. He told him of the call. "Why does he think he's running for his life?"

"Presumably, he knows the EMP weapon design has been released, and since he was working both sides, the release just flushed him out," said Grant cautiously. "With the tie to DARPA, he knows they'll let him take the fall, which was more or less planned from our end."

"What do we do with him in the meantime?"

Grant thought over the question for a minute and then answered, "His frantic nature is a liability, but since he thinks you'll save him, that is to our advantage. We should get him away from the CIA and DARPA and take him to Madagascar on the pretense that we'll hide him at the mine. In the time it takes to get there, we can decide if he should have an accident."

"Yes, that works. Set it up."

Maximillian called Bernard who answered on the first ring almost hyperventilating, "Mr. Drummond, please, you have to help me…"

Maximillian was furious at his weakness. "Bernard, quiet yourself and listen. We need to get you somewhere safe away from the CIA and DHS. I am patching you through to my head of security, who will make the arrangements. Hold please."

Grant was ready for the call. "Dr. Cummings, you must do exactly as I say. Do you understand?"

"Yes," he stammered.

"Please pack your things and after this call, shut off your phone and remove the SIM card. Dispose of it unseen. Then go directly to the Jet One terminal at the Columbus airport in two hours. Approach the main counter and ask for a man named Alfred. He will take you to a private room and give you revised travel documents and a new phone. When he does, immediately swap your current passport and driver's license with the new ones he will give you. Your new name is Dr. Bernard Maitland. Never use your real surname. When you leave the room, go back to the main counter, and introduce yourself as Bernard Maitland, using the new identification. They will take you to a waiting Gulfstream G650ER, which will bring you nonstop to Madagascar. When you land, another man will greet you as you exit the aircraft. His name also is Alfred. He will take you to the vessel *Yakka* which will bring you to the island. Is there anything you do not understand?"

"No, I think I have this. Please thank Mr. Drummond."

Grant hung up without a reply and looked over at Maximillian. "We're doing the right thing."

Director Bechtel was thinking through the recent events when his assistant knocked and came into his office. He glanced up and asked, "Anything?"

"Sir, he has two private cell phones. One was at his home office. The other is gone, but we got a trace to Columbus, Ohio, before the signal was lost. We suspect he powered it off and removed the SIM card."

"So, he's running. I'll move this up a notch. Did they get a valid location?"

"No sir. It was in a rural area with weak service, but teams were on the way to the approximate area. Also, his go-bag is no longer in his office. Security video shows him leaving our building with the bag at 9:20 a.m."

"Thanks, we'll find him. It's not like he's a field agent," Bechtel said with hope.

42

Toamasina, Madagascar

Bernard Maitland, aka Dr. Bernard Cummings, was having a third glass of exquisite champagne aboard the extended range Gulfstream, thinking how wonderful it was to travel in such style. He knew his actions had ruined his family, but they would have money to live on, as their joint accounts were attractive. Although his wife knew nothing of his alternate money sources, he would need all of that, as he suspected he could not return for some time. Eventually, he would try to explain, but he put that out of his mind for now.

By the time he arrived in Madagascar he was sporting a serious headache. Exactly as Grant had told him, a young man named Alfred picked him up and took him to a well maintained, hundred-thirty foot research vessel. It had been modified by MDE Commodities to shuttle people and rare earth metals to and from the mine. The dark blue ship with the MDE Commodities logo had been christened *Yakka*, the Australian aboriginal word for hard work and in less than thirty minutes, it was pulling away from the dock.

The captain, a well-built man in his fifties, approached him saying firmly, "Dr. Maitland, the trip to the island is not for the faint of heart I'm afraid, but we should arrive in five to six days' time. It will eventually turn cold, so in your stateroom are warm clothes and appropriate outer wear in your size. If you feel unwell, spend some time on deck and stare at the horizon. We also have an ample supply of Dramamine patches, if you prefer."

Already feeling horrible, he responded, "Thank you, Captain. I may need it."

"Very well. The mess is just below us; coffee is always fresh and there is always someone there to assist you. Mealtimes are posted."

"Yes, of course, thanks."

On the third day, Bernard was feeling seasick and put on a down parka and gloves before heading up to the deck. The seas were rolling and pitching, but this was much better than his small stateroom. He was looking out to the horizon when a member of the crew stopped by and asked in a strong Slavic accent, "Mind if I smoke?"

"No, go ahead," Bernard replied as he turned to look back at the horizon. He was feeling better. One moment is he was standing there looking out at the horizon and the next, he was hurling toward the water.

His brain had yet to register what happened, but when he hit the ice-cold water, the cold zapped him into a panic like nothing he'd ever felt in his life. After the three-meter fall from deck level, the cold shock made his heart race and simultaneously made him unable to breathe as blood vessels in his lungs constricted, all organs now trying to save themselves. He instinctively tried to turn himself to wave at the vessel, but the current was strong and was pulling him farther away. He could still see the *Yakka* between swells and he could even see the crew member smoking and looking right at him thinking, *what the hell; why aren't you trying to help me?* He tried to yell but couldn't get enough air as the water laden down clothes were now pulling him down under the surface.

In that instant, he knew. He knew he was being murdered. This was the price for betraying Maximillian Drummond.

43

MIT Campus, Boston

Dr. Zimbrean was on the phone when Maggie walked into his office and immediately became concerned as she noticed his face was pale, and his mouth slightly agape. He did not notice her as he sat listening to the voice on the phone so intently. It was almost as if he could not hear the words. Maggie thought to leave, but was so concerned she stayed. He finally spoke, "Yes, of course, this is disappointing, but I understand and await your word." He was listening again and closed with, "Thank you," and replaced the receiver in its cradle.

Maggie immediately asked, "Adrian, what on earth is the matter? You're white as a sheet."

Glancing at her, he replied, "That was the Provost and director of DARPA. They claim that the DARPA Assistant Director of Tactical Projects, Dr. Bernard Cummings is under a federal investigation and that it is likely Sara will be investigated as well."

"What possibly for? Sara is a charm."

"I agree, but if I have this correctly, the terrorists who recently attacked several targets in the EU with an EMP weapon have just released detailed drawings showing how to build it. They are saying the design was taken from the one that was in the original DARPA grant to Sara."

"But this can't have anything to do with Sara, and certainly not you, Adrian?"

"Yes, yes, I know that but as her thesis chair, should they investigate, I would have to tell her she will lose her facility access pending the investigation. This will truly break my heart."

"Oh, my God. That poor girl," mouthed Maggie.

Director Hicks was on his way out of his office when he received another call from the cyber security. "Director, Ashley Jordon from Cyber. NSA has located the IP addresses used to receive and send the detailed drawings."

"Go on?"

Ashley continued, "Bernard Cummings has a son, Thomas Randle Cummings, and his computer received an extensive file from an engineer at DARPA. Within five minutes, that same file was sent to an account we tracked to Istanbul but lost the trail there. Both the incoming and outgoing packet match the exact byte size of the UBOI drawings."

Director Hicks replied, "Nicely done. I'll have them pick up the son."

Thomas Cummings had just turned twenty-one and was a junior at Cornell university majoring in Political Science. Earlier in the day, he had talked to his mom and knew something was up with his dad, but had no details. He was just leaving his afternoon class and planned to call her once he got to his car. As he rounded the hallway which led to the student parking lot, two campus police officers and two other men walked toward him and stopped. The police stepped back and stood tall. One of the other men flashed credentials and said, "Thomas Cummings?"

"Yeah, what's going on?

"Mr. Cummings, I'm going to need you to come with us."

"Hey, is this about my dad?

"Mr. Cummings, you just need to come with us."

"Well, that's just it, I can't. I have to get home and see my mom; she's worried about my dad."

"Mr. Cummings, we are not asking. You will come with us, or campus police will arrest you and then we'll go, anyway. We're offering you an opportunity to avoid the embarrassment of a public arrest."

Defiant now, he spoke louder, "I'm not going anywhere; I'm calling my mom." As he went to pull his phone out of his pocket, both campus police officers rushed forward and pulled their sidearms aimed at his head and chest. The larger of the two shouted, "Do not move! Slowly, take your hands out of your pockets and raise both over your head. Now!"

Thomas did so in absolute fear. "Guys, what the hell. What's going on?"

"Mr. Cumming, please refrain from talking."

"Wait, this is pure crap, I..."

The campus policeman leaned forward and spoke directly into his ear, "I said, shut-the-fuck-up," as he grabbed his left hand, turned him forcefully and the other cuffed him.

Amid a small group of astonished students and a few alarmed faculty members, the campus police took him in one car and the federal agents followed in another to the campus security office. With no verbal communication, they entered the building down a narrow hall without windows to an equally stark interrogation room. The soundproof walls and lack of windows made it unnerving, but that was the point. Once there, the campus police left the room and the two federal agents sat facing Thomas, saying nothing, which created a tense silence for several minutes until the door opened and Director Hicks entered.

Still standing but moving towards the open chair he said, "Thomas, I am Director Hicks of the Department of Homeland Security. We will get to your father in a minute, but for now, this is about you. Do you know why you're here?"

"No, sir, I honestly have no idea. What the heck is going on?" Thomas asked, shaking now, almost in tears.

"Do you own an HP laptop computer?"

"No, sir, I have a chrome book. I haven't used a conventional notebook in years."

"Have you ever owned an HP laptop computer?" clarified Director Hicks.

Thomas hesitated and said, "Well, before I came to Cornell, I had a gaming laptop my parents bought me. Yeah, I think it was an HP. It's back in the garage at our house with all my high school stuff. What is this all about?"

"Someone, possibly you, used that computer to receive sensitive government information and send to an IP address in a foreign country. That information was subsequently used in a terrorist attack. Does that refresh your memory?"

"Sir, I have no idea what you are talking about. Seriously, go get the computer. My mom knows where it is, and you'll see for yourself; it hasn't been used in like three years."

Director Hicks stood and walked over to one of the federal agents and whispered something to him, and he immediately left. He turned back to Thomas and asked, "Where is your father?"

"I have no idea. My mom has called several times saying she can't get hold of him, but my mid-terms are coming up. Seriously, I couldn't deal with all the drama, so I said I would call her after class and go see her. Dad leaves all the time saying nothing, so I assumed it was just more top-secret stuff, but it's not like Mom to get this upset. When I saw you guys, I thought that was what you wanted to talk to me about. You know, my dad."

"When did you see him last?"

"I was home last Sunday. I left to come back to campus around 3:30 p.m. that day."

"Did your father seem and act normally?"

"Well, yeah, same as always. He's kind of tight ass, so you know, it's never a great time. It's just being back at home," he said, looking down.

Director Hicks and the other agent left to await any news of the search being conducted at the Cummings' house. His phone rang twenty-five minutes later.

"Director Hicks, we located three clear bins that the wife says held his high school stuff. It's all there, but there is no laptop, although there is an imprint of something heavy on a stack of clothing and appears to be the right size pattern. Nothing was in his room, either. Do you want the CIU units to go over the whole house?"

"Yes, and then head back here so we can compare notes."

Director Hicks went back to the room but entered the viewing room next to the interrogation room. Inside standing was a staff behavioral psychologist who had been observing. Director Hicks asked, "Based on what he has said, what's your opinion?"

"He is clearly nervous and worried about his mom, and to a lesser extent his dad, but at the same time he's trying to be strong.

I suspect his relationship with his father is difficult, and he resents the mother for not defending him. That said, at no time did his reactions break, leaving me to think he is saying what he knows."

"So the dad likely used his laptop, never thinking it would implicate the son."

"That sounds righter than that Thomas did it."

"Thanks." He walked out and entered the room once again with the federal agents. Thomas was having a difficult time holding it together as Director Hicks sat back down. "The computer is not there. What should we think of that, Thomas?"

"Sir, I told you I haven't seen it in years, so I honestly don't know what to say. Is this related to my dad? Has he done something wrong?"

"Thomas, we are equally concerned for him and cannot locate him, which is very odd. I am inclined to believe you don't know where the computer is or what it was used for. But son, this is an ongoing investigation. If at any time evidence reveals otherwise, you will spend the rest of your life in a federal prison for lying to me. Meanwhile, go to your mom, but don't even think of leaving town."

Back at MIT, Nadia Sadir had opened her computer and reviewed a synopsis of what she had put together regarding Sara over the last several months.

PhD candidate, Sara Ricci enters post prelim status but has her original thesis disproven by Chinese students weeks after someone hacked her MIT account and searched her office. Her mom passes unexpectedly, and she spends over a month in Italy but returns with a revised thesis. It is said her great-great-grandfather, Gilberti Ricci was a physicist murdered by the Nazis in the 1940s and his research was never found. Is her new thesis related to him? Months later, she is almost abducted, and the FBI is involved. Soon after, she is now working under a DARPA grant, but her research, which is stored at a secret offsite location, is stolen during an armed raid where the owner was shot. She is soon moved on campus and is only working in secured labs, so she has received a government clearance. How? Is she involved in weapons research? Two months later, she has been stripped of her access and is rumored to be under a

federal investigation. It is said she is now resigning
from her PhD program at MIT.

Nadia reread the synopsis and as she already knew, this was a story about the rise and fall of a young and supposedly gifted scientist. It also had deep tentacles involving the DARPA and God knows who else, but she was at a stalemate. She lacked the contacts to investigate at a government level and needed verification before she could print this. A story like this could make her career or absolutely ruin it and, although she rarely did, she thought to ask her dad for help. She had sent him a more detailed version of her summary. Hours later, she waited for him to take the video call she had arranged with his assistant.

Her father, Hassan Sadir, was almost always working or traveling, and Nadia rarely saw him or even talked to him. His large round face filled the screen. "Nadia, my child, I have but a few minutes. All is well at MIT? I have seen your summary."

"Hello father, and yes all is well. As you read, I have what appears to be a big story, but I don't have the connections to dig deeper and wonder if you did."

He looked at her. "Nadia, I admit this is intriguing, and you may very well have something, but you need to find an inside source. Any attempt to come in as an outsider will be shut down for no other reason than this is DARPA and to your point, likely others within United States Intelligence. If you can do that and get more direct evidence, I might have resources to probe further."

"So, I need someone inside DARPA?"

"That is a start. I need to go, so goodbye and good luck. All our love." As the video faded to black, Nadia sat back and wondered if she could entice the handsome Jason Sykes.

It was just before 5:00 a.m. in northeast of Yemen, as two senior commanders within UBOI sat in an old but updated two-story house. They were having Yemeni coffee, a full-bodied brew with a rich, wine-like acidic taste and had just watched international news. In the report, it had said their organization had claimed responsibility for the recent EMP attacks and the released weapon drawings that a competent engineering mind could easily build. In Arabic, they conversed.

"Someone is using UBOI as a shield. The elders will want blood."

"I agree, but does this not elevate our status? No one thinks we are capable of such technology or logistics. I think we should allow it, but kill those who authorized using our name."

"I think you are correct, but we must talk to the elders. Meanwhile, I will put out feelers to determine who is behind this. The drawings implicate the United States and their war machine, DARPA."

Arlington, Virginia

DARPA director Levin Bechtel was sitting at a small table and in front of him were a few senators, and the head of the CIA. They were grilling him as part of an official inquiry into the DARPA connection to the UBOI weapon plans. The closed-door session had been arranged in haste and was forty-five minutes underway with a participative panel. The current conversation was between Levin and Conrad Anderson, Deputy Executive Director of the CIA. He knew the real story, as did Levin, but neither would say a word of it on record.

"So, you are saying the grant was to locate atmospheric energy that could power an undeveloped space-based EMP weapon?" Anderson asked.

"Correct."

"And the idea for this and the EMP weapon was presented to you by Dr. Bernard Cummings?"

"Yes. At a normal DARPA Monday morning briefing, the proposed work of the young MIT scientist, Ms. Sara Ricci, sparked interest in several of our groups to consider her work. The most mature conversations were from the Microsystems group lead by Ralf Müller who was interested in beamed microwave energy, and Dr. Bernard Cummings who represented the tactical group. To my knowledge, Cummings dusted off a former EMP project and brought forward a grant proposal."

Anderson continued, "For the unscientific people in the room, are these two concepts beamed microwave energy and atmospheric energy related?"

"No sir. Beamed energy is deploying microwave beams from earth to space to control objects outfitted with a special receiver. Atmospheric energy in space requires locating and then converting energy to power. In Cummings' proposal, it would power an EMP weapon."

"So, they weren't competing for the same science, they were competing for the grant money?"

"Yes. I would agree."

"So, given that Dr. Cummings was successful, I can only imagine that his counterpart Ralf Müller was resentful?" Anderson said bluntly.

"Perhaps, but Müller is a DARPA veteran and as a scientist I believe he viewed Dr. Cumming's grant concept as folly." The conversation continued for another half-hour as Deputy Executive Director Anderson led the inquiry. They reviewed how the files had been transferred from a computer likely linked to Dr. Cummings to Turkey, why they might have been created and what should happen now. There was a brief discussion regarding

Sara Ricci and while Levin doubted she was involved, they needed an official inquiry, and her security clearance would be temporarily suspended. Meanwhile, the search for Dr. Cummings continued.

Deputy Executive Director Anderson finished up the session by saying rather forcefully, "Dr. Bechtel. You have some cleaning up to do within your organization to assure something like this never happens again. Thank you. That is all. Ladies and Gentlemen, we are adjourned."

46

MIT Campus, Boston

Dr. Zimbrean received the call following the inquiry the next day that on advice from the CIA, MIT had suspended Sara's clearance to restricted access until an inquiry could clear her. Nathen was not part of the inquiry and could continue research. Zimbrean walked out to Maggie who, of course, had surmised the call and he said, "This is most unpleasant, but I have no choice."

"Adrian, you are a good man and I know this concerns you. This will pass, I'm sure of it."

"Perhaps, but we have lost Sara the moment I tell her. Of this, I am certain. Such a waste."

With a heavy heart, Dr. Zimbrean stood, suddenly feeling significantly older than his age. He slowly made his way to the door before heading to Sara's office, hoping to find her alone. When he arrived, he used his fob to access the door and then again with his thumbprint to get into the hallway that led to her office. As he neared the door, he paused for a minute, and then knocked softly.

The beautiful face of young Sara filled the doorway as she opened it with a huge smile. "Wow, a visit to my office. I must have done something really wonderful or really bad." She smiled and gave a quick laugh, but it quickly turned to a frown when Dr. Zimbrean walked in. He was stoic, not smiling, and slumped into the small chair in front of her desk as she thought, *shit, what the hell have I done?*

"Sara, I think you know you are special to me," he whispered. "I see great things in your future, but we have a problem, and the school has insisted on the action I am about to discuss. This is not my belief or my doing, but as your thesis chair, I must convey this message to you."

For the next several minutes, he explained the released plans and the fact that the Dr. Bernard Cummings was on the run, had been implicated, and Sara was party to the event pending an investigation. Sara did not speak as her blood boiled. Dr. Zimbrean was near tears, so she stayed calm for him, saving her anger for others.

Sara awoke the next morning wishing the nightmare was just that, but as she made her first expresso, she knew this was really happening. Of all people, little miss do-nothing-wrong was under investigation by the federal government of the United States. They had even placed her on a no-fly list, so she couldn't even go home to Milan.

Later in the morning, she reluctantly met with Jason and Nathen. Sara was obviously upset, so Nathan tried to calm her. "Sara, we know you're being dragged into this by association with Dr. Cummings. You have nothing to do with this."

Sara glanced over at him, but focused on Jason. "I'm mad at myself. I suspected from day one there was something odd about DARPA... but I let the money cloud my thoughts and allowed that pretentious bastard to pull me in. Jason, you are truly working for an evil place and I'm not sure how you manage."

Jason was hurt, but understood where she was coming from. "Sara, I don't blame you for thinking that way, and I sure as hell cannot explain it. I never understood how Dr. Cummings could even create such a grant, and neither does my boss. The thing is, he did, and with him missing and now linked to crimes, I think your involvement is just an unfortunate step in a bureaucratic process. I'm sure this will end soon."

"Jason, I don't blame you personally, but I clearly blame MIT and DARPA for not defending me. Even if you are right, nothing else will ever be the same. My reputation as a serious scientist will be ruined. Do you have any idea how fucking hard it is for a woman to be taken seriously in this field?" Sara said as her voice cracked, and the emotion got to her.

There was nothing left to say, and they soon parted. Later Sara decided to get a drink, proclaiming herself to be officially overwhelmed, and went downstairs to the Thirsty Ear Pub. As she looked for an open seat, her eyes unfortunately settled on Nathen and Nadia, thinking, *crap, just what I need.*

She tried to look past them and walked to the back, but she knew Nathen had seen her. Finding a seat, thankfully one in the opposite direction, Sara ordered a glass of red wine, dreading they would soon come over, but they didn't.

Back at their table, both had actually seen her, but Nathen felt they should respect her privacy. Nadia was not as accommodating and said to Nathen, "You have to realize there is a huge story here."

"Nadia, this is Sara we're talking about. She's a victim and someone has set her up. I just don't know why, and neither does Jason."

Nadia took a sip of wine and responded carefully, knowing Nathen was protective, "Nathen, please consider the raw facts," as she explained the summary she had sent her father days before. When she finished she said, "Seriously Nathen, there's no way this doesn't involve her directly. I know you like her, but you're being naïve."

Nathen was shocked at how this all looked to Nadia and wisely did not react. Knowing that to change her perception, he had to reveal things he knew he shouldn't or more to the point couldn't. At the same time, he knew he had to help Sara if he could, and responding calmly. "Nadia, perhaps everything you just said is true, but there could be a lot more to this. Listen, if you're right, perhaps your story does no additional damage, but if you're wrong, she is finished at MIT because you painted her guilty before she was proven innocent. Are you absolutely sure you really have all the facts?"

Nadia paused and said honestly, "Well this clearly involves the US Government. I ran this by my dad, but he couldn't help me and said I needed someone on the inside of DARPA. Boy scout Jason wouldn't even talk to me, so I contacted a few high-level journalist friends, but they were immediately shot down. So yes, there is a cover-up of some sort, and no, I'm not sure I have all the facts."

"I cannot add more clarification, but you don't have the whole truth. Trust me."

"Nathen, if you want to help her tell me what you know. Otherwise, I will do what I think is best," she said, almost as a threat.

Neither said anything for a few minutes before the uncomfortable silence became so obvious that Nathen excused himself and headed back to his dorm. Nadia had thought that baiting him could get him to talk, but it hadn't worked. He'd get over it. She picked up her glass of wine and boldly walked over to Sara.

When Sara looked up and acknowledged her, Nadia said, "Sara, I know you just want to be alone, but I have a question, and please tell me the truth. With all that has happened, is MIT in your future?"

"Nadia, I owe you absolutely nothing but for clarity, I'm don't understand what you mean," Sara said, amazed Nadia was this brazen.

"Dr. Zimbrean comes to you tomorrow and says, oh sorry, they made a mistake. Welcome back. Do you stay at MIT?"

Sara was surprised that Nadia had stolen her exact thought. Clearly, Nadia would love it if she left MIT, but it was a valid question. She calmed and said, "I'm unnerved by the situation and furious at MIT for not even giving me a chance to defend myself, but no, I don't know exactly what I would do."

Nadia answered, "I'm conflicted, Sara. I have a story that could open this up. If it were well received, it could open doors and ask the kinds of questions that benefit you. But if you're complicit, all doors could slam shut. I'm not sure what to do."

"Oh please! You're completely self-centered and will do whatever you think helps you advance your career. You couldn't care less what happens to anyone else, especially me. Do whatever you want. I cannot be harmed more than I have been. But know this; you're actually wrong and if you print this, I suspect this will end your brief career as a scientific journalist." Sara stared at Nadia without blinking until Nadia finally backed down and walked away.

47

Isle of Skye, Scotland

Maximillian contemplated the current state of affairs. With Bernard eliminated, it would seem the world had accepted him and the UBOI's involvement and guilt, allowing Maximilian to weather the storm. Revenues at MDE Trust were up forty percent as businesses clamored to get protection, and they had already recouped sixty percent of the total cost of the EMP project. Of course, Maximillian knew this was far from over. Grants intel suggested the CIA was behind Cummings, and it was probable that they might have been in contact with UK's Secret Intelligence Service (SIS) at some point. The entire reason to release the detailed drawings was to taint DARPA and MIT in the eyes of Sara Ricci, which had worked exactly as planned but unresolved was CIA's involvement.

While he doubted any of these agencies could trace the EMP's back to MDE Defense, they might learn that the design released under the UBOI banner differed from the weapons being used in the attacks. And what if the SIS took initiative? There were still those at MDE Defense who could be questioned. He couldn't very well eliminate the entire team, but this needed to die off in the news, so the attacks presumably had to stop. A difficult financial decision.

Maximillian also thought the young researcher was vulnerable right now but that would soon change. His window to approach her was short, a month or less. But then again, should he?

The following morning, he discussed this with Grant and Bridget in his study. He opened the conversation by saying, "So, all is to plan. DARPA has pinned the release on Cummings, and Ms. Ricci has been suspended pending an investigation, and will be acquitted in possibly just a few weeks. What are our next steps?"

Bridget answered, "As I understand it, Boris will contact her and play to her victim status, suggesting she return to Italy where we can help her acceptance into Sapienza University. He will continue to facilitate her metal needs from Madagascar, if required, and I should note, we are currently locked into her invention."

"Excellent. What of her grant with DARPA and no-fly status?"

"Her NDA does not allow her to accept a second grant unless DARPA releases her." Grant said, but added, "I am told the grant can be severed if she tries to transfer it to a foreign university, which she just might do. As to leaving America, she can, of course, request to leave, but it wouldn't be approved until the inquiry is concluded. We simply need to make our intentions known and wait this out."

"I was hoping for a more decisive response, but you are probably right. I'll ask Boris to start contact and remind him of the stakes. We cannot scare her off. Grant, any word on the New York situation?"

"No sir, they have identified a large search area, but nothing has been located after two weeks of effort."

"Stay on that. Any news here in Scotland or the UK?"

"Nothing outside of the normal."

"Perhaps I need to elevate this. Thank you both, that is all."

Grant and Bridget left the study as Maximillian went back to his office. It was a risk, but he placed a call to Jocelyn Holmes, the Home Secretary whom he had known for some time. The purpose of the call was to get a sense of what the SIS might know and to what extent they may have elevated their concerns to her. She herself was a skilled negotiator, so he would have to tread lightly, hoping the unexpected call would give him an edge. Unfortunately, an aide took the call and explained she was away. He explained the purpose of the call and hoped for a return call.

Maximillian was in his study hours later when his phone rang. The aide asked him to hold for the Home Secretary, which he did, and Jocelyn Holmes came on a minute later, "Mr. Drummond, I received your call. What can I do for you?"

"Madam Secretary, thank you for the reply. I missed you at the Duke of York's presentation of 'Mary Stuart' several weeks ago in London. You were surrounded, and I thought it best to let you be. This call is not overly a concern, but I am having nearly daily agency level inquiries into my affairs by the United States. More troubling is that our own agencies, including those under your jurisdiction, seem to facilitate them. Have I not done enough for the UK as a citizen and employer?"

"Mr. Drummond, please, you have always been on someone's radar, and I suspect you rather like this, and might even stoke such fires. That knowledge makes this call uneventful unless there is another reason?"

"Well, yes, I enjoy the banter, but it is the cross collaboration with the United States agencies that bothers me. It is not as if I have to run my companies out of the UK."

"Oh, but you do, Mr. Drummond, and it would be expensive even for you to do otherwise. When your risk-taking challenges UK laws, our agencies are naturally there to keep you in check. I hardly see anything wrong with that. No one is above the law, including you."

"Yes, right? Well, perhaps this call was premature. My apologies."

"Sorry to disappoint you Maximillian. Next time I simply won't call back," and she hung up. Maximillian looked at the phone as he set it into its cradle, thinking that her confidence was a bluff or that she had something on him.

Boris Turgenev was back at the mine on Heard Island and this time of year, early July, the weather was turning nasty and cold. High thirties to low forties during the day with significant wind and rain made it harder for mine to meet the harsh environmental regulations imposed on them. He had been tasked with contacting Sara Ricci and used her previous order of the thorium like metal as the reason for the call.

Sara's phone rang, but went to voicemail, so he left a brief message. Coming back from a run not much later, she noticed the voicemail, and when she saw the contact, she smiled and called him back. When he answered, she said in Russian, "Hello Boris. This is Sara returning your call."

He replied in Russian, "Yes, hello Sara. It has been many weeks since the shipment, and I just wondered how your experiments went."

Sara switched to English, saying, "Boris, my experiment went well. I am still determining if I will require additional tests."

"So, it was successful. That is wonderful news. Did it meet your expectations? I know you wanted to consider other metals originally."

"It exceeded my expectations and I'll stay with this formulation but presently, I'm on leave pending an investigation, so I'm not sure of any future requirements."

Playing dumb, Boris said, "Sara, we are a legitimate mine backed by a very large public company. We do not deal with contraband and I can help you with any such issues."

Sara laughed. "No Boris, your metal is not under investigation. It is me they're after. The agency director who gave me the grant has done something illegal and the United States Government is investigating him, but because he gave me the grant, they are also investigating me. Of course, I have nothing to do with this, but for now I am suspended."

"I am so sorry to hear of your worries. How long do they expect you to postpone your research?"

"I wish I knew, but it doesn't matter. I could ever work with them again."

"Sara, I think you should leave America. You would be welcomed at any university. Personally, I know my alma mater, Sapienza, would gladly accept you."

Surprised, Sara replied, "You went to Sapienza University?"

"Yes, Sophia Antonion, the Managing Director for MDE Aerospace and I both attended. Of course, my Italian is not so good like your Russian." He chuckled and concluded by saying in broken Italian, "I won't keep you. I'm sorry to hear of your troubles but wish you luck. Call me if you need anything, anything at all?"

"Thank you, Boris. It's nice to hear that someone believes in me. Talk to you later." And she hung up. Based on her experience with MDE Enterprises she had to conclude she had been wrong. They were too helpful to be after her.

Boris replaced the receiver, thinking that had gone very well.

48

Almost two weeks had passed since losing her restricted access, and Sara called Maggie to set up an appointment with Dr. Zimbrean. She needed to understand how she might exit the DARPA grant. Maggie answered and said he was available in an hour. Sara agreed and when she arrived, she hugged Maggie who had tears in her eyes just as Dr. Zimbrean finished a call and waved her in.

"Sara, how are you? I am sure this will all be concluded soon, and life can return to normal." When Sara did not respond, his shoulders fell, and he added softly, "I knew this would be the outcome, but you have been a breath of fresh air to this old physicist. Perhaps it is best if we both leave."

Such a personal response was not expected and defensively Sara replied, "Dr. Zimbrean, you are the only reason I came back after my mom's passing. I'm perhaps most angry with DARPA, as they chose not to exonerate me when they knew they could, but MIT proved no better by letting everyone else fight the battle."

"I understand, Sara. It bothers me as well. Are you well? Is there anything you need?"

"I am fine I guess, but I wondered how all this works. To my understanding, the DARPA grant is not transferrable to another university, so if I resign from the MIT program, the grant will expire. But the NDA binds my thesis to DARPA for five years, which is a problem for my future research. Any advice on how to move forward?"

"Well, that is not precisely the case. Whatever university you consider, you must apply for a transfer of the grant, and DARPA must approve or deny the transfer. Because of whom this is, they would likely deny any transfer outside the United States. As far as you personally, any university, even without your substantial base of references, will accept you so far into your research. However, to get a new grant, that unfortunately is for lawyers to decide. In your favor, your NDA with DARPA is surprisingly vague. Please recall that your grant was to locate atmospheric energy. As you have done this, neither you nor they can own that knowledge. It is simply known. That you have gone a step further, to capture and convert the energy is what could be argued by DARPA as theirs, assuming you used grant monies to fund this."

"Well, yes, I did. Could I pay them back for the monies used for conversion research?"

"It is highly irregular, but it could be part of a negotiation, given what has transpired. You would have to ask."

"Okay. I'll be in touch."

"Very good. Please take care." Dr. Zimbrean rose once again, looking very sad. This had taken a toll on them both. As Sara walked out, Dr. Zimbrean made a call. He waited for several minutes before the phone was answered. "This is Dr. Adrian Zimbrean from MIT calling for Director Hicks."

Sara called her dad the following morning. She hadn't spoken to him in a while and was not avoiding him, but he could be so overprotective of her situation, sometimes it did little to help her. At the same time, she knew he was hurting too, and she needed to let him express himself.

"Dad, is this a good time?"

"For you, my special girl, it is always a good time."

Sara told him of the NDA, how she could likely break the grant and even brought up MDE Enterprises and their ties to Sapienza University and likely a grant continuation, and asked for his input.

"Sara, please be honest, how much money would be required to address repayment of the DARPA monies used in the conversion theories and finish the research to the conclusion of capturing and converting the energy? Did I say that correctly?"

She laughed. "Dad, you nailed it. I'll make you a scientist yet. There is approximately fifty thousand dollars spent to date on the theory to capture and convert, which I owe DARPA. If I can conclude my research, the remaining cost is unknown, but I expect around the same, fifty-thousand dollars.."

"Sara, come home to Italy and get into Sapienza even if it requires help from this MDE company. As to the grant, I will back your entire study so that you are no longer in the hands of anyone but yourself."

"Dad, I know you have the money, but there are many opportunities within MDE Enterprises, and I suspect this is not a big deal for them."

Responding more firmly, he said, "Sara, I'm sure that is true, but have you really considered all you have been through? I am very serious now. Gilberti started all this but was used by others, ultimately costing him his life. You have also been used by others and certainly harmed to the very point that I'm concerned for your safety. I must insist that you and only you own this."

She was shocked at his tone and commitment. "Dad, it's not that simple, but I understand what you are saying. I promise I'll give this serious thought."

When she finally hung up ten minutes later, she thought about his words and part of her could not agree more. Her own blood had started this journey seventy-five years ago, and now she was trying to finish it. Perhaps her dad was right. Why should anyone but a Ricci share the glory?

49
Washington D.C.

On the large flat screen facing DHS Director Hicks was the unremarkable face of Giles Taylor, the Assistant Chief of the UK's Secret Intelligence Service (SIS), formally known as MI6. Although in different services in different countries, they were friends and once shared a room in college.

"Giles, my friend, it's been a while. Thank you for taking the call."

Knowing the purpose of the call, Giles replied, "Greetings to you, Jeremy. I must say, this falls far outside your normal area of responsibility does it not?"

"Yes, it does. We have been following leads predicting these EMP attacks and now that it is happening, we are interested in helping if we can. Conrad Anderson, Deputy Executive Director of the CIA is heading the official inquiry, but DHS is assisting with communication."

Giles did not snicker, but was visibly insincere when he said, "And your idea of help was to call me for... help?"

Hicks didn't react to the insinuation. "The explosion in New York last month is believed to be related to a failed EMP attack likely in our financial district. In our case, a land-based scanner revealed the explosives from the fail-safe bomb which led police to go after the suspects, but they blew themselves up and injured three policemen, rather than be caught. We believe the weapons were scuttled and we're looking for them, although the grid area is large."

"I am sorry for the injuries to your policeman and thankful the attack was avoided, but I cannot see a connection until you locate evidence showing that is what it was."

"Giles, before you dismiss this out of hand, I have more intel. You already knew about the registry of the private aircraft that brought a raid team into the USA. We now know the raid itself was done with a leased helicopter, and we have a video of the raid team loading and offloading. They knew the camera was there, which made facial recognition difficult, but we got a hit on one of the raid team, a former American soldier we believe is now a mercenary. I was hoping you could run this through your own systems to see if we can identify more."

Giles understood and saw no reason not to agree. "And might I be able to gain a copy of this video?"

"Yes. You'll have it shortly."

Giles smiled but said nothing other than, "Is there anything else?"

"Given the number of EMP weapons deployed in the EU, I was also hoping you might use your extensive contacts to get better information on the fragments from other obliterated weapons. That and the facial recognition are what I meant by help."

Giles looked down in thought and said nothing before he looked up with a smile. "Jeremy, I have some information, but please have the courtesy to not take this up with anyone until I can so inform Alastair. If he knew I told a foreign agency first, he would have my head." He was referring to Alastair Evans, his boss, the Foreign and Commonwealth Secretary who, like the Home Secretary, was just one step down from the Prime Minister.

He held up a report and waved it in front of the screen. "I have a contact in Amsterdam who runs the security detail for the Port Authority. The good chaps there knew it was an EMP attack and according to my source, they brought in a forensic team from the General Intelligence & Security Service. Fortunately, one of the two EMP weapons hit the soft ground a few feet from the bunker. Although highly damaged, it left more debris, and they could describe the design and reveal some aspects of its construction. The design was quite sophisticated, comprising a ferromagnetic generator with a rare earth magnet called neodymium. This powered the primary pulse device, a flux compression generator which had a unique taper design to boost the pulse power." He paused before adding, "Before you ask, I took the liberty to send them a sample of neodymium from MDE

Commodities, but the results show the material came from the Mountain Pass mine in California."

"No match. That is unfortunate."

"Yes, well, now you know," Giles said coolly.

"Giles, the design you just mentioned does not match the design that was recently released by UBOI. It did not use a ferromagnetic generator."

"I hadn't noticed, but I'll have the boys look into it. It seems strange they would go to all the trouble to create an alternate design, although I must say, none of this fits the UBOI to the extent we know them. In any case, please reciprocate if you learn anything else." Giles rang off and immediately called to arrange some time to discuss these events with the Foreign and Commonwealth Secretary.

50

Ashdown House, MIT Campus, Boston

Sara awoke to yet another day of emptiness. For the first few weeks after losing her lab access, she did literature research and guided Nathen, but was unfocused, angry, and soon lost interest. Wearily, she made a cup of expresso and sat next to the window to observe the rare sunny day, thinking she might go for a run later. She had finished her second cup and an almond biscotti when her cell rang, and she glanced at the time. It was 7:48 a.m., and Dr. Zimbrean was calling.

She answered. "Dr. Zimbrean, is everything okay? This is early for you."

"Yes, it is Sara. I'm glad I didn't wake you."

"No, not at all. I've had my coffee and breakfast. What's up?"

"Sara, I am pleased to say that the university has completed their review in your favor based on additional evidence provided by the DHS. You are cleared and reinstated." Sara wanted to say thank you, but said nothing. Dr. Zimbrean continued, "Yes, well, we discussed this, but I wanted you to know. Sara, I'm here for you if you would like to talk further. My advice is to regain access to your materials and make adequate protections."

"Dr. Zimbrean, thank you," Sara responded affectionately. "I am here now, and it makes sense to use that time to my advantage as long as I don't use DARPA funds."

"I would agree. All privileges have been reset, so just go to the high clearance building using your fob. That will access Ms. Vassar who will reset your credentials."

"Thank you. I know this has been hard for you, too." Sara pressed end and sat wondering what she should really do now.

Hours later, both Jason and Nathen had come to see her at her request. In her cramped dorm room, she explained in more detail what had transpired, not knowing Dr. Zimbrean himself had lit the fire under DHS to get this resolved. They listened and Sara got emotional as she knew what she had to do, but had not said it out loud, as if doing so made it more real than thinking about it.

Looking at them both, with soft tears in her eyes, she said, "Guys, despite getting my access back, you know I just can't stay here. I have to leave MIT and America."

Nathen looked at Jason and both wanted to say something but were at odds who would go first. Jason acquiesced and nodded to Nathan, as in *go ahead.*

"Sara, I guess I get how you feel, but leaving MIT, that's crazy."

"Perhaps from your eyes, Nathan. Listen, only you guys and Dr. Zimbrean believed in me and I'm grateful for that, but the administration of this school wasn't there for me, so I just do not have any loyalty to them. It's just how I'm wired."

Nathan looked down as he realized this wasn't just idle conversation. Sara had decided. "Wow, I just can't imagine you not being here. I mean, I look so forward to working with you, but I also understand everything you have been through and hope you can remain my mentor and friend from a distance. I'll do everything I can to help you package up your research." Sara nodded her head in thanks.

Nathen looked over to Jason who was visually upset. Jason searched for the words before he said, "Sara, I saw this coming, but only want you to be safe and happy. If that is your decision, I support you and will always be here if you need me." No sooner had he finished than he rushed up and hugged her with all his might and then quickly walked to the door. There, he turned quickly. "It won't change the outcome, but I intend to find out what the hell is going on within DARPA," and stormed out of the door. Surprised, Nathan looked at Sara, who was looking back at him as both wondered what he meant.

Hours later, Jason arrived at Boston Logan airport. There he boarded flight AA2152 to Washington D. C. where he intended to understand what the hell had cost Sara her PhD, and in his mind, cost him Sara. He knew this could get him fired, but honestly didn't care. Something was wrong and doing nothing was no longer an option.

The next morning, Jason sat facing his boss, Assistant Director Ralf Müller, in his office at DARPA headquarters in Arlington, Virginia. Jason had not announced his trip, and Müller was accommodating, but not happy about the intrusion. "Sykes, you look like a lion ready to pounce. What's this all about?"

Jason took a moment before answering. "Sir, I need to understand what the hell is going on and why this agency more or less destroyed Sara Ricci's career."

"Perhaps you're too close to be objective and even if there was something going on, it would be way above your pay grade."

"So that's it, nothing." Jason stood quickly and in a more demanding tone added, "Tell me or I resign, effective immediately."

"Sykes, sit the fuck down and stop thinking you have any pull here. You're just going to piss me off," Müller, said with confidence.

Unsure of his next move, he sat. "Sir, I just don't understand. Why implicate her? You know her story, right?"

"I do, and none of us believe she had anything to do with this, but there is a process that must be followed given the senate inquiry. You, of all people, know this and as of yesterday, she has been exonerated. It's over, so why are you even here?"

"She is resigning from MIT and going back to Italy. The damage is done. I just want to know why."

Ralf paused and looked directly at Jason. "Leaving MIT is her decision, not ours." Ralf paused for a moment and saw the hurt in Jason's eyes. "Jason, what the hell is really going on? Nothing can change what has already happened."

"I know that, but on top of losing her, we..., we might have a larger problem. There is a journalist at MIT for the campus newsletter. Her name is Nadia Sadir, and her father sits on the board of directors for News Corp. Nadia and Sara have never gotten along, but Nadia has put together a story that depicts the rise and fall of Sara Ricci. I've read it. Besides making Sara look bad, it also includes her connection to DARPA, her security issues, FBI's involvement, and it even brings up Gilberti Ricci. I think I have a chance to stop it, but only if I understand what the hell is really happening."

Ralf was surprised, assuming, like everyone else, this would just die off, but an opinion piece in today's social media would be terrible. He looked at Jason and asked, "Can I trust you?"

"Of course."

"No, I mean it. Can I really trust you?"

"Sir, you have always been there for me. I came to DARPA because of you. You can trust me."

Ralf paused for a moment, knowing this wasn't for Jason's ears, but he needed to talk to someone. "Jason, I don't have a clue what is really happening, but I've been thinking about this for months. I believe that the DHS, as directed by the CIA, used DARPA through Sara's grant to transfer information to, and possibly from, a Scottish Industrialist, a guy named Drummond. I further believe Cummings was the one feeding the information. Based on the events involving Sara, it is reasonable to assume that he must have also been working for Drummond, a double agent so to speak. I think the detailed drawings were fabricated intentionally by the CIA or possibly Drummond to frame Cummings. Sara was honestly just collateral damage."

"Why?"

"I'm not sure, but they could have learned he was acting as a dual agent. Another possibility is that Drummond himself created the fake drawings to frame him and cause her to abandon her grant with DARPA so he can have sole access to her discoveries."

"That's bizarre, but strangely plausible. Do you think Cummings is still alive?"

"Given the resources involved in locating him, no. I suspect he is dead. He is not a trained agent, and I doubt he has the connections to stay hidden. If this Drummond got to him, he most certainly is not of the living."

"Assuming he is dead, this all dies off, but this article would blow everything right back up."

"Yes. A public message, as you have described would link DARPA to a terrorist organization in the eyes of the public, and that would gravely hurt the agency. Heads will roll."

"You mean ours?

"I'm not sure what I mean. There are possibly three levels of authority that signed off on the original grant, which makes them suspect. The other alternative is that the process was circumvented, and the only one involved is Director Bechtel. I think he and whoever is involved on the CIA or DHS side would do anything to save their skin, so yes, we would be thrown to the wolves."

"So, what the hell do we do?"

"Jason, I feel for Sara, I really do, but others are involved much higher up the food chain and I feel as if I'm being watched. Someone knows what I know, and they want to see what I do with that knowledge, but regardless, we have to stop that story from coming out. That is all that matters now."

"Are we in this alone, or can you get additional support?"

"I don't know. Stay in town for another night and I'll decide and get back to you."

Director Bechtel had been informed by DHS that Sara was going to resign from her PhD program at MIT, but didn't much care. His preference was to get all this in his rear-view mirror as soon as possible. For the record, however, he had to call her and at least try to get a continuation, and asked his assistant to locate her.

When she answered, he said, "Ms. Ricci, this is Director Levin Bechtel of DARPA. We have not met, but I allowed your grant and wanted to apologize for the actions of my former employee, Bernard Cummings. I understand you're leaving your PhD efforts?"

Sara was curt in her reply. "No Director Bechtel, I am only resigning from MIT not my doctoral efforts. Thanks to your organization, I no longer have a future in the United States."

"Well, you certainly had no problem accepting our grant and using most of the funds. Can I assume it is not possible to pick up where we left off? Your suspension was short-lived, and you have been exonerated and reinstated."

"Perhaps to you, it is that simple, but no, Director, I'm returning to Italy and will complete my PhD there."

"Very well. I will contact MIT and make the arrangements. Do you plan to request a grant transfer?

"I will request a transfer as I must, but can no longer work for DARPA in any capacity. Please note that I have already transferred all my research findings to you and have documented and reimbursed the account with all monies used on my stalled effort to convert the TGF energy."

"I'm not sure if it's that simple but understand, Ms. Ricci, DARPA has no fight with you, and I will do what I can to allow this to play out if that is your wish. When will you tell MIT about your decision?"

She had not considered the actual date but said, "I am still organizing my research, but once that is done, I will resign."

"Ms. Ricci, I'll actually need a date."

"And you will not get one, Director. I will resign when I have made my research portable."

"Very well, please know the grant is frozen and the remaining funds cannot be used."

As if not to care, Sara quipped back, "As they have been since I was suspended at your request. Goodbye Director Bechtel."

He hung up the phone, annoyed but happy this chapter was now behind him. This gal was a real firecracker. It wasn't an hour later when his assistant received a call from Ralf Müller requesting twenty minutes with him, and she set up the meeting. When he arrived, she buzzed him in.

Bechtel looked up from his desk, smiling as Ralf walked in, "Well Müller, if you're in my office, you must need money."

Ralf laughed, saying, "I actually wish that was the reason, but might I have a private conversation, Director?"

No longer smiling, Bechtel simply nodded and pressed a button, locking the door. At the invitation, Ralf sat down and explained Nadia Sadir and the story regarding Sara, leaving out none of the details, including his theory on the events and how such a story could hurt DARPA.

When he was done, Bechtel was not entirely surprised that Müller had figured this out, but the consequence of a public scandal was the bigger issue here.

"Müller, I cannot confirm or deny what if anything has transpired but appreciate this information? We are finally breathing a sigh of relief following the exploits of Cummings, and this would create significant damage. Do you have any recommendations?"

"Sir, our choices are limited. We can take this higher and create a means to deal with it once it is out or we go on the offensive and make sure the story is never revealed."

"And how do we do that?"

"With intel from the CIA, my liaison officer should be able to eliminate the threat without harm to the journalist." Bechtel nodded his head but said nothing for several seconds.

"Müller, I appreciate the offer, but I'll run with this. I thank you again and for the record, this conversation never happened."

"Understood." As he rose, the door unlocked; he walked out. Behind him, the dock clicked again as Ralf assumed it would, and he kept going.

Bechtel immediately picked up the phone and called Hicks at DHS. Knowing the call was being recorded, he spoke a code phrase. It sounded like a normal paragraph but was actually signaling a private meeting. He hung up, grabbed his coat, and proceeded to a bench on Patton Drive in the Arlington National Cemetery.

A close drive for either, they met thirty minutes later, and both sat as Hicks spoke first. "Fill me in." Bechtel did so again and, like Müller, left nothing out.

"Müller is even smarter than you assumed, and he did the right thing, but this is a problem. Stopping a journalist in today's digital age is close to impossible. I need to understand her and her father before I can suggest alternatives."

"Müller has offered for his liaison officer, Jason Sykes to do this quietly if we can supply intel."

"One approach, but an aggressive journalist with a connected father, neither of whom are Americans, likely means if we try to stop her, she'll publish just to spite us. As they say, once you know something, you can't un-know it." With that, he rose and walked back to his car.

Inspector Elis LaCour sat next to the computer screen in the wheelhouse of the NYPD vessel. For over two weeks, they had been scanning a large grid in the East River from Port Washington to the west edge of Rikers Island. Moving north to south, they had started at the explosion site and worked their way back towards Manhattan with narrowing lines. The belief was they likely scuttled the weapons at the beginning of the chase. With over three-hundred-sixty lines traveled, they had recorded several hundred pieces of debris large enough to register an interest and dove on many. But they found nothing.

As they rounded to start the last pass, the computer remained silent, and the skipper brought the boat around as they pulled up the sonar fish before heading towards home base on Rikers Island. They all knew this had been a long shot.

Sadly, had they traveled just five-hundred feet north, on the seventh to last grid line, they would have located two drones with weapons attached lying on the seabed within thirty feet of the launch ramp.

SIS Assistant Director Giles Taylor was again in a secure video room at the famous SIS building at Vauxhall Cross. Having briefed Alistair Evans, he placed a prearranged call to DHS Director Hicks who was ready in a similar room in Arlington.

"Giles, thanks for setting up this call. Any new information?"

"Jeremy, our facial recognition system verified the chap you identified, Bruce Morgan; former Army Ranger now listed as a mercenary. Our records also show he is part of the security detail to Maximillian Drummond. It may mean something, or it may simply mean he continues to hire out his skills. We also confirmed the last man to board the helicopter was a former Green Beret named Grant Aiken. He is currently the head of security for MDE Enterprises and the personal security detail of Maximillian Drummond."

"So that is a direct tie, right?" replied Hicks.

"Well, it is enough to arrest Aiken, but Drummond remains in the clear."

"At least it's something."

"Any new information regarding the EMP weapons?"

Hicks responded, "No, NYPD couldn't find anything and ended the search. They also could not identify the suspects through the limited bone and tissue samples found."

"Any news on the released design that clearly does not match the actual design? I presume this is being kept quiet," said Giles coolly.

"It is for now, as we are not sure what it means. With the DARPA Assistant Director missing and presumed dead, this caused us to end the inquiry into the MIT scientist. I'm told she is resigning their PhD program and moving back to Italy, despite being cleared and reinstated."

"Jeremy, if I didn't know better, I would suggest someone was attempting to target DARPA and possibly this director himself. Again, UBOI has no such motive. We may lack evidence to tie Maximillian Drummond or MDE into this, but it does all seem related."

"Agreed, but what we have is not enough. We'll continue our efforts to get harder evidence. Thanks for the update."

"Yes, we'll do the same, Jeremy," as Giles rang off. Hicks hung up the phone, realizing this was all spiraling out of control. Even Taylor had it figured out. He knew damn well if the story broke, it was all over for him.

It took some effort, but Sara finally managed to put her formal resignation letter into words, which she delivered to Dr. Zimbrean that same day. He was stoic, but understanding, and promised Sara he would use his influence to stay in touch wherever she may go and reiterated her entire committee would make a strong recommendation on her behalf.

She smiled sadly. "Dr. Zimbrean, you have been and always will be my friend and mentor. I promise to contact you once I get back to Milan." She stood and gave him an awkward hug.

Staying seated, he only said, "Safe travels, Sara."

Sara spent the next few days organizing her research and the millions of loose ends associated with her painful but necessary decision. Perhaps feeling guilty, DARPA had actually been generous with the release of data and Nathen and Jason had supplied hours of support. As she was preparing to leave, Nadia, Nathen, and Jason came to see her off. Nadia was beaming, but saying consolatory words, while Nathen was clearly upset. The happy couple would argue over that later.

Jason was quiet and reserved, but he ended up driving her to the airport claiming he was following DARPA's orders, although nobody believed it. For Sara, it was bittersweet to leave them all, but as far as Jason was concerned, perhaps that chapter was not over, and they vowed to stay in contact. As she went through security, she pulled her purse and backpack up onto her shoulder and went for a coffee, before she stopped herself.

She laughed for the first time in weeks, as she turned and headed for the First-Class lounge to have a glass of superb wine. New day, new life!

Back in Milan, Sara's first week home was an absolute whirlwind. She moved back into the terrace flat with her dad and by the end of the week, had organized her thoughts and contacts, enough to start the discussion of continuing her PhD at Sapienza University. When she contacted them, she was surprised to learn that the head of the acceptance committee had already been approached by both MIT and a representative of MDE Enterprises for her presumed application.

Sara had also sent a note to Boris Turgenev at MDE Commodities, formally explaining her decision to apply to Sapienza and that she must forego any financial assistance citing her NDA with DARPA.

The following day, she was surprised when her cell rang, and the incoming caller was from MDE Aerospace. Until this point, Sara had only communicated with Boris at MDE Commodities, but he had mentioned the aerospace group, so she took the call. "Hello, this is Sara Ricci."

"Ms. Ricci, this is Sophia Antonion, the Managing Director of MDE Aerospace. Am I catching you at a bad time?"

Sara's first thought was boy, are these guys aggressive, but she was also curious as this was part of MDE Enterprises. She replied, using her limited Greek, "Hello Ms. Antonion, what can I do for you?"

Sophia replied in English, "So clever. I am told you have left MIT and the United States. This is true?"

"Yes. I'm back in Milan staying with my dad. I have been in contact with Sapienza University and thanks to your company and MIT, they seem willing to assist my doctoral efforts. Can I assume your call is related to my letter to Boris Turgenev? I hope I have not undermined myself within MDE for not requiring your financial assistance?"

"Not at all. After what you have been through, you are doing exactly what I would have done in your same situation, and I understand the complexity of your NDA with DARPA. No, my reason for calling is I want to offer you a job."

"What?" Sara said, surprised.

"Ms. Ricci, I realize you are a year or more from actually working full time, so let me tell you what I am thinking. Given your work with MDE Commodities, we have a rudimentary understanding of your thesis and the teams here at MDE Aerospace and MDE Defense are quite excited about several application-based ideas. I thought it made sense to hire you as a consultant to assist their efforts in using the energy you have proven exists. I'll pay you a flat salary of fifty-thousand euros annually to help them when you can. This is your discovery, so for every application that moves forward, MDE Aerospace or MDE Defense will pay you a lump sum royalty of fifty-thousand euros if that product uses your capture/conversion concept. Do you have any interest?"

Sara was surprised, but concerned. "Ms. Antonion, I'm flattered, but I'm nowhere near having a true discovery from a commercial sense. I have only located a source of high-power gammas and, using a proxy energy, identified a method to show that some amount of conversion is possible."

Sophia replied, "Ms. Ricci, please call me Sophia, and I think you are underestimating what you have done. You have found realistic power in a smaller, more robust platform, at less cost than current methods. Second, you have found a method to slow incoming gammas which has applications worldwide. Whatever the limitations, we think you can help us solve this."

"But, in a real application, this might not work?"

"Ms. Ricci, my proposal has only two fixed outcomes. I give you fifty-thousand euros and you get a PhD from Sapienza. As far as anything else, we spend a hundred times this on basic R&D every year and believe such research ultimately creates thoughts and ideas you could never see otherwise. It's your decision of course, but I will send you the proposal. Please let us know once you are more firmly established at Sapienza." She stopped, not wanting to over sell.

"Sophia, thank you and I will look at the proposal, but my first thought is to only focus on getting into a PhD program and completing my research and dissertation. Everything else may have to wait."

"I understand, but remain hopeful," she said before switching to Greek, "And we look forward to hearing from you."

As she hung up, Sara smiled. Yes, she had been mistaken. This company was really trying to help her. She went off to find her dad and tell him the news.

Sophia Antonion replaced the receiver and stared at it for a few moments. Of course, she understood where Sara was coming from, but at the same time, MDE Enterprises appeared to have again taken a huge step backwards. She had assumed Sara would take the offer and while she still might; she had the courage to say, *I'm not interested in anything until I complete my PhD.* That could be eighteen months away, and in that amount of time, anyone could approach her. Sophia needed to confer with Maximillian. No. This just wouldn't do.

Armed with a complete dossier on Hassan and Nadia Sadir, Hicks was anything but relieved. The elder Sadir was an absolute bulldog with a reputation of being extremely well connected and a ferocious entrepreneur. Calm and well-mannered on the outside, he had a collection of enemies around the world, as it seemed he never accepted no for an answer. He simply found a way, meaning he would not be intimidated by a call from Hicks, or even the Secretary of Defense.

His daughter, Nadia, was equally tough. She became almost obsessive to anything she put her mind to and again it was doubtful that she would ever react positively to being told she needed to reconsider. It was highly likely that to her full-stop meant full-speed ahead.

Hicks thought this through, and none of the possibilities were good. The only plausible outcome was to confront her as a matter of national security. While neither she nor the father had the pull to alter that, it was a stretch if Secretary of Defense Stockdale would see this as a matter of national security. It was must easier to assume he would see this as Hick's failure and, although he might still grant the request, Hicks would pay the price. Regardless, he contemplated calling him when his assistant told him that the DARPA Director had arrived and wished for a few words.

Bechtel walked in and closed the door. "Müller called earlier. According to him, Sara Ricci's former assistant, Nathen Chase, has been dating the journalist, and convinced her not to run the story. Key points were that it would harm Ms. Ricci and possibly ruin her career given she can't verify key facts. I'm not sure how solid this is, but Sykes claims it is true and has spoken to her as well."

Director Hicks responded, "Our options were painful so for now, we'll have to accept it but have the liaison stay close to the situation. We'll need time to react if needed."

53

Isle of Skye, Scotland

Grant and Maximillian were sitting outside on a garden terrace at the rear of the residence in front of the heliport. The small area was secluded from the winds and very private as Maximillian patiently listened to Grant tell him the NYPD could not locate the intact drones and weapons.

"Your men did well to our edict. Please make sure their families are well compensated. So at least for now nothing changes," said Maximillian almost as a test.

"I have heard that fragments from Amsterdam have allowed the SIS to acknowledge the UBOI design is not the actual design. By itself, it is nothing, but all added together, it shows an orchestrated event, so I feel good about silencing the EMP attacks."

"Well, something is giving the Home Secretary confidence, so I'm inclined to think that information from SIS was important enough to reach her, but they don't have hard evidence to do anything about it."

"Angus looked into this at my request, and we believe that the United States Director of the Department of Homeland

Security, Jeremy Hicks, is the person who is driving this. More interesting is that Hicks was a college friend of current SIS Chief, Giles Taylor. They have worked together in the past and the DHS has been drawn into the various actions surrounding the scientist Sara Ricci. I conclude it is the DHS who has been trying to persuade the SIS to look into us."

"Homeland Security? Why would DHS be involved with SIS?"

"I suspect the CIA is behind this and the DHS is simply facilitating because this DHS Director Hicks has a relationship with the head of the SIS."

"That makes sense based on what we know. Make sure Angus continues to observe discreetly. I do not wish to be further surprised," Maximillian responded.

"Yes, of course. On another subject, I understand the scientist turned us down?" Grant asked.

"Sophia seems to understand her and feels after all that has happened, she is compelled to finish her PhD alone and even she thinks the NDA with DARPA would be a legal nightmare. Nonetheless, she offered her a consulting job with MDE, including a royalty arrangement, and surprisingly, she may have turned that down as well. I remain in doubt that Ms. Ricci is working on the entire scope of Gilberti's work. For the Nazis to have killed him, he must have been working on a true weapon. This young woman may know this, but is too proper to consider such thoughts. I really think we should consider getting his work papers from Milan, assuming they are there."

"That is easily done. Simply let me know if that is what you wish." Grant stood and both he and Maximillian went back into the residence.

54

Sapienza University, Rome, Italy

Sara sat with her dad under the shaded terrace surrounded again by the sounds and smells of Milan. He had just brought up the mail and as he sorted through the various letters; he smiled and handed a letter and a large envelope to Sara both from Sapienza University. She wasn't sure what the letter was since she had only applied three weeks before, but sure enough, it was a letter of acceptance.

Surprised and happy that the process had gone quickly, she now had to consider the reality of moving to Rome, almost seven-hundred kilometers away. Her thoughts were interrupted by her dad's voice who said quite pleased, "My special girl, I am so proud of you. Full circle, yes?"

Less excited, she replied, "Yes, Dad, full circle. It is kind of amazing with everything that has happened over the last three years, but here I am, right back where I initially thought I would start."

"Gilberti would be proud of you. I am proud of you."

"Really Dad? I can't imagine you saying anything less."

"Well, I just hope you can now finish your much deserved PhD in peace."

"So do I, but we can't be naïve. Whoever wants my research is still out there, and is probably following my movements."

"Perhaps we should alert Sapienza of your unique situation so we can protect you."

"Maybe. My immediate concern is that I have to move again."

"Yes, about that, I found a small terrace flat just outside the university, just two-hundred meters from the physics lab. It is a nice two bedroom, and I made an offer to purchase," he beamed.

"Dad, I just learned that I got accepted ten minutes ago and I'll likely be there less than two years. Please withdraw the offer, I can find something," she said, concerned.

"One of my colleagues from work has owned the flat for many years and wanted to retire, so I looked at this as an investment long before you even made your decision to leave America. It is a nice flat with a small terrace, and I think there will always be good rent for the more affluent student and besides, it is very much done. It has been ours for two months," Giovanni said, smiling and happy as a clam.

Sara laughed, shook her head, and marveled at the boldness of her dad, saying thank you, before giving him a hug. She didn't need to be taken care of, but it was nice to know there was always someone in her corner.

Sara led the way to track fifteen for Rome, pulling two small suitcases as she entered the Milan Central rail station weeks later. Her dad was behind her, pulling two enormous suitcases, which represented her entire collection of must have items. They boarded the Intercity fast train for Rome Terminal for a four-hour journey through the Italian countryside.

After arriving in Rome, they made their way to the street and took a taxi to the new flat less than two kilometers away. As they approached the flat, Sara was taken aback by the perfect location and impeccably manicured building that she would now call home. No doubt this had set her dad back far more than he would ever admit.

They unpacked the basics and went out for an early dinner at a local ristorante before walking back onto the campus for a quick tour.

Fresh from a light breakfast the next morning, Sara entered the Department of Physics building to meet her PhD coordinator. As she walked through the building, the sounds of Italian voices and the familiar Romanesque architecture made this feel very right. Heading to the stairs, she wondered for a moment what it would have been like to have gone here as she originally intended.

Exiting on the third floor, she walked into the room and introduced herself to the student receptionist. She then had a quick meeting with the coordinator who had helped her pick her new chairperson and would assist her as she formed her committee.

Later that day, she met Dr. Emilio Ferrera, her new thesis chair. Sitting now in his small but practical office, they were discussing where she was in her research. "Ms. Ricci..."

Sara stopped him and said, "Please it is just Sara."

"Very well. Sara, I have read your application notes and your recent paper regarding the TGFs and the outputs surrounding them. This seems to be a direct conclusion of your thesis. But I also see you have tried considerably to convert these energies. This is true, yes?"

"Yes, Dr. Ferrera. After several months of investigation and just before leaving MIT, I completed two significant experiments. The first was to establish a composite material structure that might slow or stop gamma rays, depending on their incoming energy." Sara handed him a notebook describing the experiment and then continued. "The next experiment used the worthiest variant from the first test, to coat the panels of a one-point-five meter parabolic dish that I designed to hold the gamma/matter interactions and all tertiary ones."

Dr. Ferrera reached forward to accept the second folder, which Sara had prepared to show the results.

"If you skip ahead to the conclusion page, you'll see that I used four incoming power ranges, the average from my TGF paper. This could slow or stop up to sixty percent of the incoming gammas. Although this was at the highest incoming power. The lowest power only slowed or stopped seventeen percent."

"I see, thank you. I'll go through this to determine its merit, but it sounds like you have located, quantified, and converted to energy the TGFs. Is it your intention to conclude the research phase and begin your dissertation?

Sara wasn't sure if this was a valid question or a test, so she answered honestly. "I'm actually not sure. Mathematically, the parabolic dish should have been over three meters in diameter to maximize the interactions, but I was financially constrained and elected to prove the concept rather than optimize it. I did some computer modeling and estimate the larger dish could yield an additional eighteen percent, all other things being equal. Given that I wasn't even going to include the conversion in my dissertation, I think it is reasonable to move forward without additional testing."

"Sara, let me consider this, and I'll get back to you. On the surface, I think I agree." The meeting concluded, and Sara went to her new office to consider her thoughts on the matter.

In Scotland, Maximillian had just hung up with Sophia Antonion at MDE Aerospace after getting an update on applications should the young researcher's work determine that there was sufficient space-based energy. He walked into his study and summoned Grant and Bridget to join him. Bridget entered and went to the bar while Grant sat across from Maximillian. As Bridget sat, Maximillian spoke. "Our young scientist has located and extracted the energy from these TGF events using discoveries of her own design. But the process of creating the lining of this parabolic dish is controlled by a third party. I had Angus do some research and the United States-based company, Cerium Scientific Compounds is in South Beacon Hill, Washington."

Bridget replied, "That is true and a tactical error on her part. Although in fairness, she told Boris she didn't know what she would find and likely never thought of the significance, since DARPA technically owned the discovery via their grant and NDA."

"Well, we'll need the mechanics of this process to move forward." Maximillian said, concerned.

"You could create a royalty arrangement with them." Grant suggested.

"Perhaps, but at this early date, we don't know our needs," Maximillian responded. "In its lifetime, will we require ten applications or a thousand? For now, we need to get inside information on the process. Grant, any thoughts?"

"I have a contact who can discretely research the company and determine their level of security and application secrecy before we assume next steps." Grant rose and left, noting the time so he could call Bill Adkins in Boston.

The following week, Adkins walked into the bar on the ground floor of the Four Seasons Hotel in Seattle. Immaculately dressed in a dark navy Armani suit and Churches Dubai brown oxfords, he adjusted his cuff and slightly exposed his Panerai watch. Ordering a Hendricks Gin & Tonic, he waited for a former engineer from Cerium Scientific Compounds to arrive. The engineer had worked there as one of their first employees but left last year, claiming the job had become highly repetitive.

Theodore (Ted) Gunther, the engineer had been contacted through a friend posing as a recruiter and tonight, Bill Adkins was not portraying himself, but a fictitious Vancouver based investor, William Randolph. His plan, after carefully investigating all public information on the company was to wine and dine the information out of Ted to form the basis for next steps.

Bill watched as Ted entered the bar, looking apprehensive and out of place. He asked the hostess presumably for Mr. William Randolph, and she motioned for him to follow her. She walked him to the bar and said softly, "Mr. Randolph, your guest has arrived."

Bill set down his drink and rose to his full six-foot four frame, looking down on Ted who was significantly shorter and said in his deep baritone voice, "Mr. Gunther, I'm William Randolph. Thank you for meeting with me. Please call me Bill." He shook Ted's hand.

"Sir, the pleasure is mine," Ted replied nervously. "I was hoping for a job interview, but this might help with some extra money."

Bill nodded, grabbed his drink and with Ted, followed the hostess to their table where he ordered another cocktail and Ted ordered a local draft beer.

When the drinks arrived, he said, "Ted, the reason for this meeting is that CSC wants to make a sizable investment in capital, but their financial situation, while not dire, cannot easily accommodate more debt. I am a person who makes such investments, but when I met with Dr. Boylan and his wife, Lillian, his obsession with secrecy revealed so little, I'm at a standstill. I'm intrigued by the opportunity, but I'm insecure about the risks as I learned almost nothing about the company. Rather than just walk away, which I probably should do, I decided to see if a former insider could help me understand what the company really does and why they might require this investment."

"Well, Mr. Randolph, I mean Bill, I worked there for seven years from the startup until last year. That said, as much as I need the money, I'm not sure what I can really say, as I am bound by an NDA."

"Yes, of course," Bill responded, "I assumed you were. Ted, I'm neither a scientist nor am I looking for secrets, just a better understanding of how the factory works and the risks involved to gauge my financial interest. By all means, say nothing if you're uncomfortable doing so. Although, in fairness, this is a financial transaction and what you receive in consideration is directly tied to how well I can understand Dr. Boylan and his company."

"Okay, I understand. Here is what I can say. When Dr. Boylan talks of CSC, he always uses the analogy of a gourmet chef to describe what they do. They create a recipe meant to exceed the expectation of their customer. It starts with raw materials which, in this case, are metals, metalloids, polymers, binding agents, etc., and he selects these ingredients based on purity, compatibility, and economics. Next is the mixture, as each material responds differently to each other and to heat. So, the amount of each material varies. It is never in equal parts and some ingredients are only used to accentuate the binding process or to assist other ingredients."

Ted stopped to have a sip of his beer. "After that comes the preliminary curing process, which stabilizes the mixture prior to bonding and could involve heat, cold, or just time at air temperature. This process can be suggested scientifically, but is usually completed by trial and error. Once the mixture has been stabilized, the next process is the oven. Some recipes have set ranges like X temp for Y minutes, while others have stepped ranges each getting hotter and hotter or colder and colder. These are usually developed by trial and error, and last is the final curing process, which strengthens and stabilizes the outcome. Sometimes, this is the most critical step. Does that all make sense?"

"It does and thank you; I better understand. Fascinating." He stopped as the server came to the table and they quickly ordered dinner and a nice bottle of wine before he continued. "So with these processes in place, do you suspect his need is special equipment, or perhaps just more of what they already have?"

Over the next thirty minutes and a wonderful dinner, Ted had explained much of what Maximillian would see as a concern. All equipment was operated by tablets that his wife Lillian had designed. These tablets only talked to the equipment not to the Internet or to each other. The recipes were on the tablets, so operators had no say or control. Each tablet was numbered and issued in the morning and retrieved and locked in a safe at night. Factory capacity being used was estimated at just forty-four percent and the company never operated unless the husband or wife was on site. Ted believed the reason for new capital was likely required higher temperatures. Apparently, increasing temperature could elevate the cost of the equipment.

Following that exchange, Adkins, aka Randolph, took a risk and asked, "Well, that makes sense. Liam and his wife own CSC themselves, right?"

Ted, who was now more or less intoxicated didn't shy away from the question, saying, "Almost. There were early investors, but they have all been bought out, although a friend of theirs who owns a company called Versilant Nanotechnologies still owns a portion of the company. Why do you ask?"

Bill shifted gears in order to not create suspicion and said, "Just trying to understand their internal financial leverage. So, Ted, tell me a bit about yourself. Every week I'm in a different company and perhaps there is one that needs a smart engineer?"

The evening concluded and William "Bill" Randolph thanked Ted Gunther and handed him a monogrammed envelope with $5,000 in cash for an informative evening.

55

Isle of Skye, Scotland

Grant was at his desk, having just spoken to Adkins in Seattle. He carefully reviewed his notes and took a second to think how he would present this and then sent a text to Maximillian asking for an audience. An hour later, he and Bridget were asked to come up to the study.

"Grant, you have some information regarding Cerium Scientific Compounds?"

"Yes sir, my contact located a former engineer, and they run a tight ship. There are no written plans or recipes, everything is in tablets of the owners' design. Process equipment can only be controlled by these handheld tablets, and they cannot talk to the outside world or even to each other. They are lot controlled, issued daily and placed in a vault at night. The factory never runs unless the president, Dr. Liam Boylan, or his wife are present."

"Sounds abnormal. To the extent possible, what of the processes themselves?"

"Complex and outcome dependent. All formulations are unique. Ingredients are chosen by PhDs in metallurgy or chemistry and the selection involves price, quality, and purity.

Inputs are mixed based on how the ingredients themselves interact with each other, how they interact with the binding agents, or how they are affected by heat. There is a pre-cure phase and then the actual heating process, suggested by science but completed by trial-and-error. Last is a post-curing process, always determined by trail-by-error, and is often considered the most important step."

Maximillian frowned, saying, "Perhaps we will have to approach them to purchase or create an agreement. It does not appear there is a low-risk way to get the recipe."

CI Timothy Hawkins was alone in his small office at the Police Scotland North Command HQ at the Scottish Police College in Fife. He had spoken to DCI Hughes at the Metropolitan Police in London and received a business-as-usual report from CI Stewart in N-Branch who had jurisdiction over the Isle of Skye. There was no new information except the revelation that one and possibly two members of Maximillian's security detail were identified on video from the raid in America. Like all things involving Maximillian, there was still no direct connection to him. He wondered if word had gotten to SIS involving the call from the MDE Trust informant regarding the EMP attacks and their annual sales list. His phone rang, and he lifted the receiver.

"Hawkins, a word." The phone went silent, but the voice was well known. It was his boss, Finlay Cormack, the Assistant Chief Constable. He hung up and grabbed his coat, thinking, *did old man Cormack just read my bloody mind?*

He entered the hallway that ended at Cormack's office and knocked on the outside. The door was already open. "Sir, you wanted to see me?"

"What are you working on these days, lad?"

"My normal caseload, sir. Most of my time at present is on a murder-suicide in Inverness."

"Is that so? Then why do you seem always involved with DSI Hughes at Metropolitan regarding Maximillian Drummond?"

"Sir..., I have... I mean, that's simply not true. But yes, I have been dragged in a bit given his residence is on the Isle of Skye."

"Relax lad. I know that you, Stewart, and Hughes have been sharing information with SIS who is sharing with DHS and the CIA in America. I am also aware of the video of his security team and the fact that even the SIS believes Drummond might actually be behind this nonsense. They suspect it has to do with the recent string of EMP attacks but have no proof. You are involved because I gave them your name."

"What? So, what was the exchange we just had sir?"

"Aye. That was a reminder you work for me and not the other way around. What do you have beyond what you have said?"

"Nothing. Well, maybe something."

"Spit it out son, I don't all day."

"The thing is, it is just hearsay and the only way to find out is to open it up and see what happens."

"I'm listening."

"A month back, I received a call from a senior salesperson at MDE Trust who said that all the EMP attacks match a sales target list that the company created to promote new business. MDE Trust helps companies protect electronic assets from EMPs and similar risks. Apparently, this terrorist group, the UBOI, has their list. I have since discussed this with Hughes and Stewart, but felt I needed more information to bring it forward than just a conversation with a possibly disgruntled employee."

"I understand the reason for concern given who we are talking about, but you should have at least informed me. Did this informant mention a connection to Drummond?"

"No sir. She has a great deal of respect for him and never thought he could be involved, but suspects his sister, Bridget."

"Well, I've met her. She is more than a wee nasty. I'll take this up a notch and see if we want to give it to SIS directly, which I suspect we should. If this is something, we'll have hell to pay if it is found we knew in advance."

"What about the Managing Director of MDE Trust? Can I approach her?"

"Perhaps. I'll give word once I have brought the Chief up to speed." He didn't say it, but Conor Gilkeson, the Chief Constable for Police of Scotland was the last person in the world he wanted to talk to.

The elders of the UBOI were gathered around a large square table that allowed them to view each other. They sat on small cushions and the most senior members sat in the corners. Saleh al-Ayad, the senior field leader, was standing in the only entrance facing them. He had been summoned to the gathering regarding the fact that someone had used the UBOI name to claim responsibility for the EMP attacks and design of the weapons, which was not a fact.

In Arabic, the senior most member said to Saleh al-Ayad, "Continue your quest to find those that have used our name and offer just punishment but only to the person who gave the order."

56

Millbank, London, England

The next morning, Giles Taylor rang Director Hicks at DHS to determine if they were, in fact, going to extradite Grant Aiken. Hicks' reply was predictable, "The word has not been given, but I'm fairly confident they will."

"Jeremy, as I have said before, there is no tie yet to Maximillian or MDE Enterprises. Most of his security team comprises former soldiers that have been, and sometimes still are, working mercenaries. These guys don't talk, just as they were once trained, and if you make a formal request for Grant Aiken, it will stop any inquiry into Maximillian Drummond."

"Giles, I understand and will make that argument, but given the partisan divide in my country, this DARPA mess is now bigger than me, so all I can do is effectively recommend. Other than this, any other hopeful news on your end?"

"We are trying to get authority to question the Managing Director of MDE Defense regarding the EMP weapons and the Managing Director of MDE Trust. MDE Trust is the newcomer to MDE Enterprises and protects electronic assets from a variety of threats, including EMPs. Apparently, a salesperson there contacted Police Scotland, which we only just learned, to say that a list of sales targets they made regarding potential new customers matches all the actual attacks. She felt the terrorists have their list or worse, her company was involved. For now, it is just talk. No approval has yet been given."

"Giles, this can't be a coincidence. Why do your police need government approval?"

"Apparently MDE Trust was hacked, and the list revealed. Maximillian Drummond himself broke the news and is said to be highly embarrassed because if it got out, no customer would trust them. The person who called was not aware of the hack and doesn't think he is involved, but thinks his sister, Bridget, just might be. We are treading softly because such questioning is only meant to open things up and we don't have a satisfactory response amongst agencies of what we would do if it did."

"What do we know of the sister?"

"Very little actually, except that she's tough and is often the closer between MDE Enterprises and Maximillian's private company."

"Could we have this wrong? Maximillian is just a shrewd businessperson, but his sister and Aiken are the enforcers?

"Interesting take, and perhaps. In any case, you must try to get a stay on the extradition attempt. Let's stay close to this one." Giles replied as he disconnected the call.

The next day Giles Taylor made the case to the Superintendent of the Metropolitan Police and the Chief Constable for Police Scotland. He was asking the Metropolitan Police to consider questioning the Managing Director at MDE Defense regarding the possibility that EMP weapons were made there. Police Scotland should question the Managing Director at MDE Trust regarding the hack that placed the sales target list in the hands of the terrorists to determine the story's veracity.

All felt they needed to break this open to see what happened and it might lead nowhere but might also reveal next steps.

Managing Director of MDE Trust, Candace Perez was seated in her office when she noticed the unmarked Police Scotland car pull into the drive. Two officers got out of the Vauxhall Insignia wagon and headed toward the lobby. Moments later, the receptionist entered and told Candace that CI Hawkins from Police Scotland and DCI Hughes from the Metropolitan Police were there to ask her a few questions.

"Did they say what this was about? I have a meeting in less than ten minutes."

"No, they didn't. Should I tell them you only have a few minutes?"

"Yes. Please."

The door reopened and the two inspectors walked in. Hawkins took the lead and explained himself and introduced his counterpart in London.

"Ms. Perez, thank you for speaking with us. I realize you are short on time and the faster you assist us, the faster this meeting is over. I cannot however assure you we will have concluded our business in five minutes."

"Then I'll have to ask you to leave and make an appointment for another time." Candace said curtly.

"Or we can go to the Edinburgh Station, leaving all your employees to wonder what's going on and you'll miss your meeting, anyway."

Annoyed at his cocky tone, Candace fired back, "What the hell is this about?"

"We received information that your company produced a list of sales targets, and that list matches the recent EMP attacks here and in the EU. We also learned that someone has hacked into your systems and has taken this list. Can you confirm or deny this?"

Candace was shocked to hear the words she had tried so hard to hide, but here it was. She put on her best poker face and said with courage, "I will have to discuss this with my solicitor before I can comment."

"Very well. If you could please come with us voluntarily, we'll arrange for your solicitor to join us." Both men rose, expecting her to do the same, but she remained seated. Hawkins could see the gears turning in her head. She did not want to leave and most certainly knew something.

"Gentlemen, I really have an important meeting and cannot leave. Perhaps we can arrange a meeting tomorrow."

"Or perhaps you can just answer the question." Hawkins replied as they both sat back down.

After a lengthy pause, she relented. "Yes, we produce such a list every year based on vulnerable targets and give these potential clients to the sales teams to offer our help. We noticed the connection, and it was revealed that three weeks prior, someone had hacked our systems. The CEO himself came to tell me and thankfully there have been no new attacks that I am aware of."

"And you prepare this list personally or as a team?"

"The list is created by the CEO's private staff."

"So, the CEO himself oversees its creation?" he said carefully.

"Well no. This year the project was run by his sister, Bridget, Bridget Drummond."

Hawkins used every muscle in his face to conceal his reaction and stay on the script. "So, prior to the CEO telling you of the hack, you knew your list matched the attacks. Did that not bother you?"

"Of course it did," Candace answered honestly. "This company is my life, and everything here and every decision involves me. At first, I just assumed we were good at identifying the vulnerable targets which we are, but after the second attack, there was still a direct match. I was going to discuss this with Mr. Drummond when he actually came here."

"And what did he say exactly?" Hughes asked.

"That these terrorists possibly had inside help, as that was the only file taken and he shared his absolute embarrassment that we were hacked. He all but said, *you see the irony here, our name is MDE Trust. How can someone trust us now?*"

"And what did he ask you to do about it?"

"My job was to keep the link to the attacks away from customers or the press. I immediately withdrew all copies of the target list and we stopped the formal campaign to call on them."

"And what about the possibility of an insider?"

"Mr. Drummond said that his IT staff and his head of security would handle that, but I have heard nothing of it."

"Your systems are quite safe, yes?"

"Well, I thought so. All MDE companies work on a specific data protocol that Mr. Drummond's personal team developed, and there are no exceptions. Whoever got in was very good."

"Last question, Ms. Perez. Are you aware that companies under MDE Enterprises are perfectly suited to create such weapons for the benefit of MDE Trust?"

"I think I understand what you are saying, but no. I really don't follow the other businesses because they are manufacturers.

We are a service company. Second, I'm sure you know that Mr. Drummond is a multibillionaire who I suspect could make any business succeed. Why the hell would he resort to blowing things up for the benefit of his smallest concern?"

"But MDE Trust has prospered with the attacks, has it not?"

"Yes, because most business leaders never think it will happen to them and don't wish to spend their precious capital on risk prevention."

"We'll talk again, Ms. Perez. If, on reflection, there is anything you haven't said, or anything you have said that you would like to clarify or recant, here is our contact information. It is in your best interest that we only have the truthful facts."

They rose and departed. Candace sat unnerved for several minutes before she went into her meeting, already ten minutes underway. After the meeting, she placed a private call to Maximillian and told him of the questioning, an informant from MDE Trust, and how the police seemed intent on pinning this on MDE Enterprises.

Maximillian was his normal brilliant self. "Candace, I understand this meeting upset you, but please pay it no mind. MDE Enterprises and I, by extension, are always under attack and you must admit, even I can understand why they might put things together to arrive at such a conclusion. My only real issue is how they got this information. First, we are hacked, which I feel must have involved an MDE Trust employee. Now we have a call or letter to the Police, likely from the same person. If I didn't know better, I would say one of your employees has it in for us."

"I'll look into this and get back to you."

"Please do so carefully as my team continues to work behind the scenes." Maximillian hung up and called Alexandre Arnaud, Managing Director at MDE Defense. If a DSI from London was there in Scotland, they would soon be at Arnaud's doorstep.

Bastards, they were using the poor inspectors, so when all hell broke loose, the higher ups could keep their jobs.

Two days later, DCI Hughes realized they could not surprise Alexandre Arnaud. Security to the entire premises of MDE Defense was airtight and there was no way to call on him unannounced unaware that Arnaud had advance notice of their arrival.

Hawkins and Hughes went through two checkpoints within the building before being led into a modern sitting area on the fifth floor and were told Mr. Arnaud would see them momentarily. Sure enough, two minutes passed, and a tall, deeply tanned man walked forward and introduced himself as Alexandre Arnaud. He motioned for them to follow him into his office, which overlooked the main runway at Gatwick, and as they sat, he asked, "What can I do for you inspectors?"

Hughes asked, "Mr. Arnaud, are you aware of the recent EMP attacks being carried out by the UBOI terrorist organization?"

"Yes, it made the news."

"As a company in defense, how difficult would it be to build such a weapon?"

"Building them would be easy. It is the design that is difficult. They say drones are being used to transport them and a commercial drone has a payload limit of less than one hundred kilos or roughly two hundred-fifty pounds. These devices are small but powerful."

"But MDE Defense could make them?"

"I suspect you could make them. As I said, they are easy to build, but hard to design."

"But you didn't make them."

"Make what?" Arnaud asked.

"The EMP weapons."

"What in the world gave you that idea? We make tactical equipment for the military. We don't actually make weapons per se despite the name includes the word defense."

"Of any kind?" Hughes said in surprise.

"No. It's a common misconception. We make the tactical tools that deploy weapons, hold them, cover them, etc., but with all respect, you didn't answer my question. What makes you possibly think we made these EMP weapons?"

"I only asked if you could and if you did. I take it your answer is no."

"Gentlemen, I am trying to be generous here, but let's dispense with games. They are unworthy of my time."

Hughes responded, "Mr. Arnaud my apology if that was too direct. Let me ask a different question. What is the relationship between Mr. Drummond's private companies and MDE Defense?"

"I'm not sure I really know the answer, as they are his private companies not mine. But in principle, Mr. Drummond runs an organization outside of MDE Enterprises whose job is to research and consider events, products or companies that complement the public business. As an example, if advanced wire connections were a critical technology to our business, his private company might start-up or even buy a company that does this. Once it was established, we would tuck it into our own business or, at a minimum, purchase only from this new company. All companies within MDE Enterprises are each other's largest customer."

"So, the two only come together when Mr. Drummond decides?" Hughes answered.

"Yes, I suppose that's true, although it is his sister, Bridget, who does the actual integration," Arnaud replied.

Hughes gave Hawkins a significant look. "So, Mr. Drummond never uses your employees for his private company?"

"I cannot say that. While it doesn't happen often, he has used employees from all companies within MDE Enterprises to assist him in research or due diligence for acquisitions, and I imagine he sees my employees as his own."

"Did he use your employees to design the EMP weapons, Mr. Arnaud?"

"Ah, and there you go again. If you think you have evidence of a crime, go through the proper process to serve me and perhaps we can talk again. As to this little poke and jab session, I would have to conclude we are done."

"So that is a yes, but you can't talk about it?"

Arnaud, standing now with his hands on the desk looking straight down on Hughes said, "It is a no, and if that answer is not to your liking, come back with a warrant, gentlemen."

Hughes and Hawkins walked back to the car and sat for a moment, wondering what to do next. Far more polished that Candace Perez, Alexandre Arnaud had pushed them into a corner. If they could interview his managers or people the CEO had "borrowed" from the business, they might get something, but how would they ever get such approval? One thing was for sure, this Bridget Drummond was knee deep in whatever was happening.

57

Edinburgh, Scotland

Sharon Klein, senior salesperson at MDE Trust drove her late model white BMW out of the Best One convenience store just off A701. She was headed to dinner at the Swanston Golf club to meet her date, a golf pro she had met a few weeks before. Nothing serious, just fun.

As she approached the bypass, she passed through the roundabout onto the A702. It was getting dark when her cell rang. She answered hands free, and the call was a potential windfall. The caller introduced himself as Simon Bates and although she didn't know him; she knew the account, and this could be a nice commission. Although he asked very specific questions, she knew the answers by heart, never noticing a large van not far behind her without a working headlamp.

So involved in the call, she missed the turn into the golf club and didn't realize it until she saw the sign that said the split to the A703 was just ahead. "Oh shit," she said aloud.

That prompted the caller to ask, "Is everything okay?"

"Yes, Simon, not to worry. I missed my turnoff and I'm about ready to change highways."

"Is this still a good time to talk?"

"Yes, of course. Hold on I'm going to get off this highway and turn around when I can."

"Well, perhaps just hang up. We can reconnect later."

"No Simon really, it will just take a minute." There was no way she was letting this go.

She was silent now as she tried to locate a side drive to pull in and turn around. Still going quite fast, she saw a small bridge ahead and what looked like a void space just after, but as she braked hard, the car suddenly lurched forward, going left. She immediately looked in the rear-view mirror to see the grill of a large vehicle as her BMW slammed into the post and rail of the bridge before continuing forward, flying down into the culvert. The airbags didn't deploy, leaving nothing but the seatbelt to slow her forward momentum as the steering column crushed her chest and her head snapped forward into the windshield.

Bruce Morgan, aka Simon Bates, was driving the modified van that had just tapped her off the highway as he backed up and then continued south. As he did, he flipped a switch to turn on the nonfunctioning headlamp as he braked and turned right onto Burnside Road, heading back to his shop.

At a farmhouse down the road, the owner was on his porch having a beer when he heard the crash. He grabbed his phone, knocking over his beer, and yelled "Bloody hell," as he dialed 999 to report what sounded like a horrible accident on Old Pentland

Road. With the phone still in hand, he ran across his newly plowed field towards the sound.

Maximillian Drummond demanded loyalty from his employees.

58

Vauxhall, Lambeth, England

Giles Taylor picked up the phone to answer a call from Director Hicks. "Jeremy, any new information?"

"Yes, I'm calling because the extradition request has been prepared and is being sent. I agree with you, but there it is. I just wanted you to know first."

"Thank you, Jeremy. It is amazing that despite our positions, we just take orders, but we'll make the best of it. Cheers."

He hung up the phone, paused for a few minutes, then called Maximillian Drummond, hoping to put him on notice and avoid any difficulty. Drummond came on after his aide told him who was calling, "Mr. Taylor, it has been some time since we spoke. You are well?"

"Yes, Mr. Drummond, I am fine. This is a courtesy call regarding an employee, Grant Aiken. I am told we are to receive from the United States an extradition request. He has been identified and charged in a raid and assault of a house in Montana where secrets owned by the United States were taken at gunpoint and the owner injured. He and another member of your security detail were identified using facial recognition."

"And how does this involve me? Mr. Aiken is a trusted member of my staff, but he is also very much his own man."

"Yes, of course. Perhaps you could facilitate him voluntarily turning himself in to avoid publicity and the like," Giles said with confidence.

"Mr. Taylor, that is very thoughtful, but I know him. He is not one to just give in and I doubt he would ever just accept a story from the Americans, regardless of what they think he has done. In any case, I have not seen him for days, so he is not here for me to question. As Police Scotland and the Metropolitan Police are about to meet with my solicitors on a separate matter, perhaps you can create the necessary legal documents, so I might assist you."

"Mr. Drummond, please, this doesn't have to be rough."

"Oh, but it does, Mr. Taylor. I have never understood why governments feel the need to think the very worst about their very best. It is a fallacy of a democracy I assume, but I thank you for the call. Is there anything else?"

"No Mr. Drummond, that was all." Giles clicked off and knew the process had begun. For some time, this was all he was going to work on, and heaven help him if they couldn't link this to Maximillian Drummond and the MDE Enterprises.

Maximillian spoke to Grant as it would appear they might have a problem and despite what he had said to Giles Taylor, Grant quickly offered to turn himself in to relieve pressure on Maximillian. He also explained that they were fully aware of the cameras, but he was confident their training allowed them some level of anonymity, but it was also possible they had actual evidence. Maximillian didn't care and told Grant to first not worry but to be prepared. In his view, this was sure to escalate.

Once he was alone, he noted the time and picked up the phone to call the United States Director of Homeland Security Department Jeremy Hicks. When his assistant walked in and told him who was holding, Hicks was at first shocked, but that immediately went to concern, as any call here was being recorded. That might be good or bad, but he decided it was likely best to have this evidence if needed and took the call.

"Director Hicks," Jeremy answered abruptly.

"Director, while we have not spoken previously, you seem intent on knowing me, so here we are."

"Mr. Drummond, I assume there is a purpose for this call?"

"Of course, Director, I rarely use my words for mere conversation. I would like you to please stay out of my affairs."

Jeremy chuckled and said, "Mr. Drummond, if this is regarding Grant Aiken, I can't do that. He shot a decorated Veteran, ruined his house, and stole secrets that belong to the United States Government."

"I believe your answer is short sighted, Director. Perhaps you should have a heart-to-heart talk with your decorated war veteran, as there may be a few details of this so-called raid he has not elected to share with you."

"What exactly are you saying, Mr. Drummond?"

"I merely wish you to be fully informed before starting something that cannot be undone."

"Anything you think is there does not take away from the crime, Mr. Drummond. There is nothing that can change that," Hicks replied, not at all sure what this was really about.

"I assure you, Director, you cannot answer without all the facts. I will leave you with your thoughts," and the line went silent.

Hicks waited until lunch to leave the office and once in his car, he drove to a rare and not well-maintained pay phone at a gas station several miles away. He called Richard "Rottweiler" Chase.

Chase was having lunch is his office when his assistant came in and told him he had an urgent call from the DHS Director. He

351

immediately wiped his mouth and took the call, asking her to close the door behind her as she left.

"Hicks, any news?"

"Richard, I'm at a pay phone, which gives you some idea of the situation. I just received a call from Maximillian Drummond himself. We are getting ready to extradite his chief of security Grant Aiken, and he tells me I have missed something about the raid. Something so big it is worth more than Aiken. Care to explain?"

Richard was silent, his mind immediately going to his server. Shit, his world was about to end. "I'm not sure, but I have an idea. Of the three servers taken, one was that of the scientist. One was a backup of financials to Fortitude, which is worthless. The third server was mine. I used it for private things. Things I may need some day."

"Don't sugarcoat this, what the hell does Drummond have?" Hicks yelled.

"Every job I have done for various agencies within the government," Chase hissed.

"Chase, I think I understand what you just said, but why would you have this?"

"Self-preservation. I am first and foremost a soldier. You fuck with me, and I'll fuck with you, but twice as hard. Although I will do anything for my country, I'm not naïve and the very agencies I did work for would gladly let me die to preserve themselves. It was only meant as insurance I hoped I would never need."

"And this fucking evil genius Drummond has it?"

"It was encrypted with three separate locks, so it is almost unimaginable that he could open it. The only other possibility is they cracked the encryption long enough to see it but lost it when they tripped the other failsafe losing it all."

"How sure are you of this? I mean they saw it, but don't have it,"

"I feel pretty strongly about it."

"Chase, I have no idea how this will end, but you better hope the SIS gets to Drummond first. If not, you are correct. The very agencies you helped will kill you and I can't stop it." The call ended and *oh shit,* was all Hicks could think of.

As the day ended, Hicks was in his office with the door closed having a glass of Courvoisier. He knew this could be career ending but was unsure what to do. What he should do was call Secretary of Defense Stockdale, but the moment he did, his career was over, and Chase would be arrested or worse.

If it were true that Maximillian Drummond knew something but couldn't back it up, his only way to move forward was to reveal it publicly. But theoretically, if he put the stolen evidence out there, it implicated him of a crime via Aiken. Sadly, Hicks was no better off. If he made any attempt to contact Drummond to better understand what he had, he was admitting the third server was real. His only defense was he was the good guy and Drummond was the bad guy. Fucking worthless. When all hell broke loose, nobody would care.

Hicks decided to error on the side of hope meaning, he would not call Stockdale just yet. He would wait for Drummond to call his bluff.

Foreign and Commonwealth Secretary Alistair Evans received the formal request to extradite Grant Aiken for crimes in the United States that morning. While he understood and was aware of the circumstances, he also knew in his soul that Maximillian Drummond was likely all the trouble so many said he was. A difficult thing to be the first to say it out loud. He called his counterpart, Home Secretary Jocelyn Holmes.

"Madam Secretary, it's Alistair. Do you have a moment to discuss the rumblings involving Maximillian Drummond?"

"Alistair, I dare confess to being sick of the daily rumblings of Maximillian Drummond, and despite all of his Parliamentary friends, the information from American intelligence and SIS has accelerated from annoying to troubling."

"Yes, well, that is why I called; I have received a legal, diplomatic request to extradite Drummond's head of security, Grant Aiken, for a crime in America."

"This involves the theft of the MIT researcher's information?"

"Yes. SIS confirmed that two of the raid team are members of Drummond's security detail. When you consider this together with the overall capability of MDE, the connection of the recent UBOI attacks to sales list, and the recent death of the MDE Trust salesperson who brought that intel to the police; the whole affair looks like much more than just coincidence."

"And what do you propose?"

"As I have the request to extradite, I would like to suggest the Police Scotland approach Drummond's residence to apprehend Aiken and question Drummond himself."

"We don't have to, but I suggest we pass this by the Prime Minister given his connections. I'll set it up."

Later the next day, both Jocelyn Holmes and Alistair Evans sat in front of the Prime Minister. He listened to the calm and methodical discussion, which had been carefully scripted, a fact not lost on him.

"So, if I have this correctly, Maximillian Drummond may have finally been bested, and you both believe this evidence is rock solid."

Alistair spoke first. "Sir, we only have genuine evidence against Grant Aiken. We have a plausible story and motive, but all evidence regarding Drummond or MDE Enterprises is conjecture and would not withstand a court of law."

"And you wish to go after the security chief and only question Drummond?"

"Yes, sir."

"Why the formality? Why not just approach him?"

"Giles Taylor at SIS made that call yesterday to no avail. Drummond simply launched his solicitors at us."

"And this is a police matter or something more robust?" The Prime Minister asked, knowing the likely answer.

"It is rumored that the residence, which is also Maximillian Drummond's private company has its own security force. With that in mind, we should respond with a small show of force, but only as a precaution. This is not a raid." Home Secretary Holmes replied.

The Prime Minister was clearly not excited about this but answered, "Do what you must but completely understand. You had better find something to link this to him directly."

The meeting was over and while a success; they were out on a limb and left to wonder if it was all worth it.

Sara was walking up the stairs to her flat, having just left her lab at the university, when her cell rang. She looked at the United States number, but there was no caller ID, it just said *private*. It rang again, and she answered, "Hello, who is this?"

"Ms. Sara Ricci?" Director Hicks asked to confirm.

"Yes."

"Ms. Ricci, this is Director Jeremy Hicks of the Department of Homeland Security. We met during your briefing following the DARPA grant."

"Yes, I remember you," she said vaguely surprised.

"Ms. Ricci, do you recall when I said that the entity most likely behind your security issues was a UK based organization?"

"Yes, I have puzzled over this. Do you have new information?"

"The UK organization is MDE Enterprises and specifically its principal owner and CEO, Maximillian Drummond."

"I know MDE Enterprises, and they have been very helpful to me." Her head now reconsidering her current thoughts.

"The divisions of MDE Enterprises such as Aerospace, Commodities and Defense are likely excellent businesses, and it is not they who make up this warning. To the best of our knowledge, it is the CEO and his head of security who have been behind your many security issues."

"Director, MDE Aerospace has offered me a grant and a royalty should they use my methods. And MDE Commodities have supplied key materials to my invention. Why would the man that owns the entire company be trying to harm me and at the same time, help me? This makes no sense."

"Ms. Ricci, I cannot reveal details or timing, but events are about to unfold, and all hell could break loose. I'm simply warning you to avoid any contact with any MDE business or associates until the dust settles so you are not caught in what could be a political fight."

"I suspect this is just another way for you to protect yourself once again at my expense."

"Although you don't understand my world, I have risked a great deal to give you this warning. I only hope you are smart enough to keep your head down. Good luck Ms. Ricci." The call ended abruptly.

Sara stared at the phone. Yes, even she had thought at one point MDE might be involved, but no, this was just the United States trying to screw her again.

Salah al-Ayad watched over a dozen technicians clicking away on computers as they had been for weeks. He had no idea how they did what they did, but they were narrowing down how the drawings and the first reference to UBOI had been placed on the dark web. They had traced the upload to a computer owned by Thomas Cummings whose father was Dr. Bernard Cummings of DARPA. Further investigation revealed he had sent the drawings to an IP address in Turkey.

A young computer tech, Gilad Qasim, sitting next to Salah al-Ayad had found evidence, however, that this had not been done in at the home IP address of Dr. Cummings as thought. It was actually part of an elaborate setup whose digital trail actually led to Scotland. Further, Qasim was convinced this was the work of the infamous Beithir. Pronounced, Bee-thee-uh, this code name belonged to a hacker of immense skill and was said to be Scottish, hence the reference to a Scottish mythical dragon, Beithir. The key was to determine who Beithir actually was, and they had been working on this nonstop.

At the same time, Qasim was trying not to dig too hard. Guys like this were so good they could see if someone was trying to find them. They had carefully mined blogs and dark channels to learn of his work, but so far, nothing. They had also hacked into several databases to look into criminal records but again, found no reference to Beithir. It was close to two in the morning when they found a juvenile record that had been sealed. It contained a reference to an eleven-year-old at the time, Angus Adair, who had hacked into the Government Communications Headquarters, a government agency similar to the United States NSA. He did it for fun, although authorities did not find it at all humorous. By morning, Qasim approached Salah al-Ayad cautiously and explained what they had found.

They located an Angus Adair living in the Scottish Highlands who worked for a private company belonging to a Scottish industrialist, Maximillian Drummond. Salah al-Ayad was only interested in who gave the order and assumed it was this Drummond, so he asked Qasim to focus on his whereabouts.

Grant and Maximillian sat discussing several issues including once again the secrets of Cerium Scientific Compounds. Sophia had contacted the owner and founder, Dr. Liam Boylan regarding the potential acquisition of Cerium Scientific Compounds by MDE Enterprises. She was rudely told it was not for sale at any price and not to call him again. The company attorney followed that up with a letter saying the same.

"I'm not even sure why I remain interested, as we don't even know if it is possible to harness enough power to advance our applications, but I feel this is a significant future opportunity." Maximillian said.

"It does not appear that there is easy access to Cerium Scientific Compounds, although it is rare to find a manufacturing process being controlled almost militarily. It makes you wonder why? As for the researcher, we can have someone shadow her at Sapienza. We could at least learn more about her experiments." Grant replied.

"Yes, let's do that, but she simply cannot know. I need her to think she is safe and sound in Rome."

"Okay, I'll set it up. I am not saying we should, but at some point Bridget's original recommendation might make sense. We could simply grab this Liam Boylan and Sara Ricci and get their knowledge." Grant said.

"That is a decision that, once made, cannot be reversed. Let's first see what she really has." They turned the conversation to other business not understanding that in a few hours, everything would change.

60

Isle of Skye, Scotland

Less than an hour before the sun rose to greet the Isle of Skye, twelve men and women from Police Scotland and MI5 gathered next to their vehicles in the cool dawn light. The entire mission had been unannounced, as it was believed Maximillian Drummond might likely have connections within the local Police Scotland office out of Portee. Although they did not expect resistance, rumors of the special security detail led by Grant Aiken were not to be taken lightly. Surveillance had determined the number of people there during non-business hours and they had concentrated on the road entrance. Given there was no obvious route down the steep cliffs to the beach area, they left that area unprotected.

Although they were well equipped, very few of the team members had real world experience against heavily armed resistance. This worried the overall mission leader, former special forces veteran Cameron Halladay as he addressed the teams. "Okay, we have three teams and three team leaders. Team Ronda will hold the perimeter from the residence to the route A855. No one gets in or out. Team Malcolm will head straight to the main door of the residence, which is not in the front but to the right of the heliport on the left side. Note, this is not a conventional door, but a wall of glass. Team Edward will simultaneously head to the right-side entrance, which is for staff and the security team. Questions?"

"Sir, do you think we'll get resistance and if we do, what is our response?"

"Doubtful, but it is a possibility. Once we identify ourselves, there should be no issues, but if they choose to ignore that, do whatever is necessary to apprehend Grant Aiken and secure Mr. Drummond for questioning."

"Sir, our orders are to arrest Aiken and bring Drummond in for questioning. What about the sister?"

"We don't care about the sister unless she puts any members of the team in danger."

Jack Walker, a Special forces soldier on Team Malcolm asked, "What if the doors are locked and nobody answers?"

"We do not presume that to be the case, but if it is, use your best judgment. A reminder, team: this is not a raid." He looked at each of them to get the point across. After a few minutes of silence, Halladay assumed there were no additional questions, and they climbed back into the three vehicles. They would drive to the residence and enter at 6:45 a.m.

Fifteen kilometers up the A855, the inside of the sleek dwelling was far from asleep. Most of Maximillian's working team would not arrive until well after the action, but Grant and Maximillian had both received some advanced warning about the police movement, but no explanation. Maximillian was initially surprised as he could not imagine the Home Secretary granting authorization to do this, but they were clearly on the way, and it was likely because of the extradition request for Grant.

If this were just an inquiry, with the backup as a show of force, Maximillian would meet with them to discuss whatever they wished. He knew his call to the Home Secretary weeks before had been a prerequisite to some type of action, which Giles Taylor confirmed. While he would prefer to avoid a battle in his residence, his security team was ready and waiting.

At Grant's urging, Maximillian went to his private office next to his suite to await instruction. From there, Maximillian had an escape route also known to Grant and Bridget, and they too would head there if all hell broke loose. Bridget herself would be the first to meet the intruders, as her presence usually calmed men, even aggressive ones.

Across the expanse of soft grass and moss in front of the residence, Grant watched the three vehicles approach through hidden cameras. Through the zoom lens, they were all highly armed and ready for a fight, not at all what he expected. There were only two ways into the residence, and he watched one team hold back at the road, one head toward the side entrance and the other to the main entrance next to the helipad. Grant had his team hold their internal positions, waiting to see what the authorities did.

Jack Walker was not pleased that Police Scotland was leading this, and decided to assume command as he crouched next to the helipad with all of them behind him, including the team leader. He stayed low and shuffled to the huge glass door. Not finding a normal handle or knob, he stayed off to the right and cupped his left hand to see into the glass, but saw no movement. The remaining three members were still behind him when he hit the glass hard with the butt of the gunstock, but nothing happened. He waited a few minutes as if he had just knocked. When no one came, he swung his SA-80 assault rifle at the door and sprayed the glass with over fifty rounds. The heavy glass shattered and dropped to the ground with the sound of an intense explosion. Grant watched the event electronically, which had not included an identification command from Police Scotland, and gave a single response to his team, "Security Breach, KOS," *Kill on sight.*

As Team Walker cautiously entered the residence at the opposite service entrance. The three from Team Malcolm, although happy to have Jack Walker out in front, were shocked he had shot out the glass. They reluctantly came in behind him crouched down with weapons in firing position, safety's off. Walker was now five meters into the residence when his head suddenly flew backwards and he went down. The rest of his team heard the shot and saw the high velocity round burst from the back of his head and immediately began firing in the general direction it came from.

The Team Malcolm leader, shooting an assault rifle for the first time outside of training, was firing forward when she felt a searing burn. First in her arm, and then in her leg, which spun her around. She screamed as she corkscrewed into a sitting position and crouched down further to take cover, losing her weapon as she did so. The other two members of the incoming team retreated and took cover behind her, but still outside.

On the other side of the residence, Team Edward heard the shots as they approached the side entrance. The door was unlocked, and they entered cautiously down a long hallway with no doors. As they moved into the main area of the residence, they saw the shattered glass of the door on the far side of the large room and the body of Jack Walker.

A sound came from the left, and Team Edwards' leader was closest. She readied her weapon and waited for the sound to come to her. A member of Grant's security team slowly came forward, shielded from the first team at the other side of the room and only visible to her. She stood and yelled, "Police Scotland, we have this residence surrounded! We have a warrant to search this premise for Grant Aiken and Maximilian Drum..."

She never finished as the security member raised his weapon and sprayed the width of the room, as she quickly dropped below a sleek chair for a moment. She quickly jumped up firing as the security man dropped in pain. He was likely wearing armor, but for now he was down, and she told the team to watch for him. She retreated now behind a curving sofa, held position, and waved an advance sign to those behind her.

Team Ronda heard the gunfire from the roadside unsure what to do. The team leader saw the concern on the young faces and said, "Easy lads. We hold until told to do otherwise."

"For fuck's sake, our guys are getting killed in there."

"Or Team Malcolm and Team Edward are eliminating hostiles. Stand down until I say otherwise." Just moments later, his comm blurted, "Team Ronda, need assistance. Call for backup, three down."

The leader then called Police Scotland in Portee without explanation. He turned to his team and yelled, "You two stay here to accomplish the original mission. Shoot on sight anyone leaving that house." He turned to the other and said, "You follow me," as they headed to the main entrance.

Most of Grant's security team were watching the action on video monitors in hopes of simply drawing the incoming attackers into the residence and surrounding them. The house segmented sleeping rooms from the main salons which were all ocean facing. This was accomplished with a long and curved separation wall, but like most of the residence, the doors into and out of this area did not reveal themselves.

Inside this area, Grant was working with his team to determine how to proceed. The first team had failed to identify themselves, so it was fair game, but the second team had announced they were police and why they were there. Grant would have to give a command decision soon. The team positioned on the road had likely called for backup and two of them were moving forward, although his priority was Maximillian and Bridget.

Maximillian was in his private office when Grant summoned Maximillian to abandon the residence. Maximillian did not hesitate as he grabbed a bag and headed down the long hallway. As he neared a large sweeping corner, he placed his right hand on the wall and a biometric scanner detected his presence, making the wall slide back. He entered, keyed in a command, and the wall closed just as a light came on in the small space that was actually an elevator. In a moment, the elevator descended, taking him from the residence level on the bluff down slightly over ten meters below sea level. The door opened and Maximillian exited, and from the outside, keyed a command on a wall keypad which closed the doors, and sent it back up to the top to accommodate Grant and Bridget.

He proceeded down a round, well-lit tunnel for over a hundred meters until he reached the end and sat down on the circular leather sofa and looked up at the hatch above him. He pulled out a special communicator and texted.

Maximillian soon heard a humming sound increasing in volume until the sound grew steady and a clanking metal-to-metal click followed. The center wheel in the hatch above him turned, and the hatch opened downward. A sailor reached down and said, "Sir, let me help you up." A small personal submarine had docked on top of the escape pod.

In the residence above, the standoff continued. Grant texted Bridget and told her to get to Maximillian's private study to meet him. Grant's men had semi-surrounded the remaining police, and they were in a small exchange of gunfire, some productive, some not. Three additional casualties had occurred when two policemen took cover behind a couch. The older one said, "The wall behind us must separate the living quarters from this room. They have to be there watching our every move."

"Agreed. I don't see any natural opening, but there has to be a door somewhere to the left. Cover me and I'll see if I can locate it."

Bridget was still in her office, one floor below the action, when she received Grant's message. She had to go up one level to get to Maximillian's study. There had been a lot of shooting, although she was not fully aware of what was going on, but knew Maximillian had likely been evacuated, meaning she would join Grant. The gunfire had been stopped for a while, so she saw this as her chance. She crept out of the office, eyeing the stairs that led up to the residence, wondering if she should she go up or sit there and wait it out?

Grant had assessed the situation quickly. They had decimated the police force and his team had taken hits; a few were down. Once the backup arrived, however, it would move back to police favor, and he would have to be at or close to the escape room when that happened. He gave the command for his team to engage. About to head out, the door flew open and a young policeman ran in and without hesitation, shot Grant twice before he could react. The first hit his lower abdomen where his Kevlar vest took the impact, but the second grazed the side of his left shoulder. It was going to hurt, but it would not stop him.

The young policemen walked toward Grant, gun in hand, and took out a handful of long zip ties. As he approached, he tossed Grant a zip tie. "With your hands in front of you, place this around your wrists, now!"

Grant looked at him and said, "No lad. If you want to cuff me, then do it, but I won't do it for you."

"Do it now, or I'll shoot."

"No, you won't. Listen lad, this is the only chance you'll get to save your life. Shoot me or leave, otherwise I will kill you. Do you understand?"

"Listen you crazy shit, I have a gun pointed at your bloody fucking head and you're wounded, so don't get all tough with me. Tie your hands in front of you."

"Lad, you're going to die. I will kill you; this is your last chance."

The policemen holstered his weapon in anger as he moved forward and took out another zip tie. "I'm going to make this extra tight asshole," as he bent down to wrap the zip tie. "Put your hands out in front of you."

Grant winced as he pulled his left arm off the floor. The young policemen did not see the razor-sharp tactical knife in his right hand and in an instant Grant's arm flew up, planting the knife into his sternum. Despite the pain in his shoulder, now with both hands he clenched the knife as the young man hemorrhaged and died on the end of the blade. His face was one of bewilderment and shock.

Grant softly said, "Sorry lad, I gave you every chance." Using his right arm, he pushed the policemen back and pulled himself up. Taking off his belt, he made a sling before walking out the door, thinking of how he could get to the escape room. He took a moment to text Bridget and told her he was on his way. They needed to get out now.

The two members from Team Ronda came around the heliport structure and cautiously entered the residence through the expanse of broken glass that had once been the large sliding door. Jack Walker was very much dead, and Team Edward's leader was wounded, sitting with her back against the wall. Team Ronda's leader, his SA-80 out in front of him, crouched next to her and asked if she would be okay until they could clear the scene and get her help. She was weak and pale but nodded a yes. He quickly placed a tourniquet on both her arm and leg and rose when a single shot came over his left shoulder and he quickly lowered himself to the ground. Radioing for backup, he stayed outside the main doors for now.

As he counted three, he jumped-up, spraying bullets in the general direction of the single shot and then crouched back down. Nothing, no return fire. He counted to ten and rose to do it again when another single shot hit his right shoulder, spinning him around as he went down. His partner who was just outside the door saw him take the hit and ran in, firing on automatic in the general direction of the shot. The shooter, one of the newer of

Grant's men, fell from the corner next to the glass wall. He went down hard, and his gun skidded across the floor.

On the far side of the residence where Team Edward had entered, shots had more or less stopped. In the distance, sirens could be heard, and Bridget got Grant's text. Scared, her reaction was now or never. She cautiously walked up the stairs and just as she got to the door, her fob automatically activated the door as it slid open on command. Although she had not walked into the room, she immediately screamed as right in front of her was the dead body of one of Grant's men. Just as she thought to turn and run back down the stairs, she simultaneously heard a shot and felt a hammer blow as she flew backward as if pushed. Her head slammed into the wall behind her. Immediately, a sharp burning sensation rose in her upper chest as she slowly lost strength to stand.

Without fully understanding, she tried to move, but was frozen and looked down, seeing the blood on her blouse, and realized she'd been shot. She was confused as her brain was telling her to get down the hall, but her body couldn't move, and she felt herself weakening. For a moment, she would have traded all her evil ways for another chance at life, but before she could process the thought further, everything went black.

Firing to make a path, Grant ran toward the door that led to Maximillian's suite and was surprised to see it open. He ran into the hall, closed, and locked the electronic door, and immediately saw Bridget, *oh shit! This is not good.* He checked and found a weak pulse and wondered how he was going to pull this off, but instinctively knew if he moved her, it would kill her. The bullet was close to her heart, her breathing labored. A tough call, he told her softly he would have to leave her there so she could get proper care, but wasn't sure if she heard him.

He quickly headed down the hall and disarmed the door code into the suite and walked down the massive hallway before holding his hand to the wall. It registered his biometric code, and the door opened into the elevator. He entered the small space and closed the door as he keyed the descent code. Once there, he exited the elevator, but did not return it to the surface, walking to the pickup area where he texted the submarine which arrived just minutes later. The hatch opened, and he pulled himself up and climbed in, which was difficult given his wounded shoulder. The helmsmen, seeing the wound, helped him, and said, "Mr. Drummond is safe. Have you seen Miss Bridget?"

"Yes, but she will not be joining us. Please allow me to discuss this with Maximillian personally. Say nothing to anyone. Am I perfectly clear?"

"Yes sir. I'll proceed to Churchton Bay." Once they reached the boat in the secluded bay, they surfaced. From the upper port, Grant opened it with his good arm and pulled himself out. Almost white now, they helped him into the stern of the vessel as the upper door to the sub closed and the pilot submerged.

Grant came into the wheelhouse as the captain pulled anchor to get them to Kyle where they would exit. Maximillian approached him, seeing his pale coloring and bloody shoulder.

"Grant, are you okay?"

"Yes, sir, but I will need help on the plane. Sir, Bridget..."

Realizing now she wasn't there he asked, "What about her? Where is she?"

"Sir, she was hit when she came upstairs presumably to get to your study. I came across her as I entered your hallway and she had been shot once in the upper chest, right side. She is alive with a weakened pulse, but if I tried to move her, it would kill her. There was no way I could get her to the sub safely, so I left her to save her life."

"I understand. You did what you are trained to do. She is strong and will be taken care of. It might actually be useful to have her in a position of power," Maximillian replied pragmatically and quickly told the captain to proceed.

61

Back at the residence, eight policemen from Portee arrived in full armor and met the two members from Team Ronda, quickly making their way to the residence. They came into the main salon and entered through the side door Grant had exited and several shots were fired with both sides losing a man, but fifteen minutes later, the residence was secure. Maximillian Drummond's security team had been captured except for the few not killed or wounded.

A helicopter came into view of the residence and after radio confirmation that the house was secure, it set down in the residence heliport. Finlay Cormack and Timothy Hawkins exited and approached the raid commander, Halladay. No sooner than they met, the helicopter lifted off to make room for a Life Flight helicopter that was en route.

"Status?" groused Cormack gruffly, seeing the glass and bodies.

"Significant casualties and wounded, sir. Bridget Drummond was shot but is alive, and they are preparing to Life Flight her and three others. Aiken and Drummond are nowhere to be found."

"How is that possible? What the hell happened here, Halladay?"

"We entered the residence and identified ourselves. The shooting started, and both sides defended themselves."

"Were Aiken and Drummond even here?"

"Aiken was here, but we never saw Drummond. There has to be a backdoor somewhere, although his security detail is unaware of a secret passage out, but we're searching now."

"What a royal fucking disaster!" Cormack shouted, knowing that unless evidence supported him, his twenty-seven-year career was over.

As Cormack fought to understand how all had gone wrong, Maximillian and Grant were in a helicopter sixty kilometers east of the Isle of Skye heading to Inverness where a jet awaited them. After leaving Churchton Bay on the island of Raasay, they had traveled down the inner sound into Loch Alsh. Grant jumped off early and made his own arrangements. Maximillian left the boat at Kyle and took a car down A87 where he met Grant again, and they boarded the helicopter at a remote location.

Hours later aboard the plane, Maximillian came forward to where Grant was sitting. This had been the first private moment for the two to discuss the events of the morning.

Maximillian spoke first in a calm but strained voice. "Grant, I don't understand. Why would they raid the residence?"

"Sir, I'm not entirely sure. The first detail was led by an overzealous Special Ops guy named Walker. He's just that way and apparently got antsy, which I believe started the whole affair. He did not identify himself, and I have the video and recording and left a copy for the police to find. A second team who came in through the employee hallway identified themselves about fifteen minutes later and said they had authorization to arrest me and hold you for questioning. At that point, we had the upper hand and played it out."

Maximillian replied coldly, "I hope those that allowed this will suffer."

"What do we do now?"

"Presumably, we'll have to run operations from MDE Commodities in Madagascar. They have no extradition treaty with the UK, so we can stay there until we can determine our ability to return without prosecution. Angus is en route, and he assures me they will find nothing at the residence."

The forensics team was still at the residence twelve hours later. The bodies were gone, the wounded cared for, and statements were already taken. Within days, they would get ballistics on the dead to determine which weapon had killed them and where the shots had been fired from. The video setup in the residence had been confiscated to establish "eyes" to the events that had taken place there.

Several technicians were attempting to access various systems for evidence to the EMP weapon theory one story below in the private company area. Their warrant to do so was highly limited, so while they were looking at a great deal of sensitive information, there was not much they could do with it. Having lost all credibility on the raid itself, there was little to no chance to expand the warrant.

They attempted to access various computers and tablets of general employees, but when they tried, the systems had been wiped. Apparently, there was a fail-safe program that was deployed during the raid or when they tried to access them.

Upstairs in the residence, Police Scotland was using x-ray equipment to look for secret walls in their attempt to find an elusive secret room or exit. They started on the office floors and found nothing. As the technician went down the wavy corridor leading to the bedroom, he maneuvered the wheeled unit toward the end, and the display went from dark to gray, showing a passageway. Within minutes, the end of the hall was packed with technicians and detectives as they located the almost invisible tracing of the door, which they removed to reveal the elevator shaft. It took almost an hour to bypass the manual override, allowing the elevator car to rise back up the shaft and once they did, two of the team entered and reprogrammed the elevator controls.

When they reached the bottom, they stepped out into the hall and walked down the long hallway, which slopped downward. The detective was recording with his head cam while the technician used a handheld GPS to inform the detective that they were below sea level and heading into the ocean. They continued until they arrived at a circular leather couch. Above them was a locking hatch like one found on a submarine. The technician took the coordinates and divers confirmed the hallway ended at a docking device where a small submersible could dock and open the hatch into a like atmosphere. They had found the elaborate way out.

The following morning, a dejected Finlay Cormack and CI Hawkins were seated in a conference room at Police Scotland HQ in Fife. With them was Chief Constable Conor Gilkeson. On a video link were the Superintendent and CI Hughes from the Metropolitan Police, as was the Home Secretary, Jocelyn Holmes.

The Home Secretary opened the meeting. "Chief Constable Gilkeson, please debrief us." She knew the details, but needed him to own this and sweat it out.

"Madam Secretary, three teams of four approached the residence of Maximillian Drummond on the Isle of Skye to question him and apprehend his head of security, Grant Aiken. One team stayed at the roadway while the other two went to the only known entrances at 6:45 a.m. One team came to an unlocked door and entered. The second team shot out a glass entrance to gain access. They…"

"Which team entered first?" She asked.

"Team Malcolm entered first."

"And this was through the open door?"

"No. Team Malcolm was to enter the main door off the heliport, but it is not a conventional door. Rather, it was a large, solid glass door with no handles or locks. Presumably, the door could only be opened by someone from inside."

"So, the command instruction was to shoot it open rather than knock? Was this your command?"

"No. Halladay was the commander. He gave the order."

"So, he ordered the door to be shot out."

"I am not sure if he gave that command, or the team leader acted within her authority as one of the raid leaders."

"Wait, raid? You saw this as a raid?" She demanded.

"Just a figure of speech, Madam Secretary."

"Please stop referring to it in that manner, although perhaps that is exactly why this failed the way it did. Did the leader of Team Malcolm identify herself?"

"The leader herself was taking cover when Jack Walker, one of the Special Forces guys, was killed in the line of duty before he had the chance."

"The report in front of me says Mr. Walker all but took command from the team leader, saying I quote, 'Stay back, I'm better trained. You'll just get us all killed.' He approached the door, peered inside, and then tried to break the glass with his weapon. He waited a few seconds and fired a quarter of his clip into the five-meter expanse of glass and entered the residence followed by the rest of the team. It was seven minutes from peering into the door to when he was killed, and the team leader was wounded three minutes after that. This was confirmed by video and audio from the owner's system."

"Madam Secretary, I don't understand where you are going with this?"

She held up a report to the video monitor for clarity, "Where I'm going with this, Constable, is that sixteen minutes elapsed with over two hundred shots fired before Police Scotland identified themselves. This is your bloody report, so I assume you know these details better than I."

"With all due respect, I lost nine members of my team on a mission that was supposed to be a simple apprehension and questioning. I am perhaps less concerned with these details than the strategy of the raid, I mean mission, which I do very much understand."

"So, starting a war, shooting Ms. Drummond, and not apprehending Grant Aiken or Maximillian Drummond was all part of your carefully thought-out strategy? Continue Constable Gilkeson and if you do not approve of my questioning, best consider who you are speaking with. It would take very little based on the current facts to hang this disaster on you and no one else," she all but yelled.

Gilkeson was feared within his ranks and could barely stand that he was having to put up with this shit, as he continued explaining the events of the botched raid. They had found no evidence of EMP Weapons, only some minor reference to the sales list for MDE Trust, and he explained the escape hatch as the likely way that Aiken and Drummond had escaped.

Home Secretary Holmes concluded the briefing as Gilkeson sat with a look of disdain. Next to him, the rest of Police Scotland's command looked forward with a look of resignation, knowing they were likely going to be canned.

Maximillian Drummond had beaten them. Spectacularly.

Angus Adair arrived in Inverness that morning and enjoyed a delightful meal and a few pints of Guinness. Soon he took a lift to the Inverness Dalcross airport where Grant had arranged a private plane to take him out of Scotland and eventually to

Madagascar. He would take residence there at the offices of MDE Commodities for now and the plan was for him was to set up shop and rebuild Maximillian's data vault. Apparently, Maximillian did not intend to return to Scotland anytime soon.

That was the straightforward part. The harder effort was more personal. Someone was trying to locate him through his alias, Beithir, and once he got set up, that would be his primary job. His identity had to be protected.

62

Sara had spent the last several weeks determining if she had enough research to write her dissertation. It was a tough decision because while it would appear one could always do more research, her gut told her she actually had enough.

She bounced this off several at the university and even called a surprised Dr. Zimbrean at MIT who felt that based on her findings, she could begin writing. Sara decided, however, to follow protocol and meet with her chair, Dr. Ferrera.

They sat in his office as he glanced at the various outputs before looking to Sara and asking, "Sara, I have reviewed all of your findings. While more research might round out your experience, you have clearly proved your thesis. Have you given thoughts on how you will construct your dissertation?"

Sara had not actually thought this all the way through. A dissertation was generally a six-chapter book that summarized the subject, a section on all published literature reviewed, the method and analysis of her thesis, ending with her findings and a summary. She replied honestly, "I know from my data that some TGFs have immense energy, but others have very little. Testing concluded that the conversion rate highly depends on the incoming energy. While this may be an issue in commercial applications, it is no more an issue than the encounter rate of the TGFs themselves. Everything I have mentioned has assumed a satellite could encounter one percent of all TFGs, but the real data, not the modeled data, shows just four-tenths of one percent. It was my inclination to write the dissertation around this lower encounter rate and suggest further study to increase to one or even two percent."

Dr. Ferrera answered as a statement rather than a question. "And this encounter rate cannot easily be increased because the fixed position of the satellite and wide path of the TGF zone cannot be forced to capture more than this random chance estimate. To use multiple satellites at different angles would help, but the amount of energy available may be too small to warrant the expense."

Sara responded, "Yes, perhaps."

"I cannot fault your logic and yes, proceed as you have planned. I would like to see a draft of your summary once you get there." Dr. Ferrera concluded.

As Sara left his office, she was elated. She had done it. She had proven Gilberti's theory and was done with her research. As she headed to her office to call her dad, she was almost skipping.

63
Aberdeen, Scotland

Bridget Drummond felt a pounding in her head and her body felt heavy, as if her limbs were made of stone. She felt as though she were falling through the sheets into a void when suddenly, her mind reflected on this thinking, *sheets? If I'm dead, why am I on sheets?* She tried to reconcile this, but could not.

From the nurse's station, Mackenzie Fraser, a twenty-eight-year trauma nurse noticed the rapid change in vitals for the mysterious Bridget Drummond and immediately paged the attending doctor to the room. She then ran across the hall to the surprised Police Scotland officer sitting outside her door.

He jumped up and asked, "What's going on?"

Mackenzie shouted, "I'm not sure. Stay back, please. The doctor is on his way." Fraser entered the room. Bridget was not in distress and did not seem awake, but her eyes were fluttering, and her vitals were skyrocketing. Nurse Fraser adjusted her sedative just as the doctor came fast into the room.

He had operated on Bridget four days before, and she had been unresponsive since, an unexpected concern. Although the circumstances were vague, a police bullet struck her a few centimeters to the left of her heart, piercing her lung and nicking her pulmonary vein. She was, thankfully, in excellent physical shape and the EMTs had done a great job stabilizing her. A Life Flight helicopter had brought her and two policemen here to the Major Trauma Centre at Forester hill, Aberdeen.

"Did this just happen?" the doctor asked to Nurse Fraser.

"Yes. As soon as the monitor moved, I paged you and ran in just four minutes ago. She was not awake, unmoving, but her eyelids fluttered, and the vitals suggest her mind was highly active. I decreased the morphine solution twenty-five percent just as you came in."

"Okay, this is a good sign. She should have come out of this days ago, but she had a large contusion on the back of her head as though she might have been thrown back into the wall. Her lung is functioning normally, as is the pulmonary vein since the repair. Monitor her. I suspect she'll wake soon."

"Yes, Doctor," as Mackenzie returned to her nursing station. Twenty minutes later, the monitor went off, and she rushed back into the room. Bridget's eyes were open slightly and Mackenzie said softly, "Bridget, can you hear me? Bridget, can you hear my voice?"

She nodded and said nothing. As she heard the voice, she realized she was in a hospital room. She looked over, saw Nurse Fraser, and tried to speak, but nothing came out. Mackenzie immediately gave her a small amount of water and rubbed some ointment on her lips. Bridget had been intubated for two days following surgery and the body needed to be reminded the tube wasn't still in place. Bridget tried again and said hoarsely, "Where am I?"

"You were shot and airlifted here to the Major Trauma Centre in Aberdeen."

Bridget nodded and asked defiantly, "Who shot me?"

"I am told by the police, although they claim it was accidental. Do you remember anything?"

"No. I remember thinking I was dying. Someone was talking to me, but the words were fading, so I assumed I was dying but I'm not dead, am I?"

The doctor came back into the room just as she had spoken and replied, "No Ms. Drummond, you are very much alive." He checked her vitals and asked if she was in pain, and she said no. Reducing the morphine another twenty-five percent, he asked her a few questions to test her memory and responsiveness. She was going to be fine.

Outside the door to Bridget's room, the young policemen standing guard had immediately called CI Hawkins to tell him Bridget Drummond was awake and talking with the doctor. Hawkins was out the door immediately to make the one-hundred-fifty kilometer drive from Fife to Aberdeen, which he did in record time. He made his way onto her floor and not a minute later, a protective Nurse Fraser was there right next to him. "I'm not sure who you are, but the patient cannot be questioned at this time, so don't think for a second you are going in there."

"Nurse..." He eyed her nametag, "Nurse Fraser, I am CI Hawkins of Police Scotland. I realize the situation, but you must equally realize this woman is eyes and ears to a crime."

"Yes, well, you'll have to figure out which of your boys shot her once the doctor approves it, and he has not." Seeing this was not going anywhere, he left.

Hawkins expected the delay and had brought an overnight bag. While he waited, he spent his time working leads on how Aiken and Drummond might have left the submarine, but there were no clues or witnesses.

Two days later, he could finally speak to her, although it was clear the trauma center staff was on her side, not his. Having never met her, he was taken aback by how beautiful she was as he walked into the room. She appeared taller than him, with a fair complexion and shoulder-length blond hair. Even after days in the hospital and no make-up, she looked like a model.

Her bed was raised, and as she eyed him, he introduced himself. "How are you Ms. Drummond? I'm CI Hawkins from Police Scotland and I have a few questions. Is that all right?"

"Did you shoot me?" she asked coldly.

Not expecting that response, he stuttered for a moment before replying, "Well no, and we still don't know who did. We only know the bullet was from a tactical rifle used by the Police Scotland team. Ms. Drummond, do you recall the events of that day? It might help us understand?"

"Where is my brother?"

"We don't know. He and Grant Aiken escaped, and I assume you would have too had you not been shot. Ms. Drummond, do you recall the events of that day?"

"More or less up to that moment I realized I had been shot."

"Might I hear your recollection?" he asked.

She paused for a moment before reiterating the details of the raid although she had limited information because she had gone downstairs. "After maybe twenty to thirty minutes, the shooting finally stopped, and I came upstairs but the fob in my purse accidentally activated the door. When it opened, I screamed at the sight of one of our security staff, dead on the floor, and suddenly, I was thrown back against the wall. Someone shot me, but I saw no one. I recall nothing else."

"They left you behind. That has to make you mad," Hawkins said sharply.

"I wasn't abandoned, Inspector; I was left purposely. Grant knew if he moved me, I was dead, so he didn't. He's a perfect machine you know."

"Where was your rendezvous point?" he asked.

"I have no idea. My only plan was to find Grant."

"So, you will not tell us how he got out or where he is? You realize you can be arrested if we feel you are hindering this investigation."

Bridget laughed even though it hurt badly to do so. Looking at him straight in his eyes with an unwavering stare she said, "I dare you."

64

Antananarivo, Madagascar

Maximillian hung up, having heard from Angus that Bridget was awake and was being moved out of intensive care. Shortly after, he got an update regarding the conclusion of Sara's research and that she had begun her dissertation, meaning she had done it. She had located the energy and converted it.

The final amount of energy converted meant little to him, but he was told that while it was perhaps just a single second of output of a nuclear power plant, it is highly comparable to satellite solar sails, in a smaller, cheaper, and more durable package.

Maximillian looked over to Grant who had just walked in and said, "Well, her research is over and was conclusive. Perhaps not a tremendous amount of energy. It is enough to consider methods to increase this potential and use it in productive ways. Let's get Gilberti's original works and the researcher."

"I'll take care of it," Grant replied with confidence.

65

Rome, Italy

Days later, Sara had stopped in a small trattoria for a light meal and a glass of wine to celebrate. In the time since, she had buttoned up her research and organized the many notes which she would need as she began the tedious process of drafting her written dissertation. The server came and took her dishes as she finished her glass of riserva chianti. Not long after, she started the walk back to her flat, which was nearby. It was getting cold as Sara rounded the narrow street that went toward her parking area.

As she pulled up her shawl, she was immediately grabbed from behind, feeling a prick on the back of her neck and a cloth pulled to her mouth. She tried violently to get away, but the person holding her was very strong and had his arms and a leg around hers effectively subduing her. She continued to struggle, but the harder she fought, the less she could get out a scream. A few more seconds she felt numb. Someone was still holding her from behind and she tried to break free one last time when she saw through fuzzy eyes the back of the mini-van before her world spun into darkness.

At Maximillian's request, Grant had set up the abduction to get her to a private airport outside Rome where a nurse would regulate drugs to make her sleep. A separate team had already located Gilberti's crate in the basement of Giovanni Ricci's Milan flat. It was due to arrive in Madagascar hours before the plane with Sara and the nurse would touch down. Once it did, all would travel to the mine aboard the *Yakka* with Grant and several of his men. Maximillian, dressed as a researcher, would fly with Dr. Berniece, his own physicist, to Wilkins Aerodrome, Antarctica, and sail to the mine aboard a hired vessel.

At Sapienza University, an agitated Dr. Ferrera texted Sara from the plasma lab, but she didn't reply. He then called her, but it went straight to voicemail. They were to have met thirty minutes before and she was always very punctual but enough was enough, as he left and headed back to his office.

Unknown to him or anyone else, Angus Adair sat at a computer desk in Madagascar, holding Sara's phone, which had been taken apart and now had several wires coming from its electronics. The other end was attached to a computer that allowed him to mimic her phone. He had access to see who was calling and if authorities should try to trace the signal, they would think the phone was still in Rome. People were now trying to get hold of her. The game had begun.

The following morning, Sara was still nowhere to be found and Dr. Ferrera was now highly alarmed. He had campus security check her flat and her car was there, but the doors were locked, and her neighbor had not seen her now in several days. Dr. Ferrera, knowing of the events in America, erred on the side of caution and called the Carabinieri, and now at almost 3:00 p.m., his office was full of Police. In less than two hours, they had determined she was last seen at 9:47 p.m., two nights before leaving a trattoria close to her flat. Her cell phone provider, Vodafone, said the phone was on and the signal showed it was in Roma Tiburtina, the large railway station near the University. Perhaps she had simply gone on holiday. Teams were dispatched to retrieve the phone, which, of course, was not actually there.

Sara momentarily opened her eyes as she was awakened, feeling weak, nauseous, and alarmingly tired. Her eyes tried to focus on a slight woman in white, a nurse she thought. The moment she did, the room spun as her last thought before she again slept was that she must be in a hospital.

Although she had no idea, she was actually on day four of the six-day voyage aboard the *Yakka*. They would arrive at the mine on Heard Island in less than forty-eight-hours.

66

10 Downing Street, London

Foreign and Commonwealth Secretary Alistair Evans and Home Secretary Jocelyn Holmes sat in the outer chamber waiting to be seen by the Prime Minister. Only because he wished it, they remained there for twenty-five minutes before they were allowed into the room. The Prime Minister was seated but did not rise, and simply pointed to two empty chairs before him.

As they sat, he said bluntly, "Please give me a concise and unscripted account of what happened, hoping to get me back on your side."

Jocelyn Holmes took the lead and quickly responded, "The calling on the residence of Maximillian Drummond was a disaster because the leaders perceived this as a raid. We gave no such order, and we'll clean house at Police Scotland. Regardless of this, Grant Aiken is wanted for serious crimes as nine police are dead, along with five from Aiken's security force and another five wounded."

The Prime Minister understood but was not biting just yet as he said likely knowing the answer, "And evidence linking Drummond or his company to the EMP attacks?"

"We found nothing, which is the truth, or he was forewarned and knew to clean up. It has been established that much of the house was awake and saw the first team approach the door. That team, however, failed to identify themselves and set off a bloodbath."

With no hint of protocol, he said, "How do you propose to clean this up? Maximillian Drummond might be everything people say of him, but he is revered in many circles in which we take part and with no evidence to the contrary, we appear to have seriously overstepped. In my view, he bested you spectacularly."

"Yes, he did, sir." Jocelyn answered honestly as she looked down.

Alistair Evans spoke now. "Prime Minister, Maximillian Drummond has the resources to live comfortably wherever he is, and I suggest we let him do so until he wishes to come out of hiding and confront these realities. Meanwhile, Jocelyn is correct, Grant Aiken is a horse of a different color, and we must punish him for the deaths of our police. The story must be that we attempted to arrest him and question Maximillian for matters we cannot discuss. But Aiken watched them come up the drive, knew they were police, and took aim to kill them all. Details to the contrary are not relevant as our story will rise solely on the back of public opinion. This man and his private army killed our beloved police. We'll have a press conference and stress these facts. Maximillian need not even be mentioned."

The Prime Minister with a weak smile, said, "Very well then. Make this stick and kill that bastard wherever he might be."

Jocelyn Holmes waited a moment and said, "Prime Minister, we are unaware of their actual whereabouts, but MDE Enterprises owns a company called MDE Commodities. They operate a small mine on an island in the Southern Ocean. A territory of Australia. It is a six-day trip from Madagascar and our analysts suspect this is precisely where they have fled."

"Why do you think this?"

"The MDE Commodities vessel *Yakka* leaves Madagascar once every eight weeks to take the Managing Director to the mine. He returns after that and is in Madagascar for two weeks. This same vessel left for the mine three days ago, ten days before it should have, and we suspect they are on that ship and will arrive on Heard island in just a few days. I intend with your approval to divert the HMS *Dauntless* from exercises in the Southern Ocean with the United States Navy to arrive on the island. They have a small contingent of troops from the Royal Marines and could arrive two to three days after the *Yakka*. Admiral James Cotton on the *Dauntless* only awaits your word, and the USS *Jackson* has offered to assist."

The Prime Minister said without hesitation, "Start the media campaign immediately. How many souls live on this island?"

"Sir, there are as many as a dozen researchers on the island this time of year and the mine can only employ a maximum of fifty persons, so the worst case is sixty-two. This would be a swift attack on the main office, not likely the mine, and certainly not the highlands where the researchers are camping." Jocelyn stated.

"And you say Royal Marines are aboard the *Dauntless?*"

"Yes, Prime Minister, we have fourteen troops. Should we accept the American's assistance, they can supply an additional ten troops from the USS *Jackson*. And certainly, more firepower than is necessary."

"This seems to be our mess and not the Americans. Must we include them?"

"We have no intel as to the size of the security force on the island and Admiral Cotton believes their help would assure success and can be approached as part of their joint drills."

"Very well. Jocelyn, I am fond of you, and you have my blessing, but should you muck this up and lose control again, I'll expect your resignation without hesitation. Alistair's message will only hold if you capture or kill Mr. Aiken."

Angus completed setting up his computer lab in Madagascar using robust firewalls to protect his location and identity. He had quickly developed a system to feed critical information to Maximillian and Grant and began the tedious job of recreating Maximillian's vast library. With parts of the library being recreated by automation, Angus redirected his sights on finding who was after his alias, Beithir.

He began his search by reaching out to loyal contacts in the dark cyber world who had access and knowledge of highly clandestine code names and their methods. Through his network, they located an individual using the codename Aladdin. Angus was relieved that Aladdin was not affiliated with the United States NSA or Britain's GCHQ, but he was dismayed to learn that Aladdin appeared to be with the United Brotherhood of Islam (UBOI). His real name was Gilad Gasim.

Angus immediately sent a note to Maximillian and Grant, telling them to watch their backs as it was possible that the UBOI was looking into them, although he couldn't explain how.

There was no way for Angus to know that the communication system on the island was down. The message never got through because the satellite receiver on the island that fed all phones and computers was not operating.

67

Heard Island, Antarctica

Sara awoke feeling tired but thankful the room was not moving although she was still nauseous. She took stock of herself and seemed intact. The nurse, who was likely monitoring her, suddenly came in carrying a small plate of food and asked Sara if she was feeling better.

Sara responded, "Yes actually, but where am I? I don't seem to have any idea."

"I'm not entirely sure my dear. I'm simply here to help you and make sure you're healthy."

"But this is a hospital. You are a nurse. Where am I?" Sara shouted.

"Sara, I am a nurse; my name is Luna Parodi, but you are not in a hospital. As I have been told, you were found unconscious in Rome, and I have been working to stabilize you. Those who hired me have brought us here to protect you."

"Unconscious... I think someone attacked me." Sara said not really understanding her recollection.

"I was told that you were attacked and drugged near your home. The people who hired me saved you and brought you here out of harm's way. As to this location, we are on an island somewhere between Africa and Australia."

Highly alarmed if not only because of the physical distance from Rome, Sara asked, "Luna, who are the people who hired you?"

Just as the words left her mouth, the door opened, and a middle-aged man dressed in business casual attire walked in and sat next to her bed.

He smiled and said, "Sara, I'm so happy to meet you in person and find you safe and well. When you first arrived, I was very concerned." Sara's expression didn't change, although his voice sounded familiar. Boris Turgenev realized she had no idea what he actually looked like before saying in Russian, "Sara, it is me, Boris. Boris Turgenev of MDE Commodities."

Sara smiled somewhat. "Boris? Why are you here? Wait,... Are we in Madagascar?"

"No, Sara, we are at the mine on Heard Island. You arrived by boat yesterday and Nurse Luna has been working to assure you are heathy."

"The mine? Why am I at the mine?"

"I only know that you were found unconscious in Rome by a member of the security team of MDE Enterprises. They rescued you from the assailants and were told to arrange transport here to assure your safety."

"Where is this mine again?" Sara said now confused.

"We are approximately three-thousand kilometers from Madagascar, four-thousand kilometers from Perth, Australia and one-thousand kilometers from Davis Station, Antarctica."

"Boris, I don't understand. Why the mine? Why so far from Rome? I need... a phone, get... me... phone..." As they were talking, Nurse Luna had re-administered the drugs into her IV and again Sara had drifted off. Boris rose, nodded to Nurse Luna, and walked out of the room.

Back in Arlington, Virginia, word of the joint raid on the island to apprehend Grant Aiken made its way to Hicks who shared that with Bechtel at DARPA. In their own attempt to understand the situation, Bechtel arranged for Jason Sykes to represent them. He was on his way to intercept the USS *Jackson*, an Independence

Class Littoral Combat Ship doing joint military exercises in the Southern Ocean with the UK troops aboard the HMS *Dauntless*. Once there, Jason would join the Navy Seals already aboard and assist in the apprehension. He also felt that Sara, missing now for eight-days might be on the island. To that end, Hicks had been in contact with the Carabinieri, who, without many details had also explained this to a frantic Giovanni Ricci.

68

Atlas Cove, Heard Island, Antarctica

The northwest end of Heard Island forms a tidal area and flatland where the primary volcano, Mawson Peak, meets the smaller volcano, Mount Dixon, on Laurens Peninsula. Although Atlas Cove is one of the few places to safely approach the island, the tidal area was too shallow for the deep draft vessels that can actually make the journey there. As such, the only way to land by sea was to anchor just outside the area and boat in.

From his small outpost at the dock, one of Grant's security force, Dmitri Kozlow, watched as a large research vessel appeared and was now setting anchor just outside the inlet. He grabbed his sight glass and noted the Australian flag and immediately recognized the vessel as that of the Australian Regulatory Agency.

The vessel had been on the island a few months earlier doing a quarterly environmental assessment of the mine and monitoring permits of the few researchers. Kozlow thought it was odd they were back a month early, but he was not alarmed and continued to observe them. Soon a small launch was heading towards him. Thinking he recognized a few of researchers, he headed out onto the small dock and waved as they approached. Several waved back.

Up on the bluff in the main building, three-hundred meters down from the mine, the inlet could be seen clearly, but not the actual dock. A camera was mounted there, which another of Grant's men was watching. On the monitor it showed Kozlow on the dock, waiting to assist an incoming launch. He saw them exchange a wave and, assuming these were researchers, switched cameras back over to the mine itself.

The launch was slowing now, and Kozlow prepared a line for them. He tossed it to the awaiting hands of the deck mate and tied it off. As he looked up with a smile, he quickly frowned when he saw a tall, dark-skinned man aiming a crossbow at him. Before he could react, the dark-skinned man shot an arrow directly into his heart, killing him instantly. Two of them jumped out of the launch and grabbed his limp body, holding him upright between them, and went down the dock into the small guardhouse, dropping his body as they turned and left. All others fanned out at the base of the small hill and hiked the long way around out of direct sight to the main office, over three kilometers away.

Aiken, inside the main building, was pacing as he had asked Koslow earlier to assist with the repair to the receiver that had taken down their communication system. He would have someone else cover the water and asked the video tech to cut to the dock. All was quiet as Grant observed the empty launch and the tech told him Dimitri had helped to usher in a new bunch of researchers. Aiken thought it was odd no one was there, as it usually took a while to unload. He reached for a handset to call before he remembered the phones didn't work.

Aiken slammed down the phone and turned to Bruce Morgan, his second in command with concern. "Let's go down to the dock. Something's not right." They both walked toward a large gun cabinet when the door flew open. A man calmly walked in, followed in haste by four men, all with assault rifles aimed directly at Aiken and Morgan. Everyone stopped. The intruders all wore white thobes, loose ankle length garments with long sleeves, white turbans with a hint of yellow, and in their sash, was a jambiya, the famous Yemeni dagger.

Maximillian, who was seated at a desk in the corner, froze and kept his eye on Grant who immediately realized with anger, the sentry outside and Kozlow must be dead. The man in the center stepped forward and said in perfect English, "Although it is not important, I am Salah ibn Abdulaziz ibn Tariq al-Ayad.

409

Which of the three of you gave the order to implicate the United Brotherhood of Islam for the EMP attacks? I am only interested in the person who gave that order." He stared at Maximillian.

Grant stiffened and approached Salah al-Ayad who did not flinch although two of his men covered him carefully. The other two covered Maximillian and Bruce who had not moved. Grant said casually, "You are UBOI?"

Salah al-Ayad barked, "I do not answer to you, solider."

Grant thought quickly about how he could buy some time. His team could easily overcome this small group of men, but only if he could make some noise to alert them. "What makes you think any of us gave such an order? We are a security detail."

"Perhaps you are, but the pale one is not." As his eyes looked past Grant to Maximillian, still seated at the desk. "You are Maximillian Drummond, CEO of MDE Enterprises, a man who makes many decisions. Did you give the order to implicate the United Brotherhood of Islam for the EMP attacks?"

Before Maximillian could speak, Grant spoke quickly to get Salah al-Ayad's attention away from Maximillian. "I gave the order."

Maximillian was listening to the words in surprise when, in the flash of his eye, Salah al-Ayad reached across his body. With his right hand, he withdrew a karabela hilted sword from its sheath at his waist and expertly pulled it out and upward through the air, decapitating Grant Aikens in seconds.

Grant's head fell and his body convulsed as it collapsed to the floor. Morgan jumped forward in rage and Maximillian screamed in terror but the four UBOI rifles stopped them. Salah al-Ayad calmly wiped the blade and placed it back into the sheath as if nothing had happened. He then said softly, without emotion, "That is the punishment for desecrating the name of the United Brotherhood of Islam."

69

Atlas Cove, Heard Island, Antarctica

Maximillian was almost hyperventilating as tears rolled down his cheeks. He couldn't stop crying as he noticed Grant's killer moving towards him. He knew in that instant, this was it. A lifetime of success ended with a decision that was almost an afterthought. Grant had not wanted to do this, and now he was dead. It was his fault and now Maximillian, too, was going to die in this most savage way.

Salah al-Ayad faced him directly and then stopped a meter away. "Remove your fear pale one. Only the decision maker dies. Should you consider such a decision again, I will find you, and..."

He never finished the sentence as his head burst in a red mist, throwing him forward and stopping his voice as the weight of his body pulled it to the ground at Maximillian's feet.

Maximillian screamed again and covered his face, but it was too late as blood sprayed above and across him. He looked up toward the open door to the building where one of the security team had stood with an assault rifle. He was immediately cut down by the four UBOI fighters who had just spun around toward him, shooting all at once to avenge the death of their leader. They ran outside, firing at unknown targets. In that moment, all hell broke loose as Morgan ran toward the gun cabinet and shouted to Maximilian, "Sir, take cover and do not leave this building!" He ran out the door.

A minor war was now underway between the UBOI, trying to retreat to the dock and MDE security forces. With relatively few men on either side, the MDE men were on higher ground and killed the UBOI forces, but not before the warriors killed three of the security team.

Morgan reentered the room and paused at the sight of Aikens' body. All soldiers face death, but he admired this man. Before he went to the next room, he placed a blanket over Grant's body. When he found Maximillian, he explained what had just happened, but Maximillian hardly listened to the words. He was still in shock and feeling the weight of his guilt in his role that brought the UBOI to their doorstep.

In the room down the hall, Sara was resting as Nurse Parodi sat reading. She heard yelling and wondered what it was when the first shot was fired. She immediately rushed over to Sara who awoke immediately. Nurse Parodi helped Sara quickly get out of bed and they rushed toward a storage room, the only place to hide, and pulled the door shut just as the fire fight outside became intense.

Nurse Parodi said in a whisper, "What the hell is going on?"

Sara was still in a fog but highly alarmed as she looked at her and said, "I know exactly what's happening. They're after me again. Whoever they are, they won't be happy until I'm dead. Even here in the middle of fucking nowhere."

There was a knock at the door, and Boris entered the room and called for Luna and Sara. From the closet, Luna came out, and seeing Boris, brought out Sara. He explained to them about a terrorist attack which had been stopped by the mine's security force, but there were many casualties on both sides. He kindly asked them to stay in their room for now, and they happily complied.

Elsewhere on the island, the mine workers also were aware of the incident and casualties. Upon Aikens' death, Maximillian had placed Morgan in charge of the remaining security team and moved into the other room. He could not bring himself to congregate in the place where Grant had died.

As he sat with Dr. Berniece, Morgan said, "Sir, it is doubtful that the UBOI forces could man the Australian vessel in these waters unaided. I suspect there are UBOI soldiers still on board, holding some or all of the actual crew of that ship hostage. I would like to return to the ship on their launch and eliminate that threat."

"How many do you suspect there are?" Maximillian asked.

"Likely two to three. It should not be difficult, as they will think it's their launch and their members returning."

"Do nothing for now. Their launch is at our dock. We can watch it from here or with our cameras. I understand the threat, but the last thing we need is the actual crew to contact authorities or worse, try to come ashore. Please have Boris summon Nurse Parodi and when she leaves the room, detain her until I say otherwise. I need Ms. Ricci alone."

"Yes sir," as Morgan walked out of the room, closing the door behind him.

Maximillian looked over to Dr. Berniece. "Our presence on the island is no longer safe, so our time here is short. My original intent was to get Ms. Ricci on our side with the story that we have saved her to establish loyalty, but losing Grant has changed everything. I cannot risk anymore and simply need to understand her invention and Gilberti's true research. We must meet with her now and then make plans to vacate the island."

"Very well. I'll have security get Gilberti's crate." He went off to bring it into the room as Maximillian went to meet Sara Ricci for the first time.

At that moment, the HMS *Dauntless* and the USS *Jackson* had just sailed into Corinthian Bay at Heard Island. Previous satellite photos had shown that Atlas Cove was easily viewed by the mine and possibly the main building down from it. The plan, therefore, was to anchor in Corinthian Bay on the north side of the island. Both teams would launch from there to the rugged shoreline and climb the glacier and hike overland to take high ground positions around the mine and down to the main building.

Sara paced. Nurse Parodi had left, saying she would be right back, but she had been gone for over twenty minutes. She tried the door, but it was locked, and her mind was now going wild. Why was she being held here? Who had really hired Nurse Parodi? If the Drummonds security force had saved her, as Boris claimed, that meant they had been following her. Why? Was MDE Enterprises really involved in all this, after all? Had she just been kidnapped? It was then that she gasped and thought aloud, *oh my god, my poor dad, he has no idea where I am. He must think he has lost me as well.*

In that moment, Sara, now frantic went back to the door and pulled with all her might, but the door was solid. She turned and looked at the window, which was all glass that did not open. She immediately thought she could break it as she eyed the IV stand.

If she could get out, her plan was to get hold of a satellite phone and call her dad. She turned to grab the IV stand when the door opened. In walked an older man, impeccably dressed, wearing a look of concern on his face.

"Who are you?" Sara shouted, setting down the stand.

"Ms. Ricci, allow me to introduce myself. My name is Maximillian Drummond, the CEO and founder of MDE Enterprises. Boris Turgenev and Sophia Antonion work for me."

Alarm filled her senses. She looked at Maximillian Drummond, recalling all her own thoughts and the warning from Director Hicks before shouting, "You. You really are trying to kill me."

The door opened again, and two men brought in Gilberti's crate and set in on the floor. Sara screamed at seeing the crate. Her first thought was that they had harmed her father to get it. Another man walked in as the security guys left and the door was closed and relocked with a loud click.

Maximillian said firmly, "Ms. Ricci, this is a fellow physicist. Please calm yourself. I need you to help us understand the coating that Cerium Scientific Compounds applies to your invention. First, however, you are going to locate for me the papers that define the weapon that Gilberti Ricci was trying to develop before he was killed."

"What? Are you out of you mind? There is no weapon—only the possibility that energy exists," she yelled.

"I am quite sane, thank you, and do not use that tone with me again. I am trying to be reasonable, but it is simply not logical that the Nazis would kill him without reason. Atmospheric energy is not such a reason. You will find the weapon concept for me, or I promise you, you'll never leave this island alive. Do you completely understand?"

Sara's mind was in overdrive. She had gone through every single paper in this crate and knew there was no such thing, but she needed to buy some time. While these men were no doubt evil, they looked a tad soft, and Sara thought she might fend for herself if need be.

If she repeated the truth that there was no such thing, and that Gilberti had killed himself, this madman might just have her killed, but if she agreed, she could take hours going through the papers and that time might provide an opportunity to escape. She lowered her head in an act and said softly, "It will take some time to locate them. There is no organization to this material."

"Then you best start. You have less than four hours," he responded coldly.

Sara took a screwdriver they had brought her and loosened the top of the crate. The smells of the oils and long-gone machinery brought her back to Milan and she cried before she stopped and looked right into Maximillian's eyes. "Did you harm my father?"

"No, Ms. Ricci, I doubt he even knows this is gone from his basement. Please proceed. I have no wish to harm you, but our time is short, and the situation is escalating. There is no telling what could happen."

Finding her courage, Sara said loudly, "What the hell does that mean? What is wrong with you? Why would you give me fifty-thousand euros of free minerals, offer to fund my research, and most recently, offer me a job if you are so hell bent to kill me? Are you even aware of what your own empire is doing?"

"Ms. Ricci, you are trying my limited patience and I will not warn you again regarding your tone. As for my empire, I actually know everything about it; I have an eidetic memory. It is my gift. You, however, are still young and reactionary, and do not understand the concept of insurance, but I digress. I gave you a simple task. Please complete it now. Silently. You will do what I asked with no consideration, or I will, in fact have you killed. It is up to you, Ms. Ricci."

Sara realized he was probably crazy and said nothing as she took out the last two screws and pushed the lid back. She was on her knees and fifteen feet away; the physicist was standing with his back to her, and Maximillian Drummond was standing behind him to the right. She couldn't hear what they were saying and as she looked into the crate, realized their view of her hands was blocked by the lid. Her eyes skimmed over the papers and fixated on the small box to the left. She recalled its contents and reached in, slowly opening it. Her eyes immediately went to the gun, Gilberti's gun. She looked up to see if they were watching her; her panicked expression was a dead giveaway, but thankfully they were not.

Nerves were getting to her, and for a second, she thought she would vomit. What the hell was she thinking? She had never held a gun in her life, but this bastard, this bastard caused everything. A quick breathing exercise calmed her down. She slowly put the gun into her hand as it shook. Maximillian was standing slightly to the right of the physicist now as she brought up the pistol and fired with no warning. She fired again and then again and again as both men dropped to the ground.

Without thinking, she dropped the gun, jumped up, grabbed the IV stand, and rammed it through the window. Running back to the bed, she grabbed a pillow and quickly placed it on the windowsill to avoid getting cut and climbed out. Dropping to the ground, her adrenaline was so high she hadn't yet noticed the cold. Colder than Boston cold. Wearing just hospital scrubs and socks, she ran down the hill, then froze. Standing in front of her were two soldiers dressed in white and tan camouflage and one had a rifle pointed right at her. She dropped to her knees in resignation.

Perhaps it was the cold, which was now making her shiver, or maybe the shock that she had just killed someone, or even perhaps that they had finally won. They would certainly kill her now. At that moment, her amazing mind reached its limit, and she felt herself let go and fainted.

The soldier pushed his weapon over his shoulder, and the one behind him rushed forward and raised his protective goggles. He picked Sara up in his arms and brought her back behind the building for cover as light gunfire erupted on the other side of the larger building to the right. Holding her, he said calmly, "Sara. Sara, it's me."

Sara was limp, but her subconscious heard the sound. What had she just heard? She knew this voice. Her eyes opened, and she felt herself in the arms of the soldier who was now seated. He was holding her like a baby, and looked up to see Jason's eyes and next to him, a Royal Marine standing guard over them. She yelped and wrapped her arms around Jason and kissed him before she cried again, holding him for dear life. The Royal Marine glanced over, shocked at the sudden burst of passion, with no idea they knew each other, but did not move or say a word.

After several silent minutes, Sara looked at Jason and said, "How are you here?"

He glanced down and said, "UK and US special forces came to apprehend the head of security for MDE Enterprises. DARPA convinced them to let me come on my hunch that you might be here. I have never been so thankful to be right."

"Jason, I shot them. I killed them. Believe me; they were going to kill me!"

Confused, he said in alarm, "Whoa, whoa, Sara, who did you shoot? Who did you kill?"

"The CEO of MDE Enterprises. He said his name was Maximillian Drummond and a physicist who was with him. They said I would never leave this island alive."

"Where?"

Sara looked over his shoulder and pointed to the building without the window. "There. They held me in there," as the Royal Marine left them to check it out.

Aboard the HMS *Dauntless*, Admiral James Cotton was preparing to brief Giles Taylor having just received an update from the ground commander, who was still on the island. As they ended their conversation, Cotton went to the bridge to access the communications room. The technician rang Taylor on the secure satellite video receiver. "Sir, please hold for Admiral James Cotton." The tech then said, "Sir, you are live on comm three."

"Director Taylor, Admiral James Cotton."

"Admiral, I am here with Home Secretary Jocelyn Holmes and Foreign and Commonwealth Secretary Alastair Evans. What do you have for us?"

"Sir, we successfully engaged active forces on the island with no loss of life to our troops. Of the mine security force, there are five dead, including Grant Aiken and three wounded. All but two UBOI terrorists are dead and the two are being detained as are the remaining six members of the island security team."

"Admiral, did you say UBOI terrorists?" Giles asked in astonishment.

"Affirmative, sir."

"Do we know why they were there?" Giles asked still in shock.

The admiral answered, "The acting head of the security force, who was in the room when Aiken was killed has said that the UBOI killed him because he had desecrated the UBOI name by blaming the EMP attacks on them."

"And Maximillian Drummond?"

"Sir, before I get to that, besides who we expected here, there are also three civilians unrelated to mining operations or the research on the island. One is an Italian nurse who was hired by Aiken to look after a patient, another Italian named Sara Ricci who claims to be a PhD candidate at Sapienza University in Rome. She says she was kidnapped by Maximillian's security team in Rome and just before our arrival. Apparently, Drummond, and a Scottish physicist, forced her to locate from old papers related to her great-great-grandfather, Gilberti Ricci, a theoretical WWII weapon. They said they would kill her if she didn't, and she claims she shot them both. We investigated and found the gun inside a crate of old papers. It had been recently fired and her fingerprints were on the gun. Ten feet away was the body of Maximillian Drummond. He had been shot once in the head. Next to him was the physicist who has been identified as Dr. Christopher Berniece. He sustained serious injury but is alive aboard the HSS *Dauntless* in stable condition."

Giles, momentarily astonished, replied, "My God. The plot thickens. This young researcher disappeared from Rome under mysterious circumstances ten days ago and we have feared the worst, although our US counterparts thought she might be there. There is quite a story surrounding her, but you say she claims she killed Drummond."

"Yes sir. She is claiming self-defense and the Managing Director of the mine, the nurse, and the physicist have all collaborated her story.   Based on this, what is your recommendation regarding the detainees and the civilians?"

Taylor replied, "Admiral, secure the two UBOI warriors, the security head, the nurse, Dr. Berniece, and Ms. Ricci and bring them to Davis Station, Antarctica. We'll arrange military flights under guard to London. We will have a medical team there for the physicist. Please assure that the crate with the research papers is included. I think it is best to leave the remaining security force with the miners."

"Very good, sir."

"Despite these revelations, for myself, please congratulate the team for a job well done and please send a final report within twenty-four-hours. Right Honorable Secretary, Madam Secretary, do you have questions for the Admiral?"

Alistair Evans spoke. "Admiral, please send the encrypted report to Director Taylor's eyes only. Bring everyone together and assure that the UBOI presence and their murder of Grant Aiken is a mission detail only. Until we can interrogate Ms. Ricci, the death of Maximillian Drummond is also a mission detail. I am quite serious. There can be no mention of this, and we will so inform the US commander."

"Yes mam, I understand. Will there be anything else?"

"No, that is all. Signing off," and the satellite connection ceased. Jocelyn Holmes turned to Alastair Evans once the video ended. "So, the UBOI killed Aiken, believing he was behind the EMP attacks although he was likely covering for Drummond. And Drummond, in a rare act of desperation, has the young scientist kidnapped and is now dead by her hand. We'll have to contemplate our next steps?"

Alastair Evans replied almost in dread, "I cannot explain any of this, but thankfully, we succeeded in our primary objective. Drummond was a bonus." He shook his head and cupped his face in his hands as he added, "I have a feeling though that the ghost of Maximillian Drummond will hang over our heads for some time."

"Yes... Perhaps I should just resign. It would be better for my health." Jocelyn Holmes chuckled nervously.

Epilogue

Giovanni Ricci stood near the door holding a glass of wine. He had been talking with one of the many grad students who had showed up for a party in honor of Sara's safe return and completion of her PhD research phase. He watched his daughter in awe, knowing all she had gone through and now just weeks later, she seemed back to normal as if nothing had happened. So confident, so strong, just like her mother.

It had taken five days of travel for Sara to reach London. There, she was medically examined and determined to be healthy, except for some deep cuts and bruises. She was then brought under guard to SIS headquarters and questioned extensively for hours, but released with no charges. Although Nurse Parodi and Dr. Berniece would face charges for their role in her abduction, they corroborated Sara's version of events. She was then flown to Rome where she was again questioned by the Carabinieri who officially closed her case before she was finally reunited with her dad. It was a moment neither would ever forget.

The story released to the world had been highly scripted by both United Kingdom and Italian Intelligence. It said that the private security forces of industrialist Maximillian Drummond had abducted the PhD student close to her home in Rome, hoping to steal the secrets of her research. Forces from the United Kingdom and the United States, in the area on training exercises, were diverted to an island off the coast of Antarctica. Their mission, to apprehend the murderer Grant Aiken, rescue the PhD student, and to question Maximillian Drummond on events that happened in Scotland. Security forces on the island put up a brief fight during which Grant Aiken and Maximillian Drummond were killed.

Relieved and proud, Giovanni did not really understand what had happened on the island, as Sara had been told by Giles Taylor that her silence was a prerequisite to avoid any consequence of her actions. All Giovanni knew was that his daughter was home, safe and could now prepare her dissertation. He was not at all worried. His special girl always came through.

The air was crisp following the lightning storms the night before. As those clouds rapidly moved east, it left the skies without insulation, dropping the temperature considerably. Bridget Drummond had just returned to their company owned flat in London kept for special guests. Released from the hospital a few days before, she entered, reset the security system, and worked with the thermostat to adjust the temperature. It was freezing inside the rarely used flat that she would now temporarily call home. The residence on the Isle of Skye, now a crime scene, was still not cleared by Police Scotland to consider renovations.

Although she had heard the public story, at her request, Angus Adair was trying to give her a clearer picture of the events at the mine. While Maximillian and Grant were both killed along with several others, there was information to suggest it was not by special forces. Several sources pointed to the United Brotherhood of Islam, and Angus, who now worked for Bridget, would continue to dig until she knew exactly what had happened.

At that exact moment, however, she was not bitter, not grieving, nor was she overly concerned. She felt euphoric, and her thoughts were quite simple.

This was her moment. After years in the shadows, she was now the only one standing. She smiled as she poured a glass of Maximillian's two-hundred-year-old scotch into a glass as she looked out at the lights of London.

Sara Ricci returns in Deadly by Design to help Jason when a deadly secret is uncovered at Versilant Nanotechnologies that may kill them all.

Sara Ricci Scientific Thriller Series

Deadly Dissertation (Book 1)

Deadly by Design (Book 2)

Deadly Discovery (Book 3)

Deadly Dilemma (Book 4)

Deadly Diplomacy (Book 5)

Deadly Desire (Book 6, Coming 2024)

Made in the USA
Coppell, TX
24 June 2024

33891865R00243